Lost in the Fog

James De Mille

Contents

LOST IN THE FOG

BY

James De Mille

I.

Old Acquaintances gather around old Scenes.--Antelope, ahoy!--How are you, Solomon?--Round-about Plan of a round about Voyage.--The Doctor warns, rebukes, and remonstrates, but, alas! in vain.--It must be done.--Beginning of a highly eventful Voyage.

It was a beautiful morning, in the month of July, when a crowd of boys assembled on the wharf of Grand Pre. The tide was high, the turbid waters of Mud Creek flowed around, a fresh breeze blew, and if any craft was going to sea she could not have found a better time. The crowd consisted chiefly of boys, though a few men were mingled with them. These boys were from Grand Pre School, and are all old acquaintances. There was the stalwart frame of Bruce, the Roman face of Arthur, the bright eyes of Bart, the slender frame of Phil, and the earnest glance of Tom. There, too, was Pat's merry smile, and the stolid look of Bogud, and the meditative solemnity of Jiggins, not to speak of others whose names need not be mentioned. Amid the crowd the face of Captain Corbet was conspicuous, and the dark visage of Solomon, while that of the mate was distinguishable in the distance. To all these the good schooner Antelope formed the centre of attraction, and also of action. It was on board of her that the chief bustle took place, and towards her that all eyes were turned.

The good schooner Antelope had made several voyages during the past few months, and now presented herself to the eye of the spectator not much changed from her former self. A fine fresh coat of coal tar had but recently ornamented her fair exterior, while a coat of whitewash inside the hold had done much to drive away the odor of the fragrant potato. Rigging and sails had been repaired as well as circumstances would permit, and in the opinion of her gallant captain she was eminently seaworthy.

On the present occasion things bore the appearance of a voyage. Trunks were passed on board and put below, together with coats, cloaks, bedding, and baskets of provisions. The deck was strewn about with the multifarious requisites of a ship's company. The Antelope, at that time, seemed in part an emigrant vessel, with a dash of the yacht and the coasting schooner.

In the midst of all this, two gentlemen worked their way through the crowd to the edge of the wharf.

"Well, boys," said one, "well, captain, what's the meaning of all this?"

Captain Corbet started at this, and looked up from a desperate effort to secure the end of one of the sails.

"Why, Dr. Porter!" said he; "why, doctor!--how d'ye do?--and Mr. Long, too!--why, railly!"

The boys also stopped their work, and looked towards their teachers with a little uneasiness.

"What's all this?" said Dr. Porter, looking around with a smile; "are you getting up another expedition?"

"Wal, no," said Captain Corbet, "not 'xactly; fact is, we're kine o' goin to take a vyge deoun the bay."

"Down the bay?"

"Yes. You see the boys kine o' want to go home by water, rayther than by land."

"By water! Home by water!" repeated Mr. Long, doubtfully.

"Yes," said Captain Corbet; "an bein as the schewner was in good repair, an corked, an coal-tarred, an whitewashed up fust rate, I kine o' thought it would redound to our mootooil benefit if we went off on sich a excursion,--bein pleasanter, cheaper, comfortabler, an every way preferable to a land tower."

"Hem," said Dr. Porter, looking uneasily about. "I don't altogether like it. Boys, what does it all mean?"

Thus appealed to, Bart became spokesman for the boys.

"Why, sir," said he, "we thought we'd like to go home by water--that's all."

"Go home by water!" repeated the doctor once more, with a curious smile.

"Yes, sir."

"What? by the Bay of Fundy?"

"Yes, sir."

"Who are going?"

"Well, sir, there are only a few of us. Bruce, and Arthur, and Tom, and Phil, and Pat, besides myself."

"Bruce and Arthur?" said the doctor; "are they going home by the Bay of Fundy?"

"Yes, sir," said Bart, with a smile.

"I don't see how they can get to the Gulf of St. Lawrence and Prince Edward's Island from the Bay of Fundy," said the doctor, "without going round Nova Scotia, and that will be a journey of many hundred miles."

"O, no, sir," said Bruce; "we are going first to Moncton."

"O, is that the idea?"

"Yes, sir."

"And where will you go from Moncton?"

"To Shediac, and then home."

"And are you going to Newfoundland by that route, Tom?" asked the doctor.

"Yes, sir," said Tom, gravely.

"From Shediac?"

"Yes, sir."

"I never knew before that there were vessels going from Shediac to Newfoundland."

"O, I'm going to Prince Edward's Island first, sir, with Bruce and Arthur," said Tom. "I'll find my way home from there."

The doctor smiled.

"I'm afraid you'll find it a long journey before you reach home. Won't your friends be anxious?"

"O, no, sir. I wrote that I wanted to visit Bruce and Arthur, and they gave me leave."

"And you, Phil, are you going home by the Antelope?"

"Yes, sir."

"You are going exactly in a straight line away from it."

"Am I, sir?"

"Of course you are. This isn't the way to Chester."

"Well, sir, you see I'm going to visit Bart at St. John."

"O, I understand. And that is your plan, then?"

"Yes, sir," said Bart. "Pat is going too."

"Where are you going first?"

"First, sir, we will sail to the Petitcodiac River, and go up it as far as Moncton, where Bruce, and Arthur, and Tom will leave us."

"And then?"

"Then we will go to St. John, where Phil, and Pat, and I will leave her. Solomon, too, will leave her there."

"Solomon!" cried the doctor. "What! Solomon! Is Solomon going? Why, what can I do without Solomon? Here! Hallo!--Solomon! What in the world's the meaning of all this?"

Thus summoned, Solomon came forth from the cabin, into which he had dived at the first appearance of the doctor. His eyes were downcast, his face was demure, his attitude and manner were abject.

"Solomon," said the doctor, "what's this I hear? Are you going to St. John?"

"Ony temp'ly, sah--jist a leetle visit, sah," said Solomon, very humbly, stealing looks at the boys from his downcast eyes.

"But what makes you go off this way without asking, or letting me know?"

"Did I, sah?" said Solomon, rolling his eyes up as though horrified at his own wickedness; "the sakes now! Declar, I clean forgot it."

"What are you going away for?"

"Why, sah, for de good oh my helf. Docta vises sea vyge; sides, I got frens in St. John, an business dar, what muss be tended to."

"Well, well," said the doctor, "I suppose if you want to go you'll find reasons enough; but at the same time you ought to have let me known before."

"Darsn't, sah," said Solomon.

"Why not?"

"Fraid you'd not let me go," said Solomon, with a broad grin, that instantly was suppressed by a demure cough.

"Nonsense," said the doctor; and then turning away, he spoke a few words apart with Mr. Long.

"Well, boys," said the doctor, at last, "this project of yours doesn't seem to me to be altogether safe, and I don't like to trust you in this way without anybody as a responsible guardian."

Bart smiled.

"O, sir," said he, "you need not be at all uneasy. All of us are accustomed to take care of ourselves; and besides, if you wanted a responsible guardian for us, what better one could be found than Captain Corbet?"

The doctor and Mr. Long both shook their heads. Evidently neither of them attached any great importance to Captain Corbet's guardianship.

"Did you tell your father how you were going?" asked the doctor, after a few further words with Mr. Long.

"O, yes, sir; and he told me I might go. What's more, he promised to charter a schooner for me to cruise about with Phil and Pat after I arrived home."

"And we got permission, too," said Bruce.

"Indeed!" said the doctor. "That changes the appearance of things. I was afraid that it was a whim of your own. And now, one thing more,--how are you off for provisions?"

"Wal, sir," said Captain Corbet, "I've made my calculations, an I think I've got enough. What I might fail in, the boys and Solomon have made up."

"How is it, Solomon?" asked the doctor.

Solomon grinned.

"You sleep in the hold, I see," continued the doctor.

"Yes, sir," said Bruce. "It's whitewashed, and quite sweet now. We'll only be on board two or three days at the farthest, and so it really doesn't much matter how we go."

"Well, boys, I have no more to say; only take care of yourselves."

With these words the doctor and Mr. Long bade them good by, and then walked away.

The other boys, however, stood on the wharf waiting to see the vessel off. They themselves were all going to start for home in a few minutes, and were only waiting for the departure of the Antelope.

This could not now be long delayed. The tide was high. The wind fresh and fair. The luggage, and provisions, and stores were all on board. Captain Corbet was at the helm. All was ready. At length the word was given, the lines were cast off;

and the Antelope moved slowly round, and left the wharf amid the cheers of the
boys. Farther and farther it moved away, then down the tortuous channel of Mud
Creek, until at last the broad expanse of Minas Basin received them.

For this voyage the preparations had been complete. It had first been thought
of several weeks before, and then the plan and the details had been slowly elabo-
rated. It was thought to be an excellent idea, and one which was in every respect
worthy of the "B. O. W. C." Captain Corbet embraced the proposal with enthusiasm. Letters home, requesting permission, received favorable answers. Solomon at
first resisted, but finally, on being solemnly appealed to as Grand Panjandrum, he
found himself unable to withstand, and thus everything was gradually prepared.
Other details were satisfactorily arranged, though not without much serious and
earnest debate. The question of costume received very careful attention, and it
was decided to adopt and wear the weather-beaten uniforms that had done service
amidst mud and water on a former occasion. Solomon's presence was felt to be a
security against any menacing famine; and that assurance was made doubly sure by
the presence of a cooking stove, which Captain Corbet, mindful of former hardships, had thoughtfully procured and set up in the hold. Finally, it was decided that
the flag which had formerly flaunted the breeze should again wave over them; and
so it was, that as the Antelope moved through Mud Creek, like a thing of life, the
black flag of the "B. O. W. C." floated on high, with its blazonry of a skull, which
now, worn by time, looked more than ever like the face of some mild, venerable,
and paternal monitor.

Some time was taken up in arranging the hold. Considerable confusion was
manifest in that important locality. Tin pans were intermingled with bedding, provisions with wearing apparel, books with knives and forks, while amid the scene
the cooking stove towered aloft prominent. To tell the truth, the scene was rather
free and easy than elegant; nor could an unprejudiced observer have called it altogether comfortable. In fact, to one who looked at it with a philosophic mind, an air
of squalor might possibly have been detected. Yet what of that? The philosophic
mind just alluded to would have overlooked the squalor, and regarded rather the
health, the buoyant animal spirits, and the determined habit of enjoyment, which
all the ship's company evinced, without exception. The first thing which they did
in the way of preparation for the voyage was to doff the garments of civilized life,

and to don the costume of the "B. O. W. C." Those red shirts, decorated with a huge white cross on the back, had been washed and mended, and completely reconstructed, so that the rents and patches which were here and there visible on their fair exteriors, served as mementos of former exploits, and called up associations of the past without at all deteriorating from the striking effect of the present. Glengary bonnets adorned their heads, and served to complete the costume.

The labor of dressing was followed by a hurried arrangement of the trunks and bedding; after which they all emerged from the hold and ascending to the deck, looked around upon the scene. Above, the sky was blue and cloudless, and between them and the blue sky floated the flag, from whose folds the face looked benignantly down. The tide was now on the ebb, and as the wind was fair, both wind and tide united to bear them rapidly onward. Before them was Blomidon, while all around was the circling sweep of the shores of Minas Bay. A better day for a start could not have been found, and everything promised a rapid and pleasant run.

"I must say," remarked Captain Corbet, who had for some time been standing buried in his own meditations at the helm,--"I must say, boys, that I don't altogether regret bein once more on the briny deep. There was a time," he continued, meditatively, "when I kine o' anticipated givin up this here occypation, an stayin to hum a nourishin of the infant. But man proposes, an woman disposes, as the sayin is,--an you see what I'm druv to. It's a great thing for a man to have a companion of sperrit, same as I have, that keeps a' drivin an a drivin at him, and makes him be up an doin. An now, I declar, if I ain't gittin to be a confirmed wanderer agin, same as I was in the days of my halcyon an shinin youth. Besides, I have a kine o' feelin as if I'd be a continewin this here the rest of all my born days."

"I hope you won't feel homesick," remarked Bart, sympathetically.

"Homesick," repeated the captain. "Wal, you see thar's a good deal to be said about it. In my hum thar's a attraction, but thar's also a repulsion. The infant drors me hum, the wife of my buzzum drives me away, an so thar it is, an I've got to knock under to the strongest power. An that's the identical individool thing that makes the aged Corbet a foogitive an a vagabond on the face of the mighty deep. Still I have my consolations."

The captain paused for a few moments, and then resumed.

"Yes," he continued, "I have my consolations. Surroundins like these here air a consolation. I like your young faces, an gay an airy ways, boys. I like to see you enjoy life. So, go in. Pitch in. Go ahead. Sing. Shout. Go on like mad. Carry on like all possessed, an you'll find the aged Corbet smilin amid the din, an a flutterin of his venerable locks triumphant amid the ragin an riotin elements."

"It's a comfort to know that, at any rate," said Tom. "We'll give you enough of that before we leave, especially as we know it don't annoy you."

"I don't know how it is," said the captain, solemnly, "but I begin to feel a sort of somethin towards you youngsters that's very absorbin. It's a kine o' anxious fondness, with a mixtoor of indulgent tenderness. How ever I got to contract sech a feelin beats me. I s'pose it's bein deprived of my babby, an exiled from home, an so my vacant buzzom craves to be filled. I've got a dreadful talent for doin the pariential, an what's more, not only for doin the pariential, but for feelin of it. So you boys, ef ever you see me a doin of the pariential towards youns, please remember that when I act like an anxious an too indulgent parient towards youns, it's because I feel like one."

For some hours they traversed the waters, carried swiftly on by the united forces of the wind and tide. At last they found themselves close by Blomidon, and under his mighty shadow they sailed for some time. Then they doubled the cape, and there, before them, lay a long channel--the Straits of Minas, through which the waters pour at every ebb and flood. Their course now lay through this to the Bay of Fundy outside; and as it was within two hours of the low tide, the current ran swiftly, hurrying them rapidly past the land. Here the scene was grand and impressive in the extreme. On one side arose a lofty, precipitous cliff, which extended for miles, its sides scarred and tempest-torn, its crest fringed with trees, towering overhead many hundreds of feet, black, and menacing, and formidable. At its base was a steep beach, disclosed by the retreating tide, which had been formed by the accumulated masses of rock that had fallen in past ages from the cliffs above. These now, from the margin of the water up to high-water mark, were covered with a vast growth of sea-weed, which luxuriated here, and ran parallel to the line of vegetation on the summit of the cliff. On the other side of the strait the scene was different. Here the shores were more varied; in one place, rising high on steep precipices, in others, thrusting forth black, rocky promontories into the deep channel; in others again, retreating far back, and forming bays, round whose sloping shores appeared places fit for human habitation, and in whose still waters the storm-tossed bark might find a secure haven.

As they drifted on, borne along by the impetuous tide, the shores on either side changed, and new vistas opened before them. At last they reached the termination of the strait, the outer portal of this long avenue, which here was marked by the mighty hand of Nature in conspicuous characters. For here was the termination of that long extent of precipitous cliff which forms the outline of Blomidon; and this termination, abrupt, and stern, and black, shows, in a concentrated form, the power of wind and wave. The cliff ends abrupt, broken off short, and beyond this arise from the water several giant fragments of rock, the first of which, shaped like an irregular pyramid, rivals the cliff itself in height, and is surrounded by other rocky fragments, all of which form a colossal group, whose aggregated effect never fails to overawe the mind of the spectator. Such is Cape Split, the terminus of Cape Blomidon, on the side of the Bay of Fundy. Over its shaggy summits now fluttered hundreds of sea-gulls; round its black base the waves foamed and thundered, while the swift tide poured between the interstices of the rugged rocks.

"Behind that thar rock," said Captain Corbet, pointing to Cape Split, "is a place they call Scott's Bay. Perhaps some of you have heard tell of it."

"I have a faint recollection of such a place," said Bart. "Scott's Bay, do you call it? Yes, that must be the place that I've heard of; and is it behind this cape?"

"It's a bay that runs up thar," said the captain. "We'll see it soon arter we get further down. It's a fishin and ship-buildin place. They catch a dreadful lot of shad thar sometimes."

Swiftly the Antelope passed on, hurried on by the tide, and no longer feeling much of the wind; swiftly she passed by the cliffs, and by the cape, and onward by the sloping shores, till at length the broad bosom of the Bay of Fundy extended before their eyes. Here the wind ceased altogether, the water was smooth and calm, but the tide still swept them along, and the shores on each side receded, until at length they were fairly in the bay. Here, on one side, the coast of Nova Scotia spread away, until it faded from view in the distance, while on the other side the coast of New Brunswick extended. Between the schooner and this latter coast a long cape projected, while immediately in front arose a lofty island of rock, whose summit was crowned with trees.

"What island is that?" asked Tom.

"That," said Captain Corbet, "is Isle o' Holt."

"I think I've heard it called Ile Haute," said Bart.

"All the same," said Captain Corbet, "ony I believe it was named after the man that diskivered it fust, an his name was Holt."

"But it's a French name," said Tom; "Ile Haute means high island."

"Wal, mebbe he was a Frenchman," said Captain Corbet. "I won't argufy--I dare say he was. There used to be a heap o' Frenchmen about these parts, afore we got red of 'em."

"It's a black, gloomy, dismal, and wretched-looking place," said Tom, after some minutes of silent survey.

II.

First Sight of a Place destined to be better known.--A Fog Mill.--Navigation without Wind.--Fishing.--Boarding.--Under Arrest.--Captain Corbet defiant.--The Revenue Officials frowned down.--Corbet triumphant.

The Antelope had left the wharf at about seven in the morning. It was now one o'clock. For the last two or three hours there had been but little wind, and it was the tide which had carried her along. Drifting on in this way, they had come to within a mile of Ile Haute, and had an opportunity of inspecting the place which Tom had declared to be so gloomy. In truth, Tom's judgment was not undeserved. Ile Haute arose like a solid, unbroken rock out of the deep waters of the Bay of Fundy, its sides precipitous, and scarred by tempest, and shattered by frost. On its summit were trees, at its base lay masses of rock that had fallen. The low tide disclosed here, as at the base of Blomidon, a vast growth of black sea-weed, which covered all that rocky shore. The upper end of the island, which was nearest them, was lower, however, and went down sloping to the shore, forming a place where a landing could easily be effected. From this shore mud flats extended into the water.

"This end looks as though it had been cleared," said Bart.

"I believe it was," said the captain.

"Does anybody live here?"

"No."

"Did any one ever live here?"

"Yes, once, some one tried it, I believe, but gave it up."

"Does it belong to anybody, or is it public property?"

"O, I dare say it belongs to somebody, if you could only get him to claim it."

"I say, captain," said Bruce, "how much longer are we going to drift?"

"O, not much longer. The tide's about on the turn, and we'll have a leetle change."

"What! will we drift back again?"

"O, I shouldn't wonder if we had a leetle wind afore long."

"But if we don't, will we drift back again into the Basin of Minas?"

"O, dear, no. We can anchor hereabouts somewhar."

"You won't anchor by this island,--will you?"

"O, dear, no. We'll have a leetle driftin first." As the captain spoke, he looked earnestly out upon the water.

"Thar she comes," he cried at last, pointing over the water. The boys looked, and saw the surface of the bay all rippled over. They knew the signs of wind, and waited for the result. Soon a faint puff came up the bay, which filled the languid sails, and another puff came up more strongly, and yet another, until at length a moderate breeze was blowing. The tide no longer dragged them on. It was on the turn; and as the vessel caught the wind, it yielded to the impetus, and moved through the water, heading across the bay towards the New Brunswick shore, in such a line as to pass near to that cape which has already been spoken of.

"If the wind holds out," said Captain Corbet, "so as to carry us past Cape d'Or, we can drift up with this tide."

"Where's Cape d'Or?"

"That there," said Captain Corbet, pointing to the long cape which stretched between them and the New Brunswick shore. "An if it goes down, an we can't get by the cape, we'll be able, at any rate, to drop anchor there, an hold on till the next tide."

The returning tide, and the fresh breeze that blew now, bore them onward rapidly, and they soon approached Cape d'Or. They saw that it terminated in a rocky cliff, with rocky edges jutting forth, and that all the country adjoining was wild and rugged. But the wind, having done this much for them, now began to seem tired of favoring them, and once more fell off.

"I don't like this," said Captain Corbet, looking around.

"What?"

"All this here," said he, pointing to the shore.

It was about a mile away, and the schooner, borne along now by the tide, was slowly drifting on to an unpleasant proximity to the rocky shore.

"I guess we've got to anchor," said Captain Corbet; "there's no help for it."

"To anchor?" said Bruce, in a tone of disappointment.

"Yes, anchor; we've got to do it," repeated the captain, in a decided tone. The boys saw that there was no help for it, for the vessel was every moment drawing in closer to the rocks; and though it would not have been very dangerous for her to run ashore in that calm water, yet it would not have been pleasant. So they suppressed their disappointment, and in a few minutes the anchor was down, and the schooner's progress was stopped.

"Thar's one secret," said the captain, "of navigatin in these here waters, an that is, to use your anchor. My last anchor I used for nigh on thirty year, till it got cracked. I mayn't be much on land, but put me anywhars on old Fundy, an I'm to hum. I know every current on these here waters, an can foller my nose through the thickest fog that they ever ground out at old Manan."

"What's that?" asked Bart. "What did you say about grinding out fog?"

"O, nothin, ony thar's an island down the bay, you know, called Grand Manan, an seafarin men say that they've got a fog mill down thar, whar they grind out all the fog for the Bay of Fundy. I can't say as ever I've seen that thar mill, but I've allus found the fog so mighty thick down thar that I think thar's a good deal in the story."

"I suppose we'll lose this tide," said Phil.

"Yes, I'm afeard so," said the captain, looking around over the water. "This here wind ain't much, any way; you never can reckon on winds in this bay. I don't care much about them. I'd a most just as soon go about the bay without sails as with them. What I brag on is the tides, an a jodgmatical use of the anchor."

"You're not in earnest?"

"Course I am."

"Could you get to St. John from Grand Pre without sails?"

"Course I could."

"I don't see how you could manage to do it."

"Do it? Easy enough," said the captain. "You see I'd leave with the ebb tide, and get out into the bay. Then I'd anchor an wait till the next ebb, an so on. Bless your hearts, I've often done it."

"But you couldn't get across the bay by drifting."

"Course I could. I'd work my way by short drifts over as far as this, an then I'd gradually move along till I kine o' canted over to the New Brunswick shore. It takes time to do it, course it does; but what I mean to say is this--it CAN be done."

"Well, I wouldn't like to be on board while you were trying to do it."

"Mebbe not. I ain't invitin you to do it, either. All I was sayin is, it CAN be done. Sails air very good in their way, course they air, an who's objectin to 'em? I'm only sayin that in this here bay thar's things that's more important than sails, by a long chalk--such as tides, an anchors in particular. Give me them thar, an I don't care a hooter what wind thar is."

Lying thus at anchor, under the hot sun, was soon found to be rather dull, and the boys sought in vain for some way of passing the time. Different amusements were invented for the occasion. The first amusement consisted in paper boats, with which they ran races, and the drift of these frail vessels over the water afforded some excitement. Then they made wooden boats with huge paper sails. In this last Bart showed a superiority to the others; for, by means of a piece of iron hoop, which he inserted as a keel, he produced a boat which was able to carry an immense press of sail, and in the faint and scarce perceptible breeze, easily distanced the others. This accomplishment Bart owed to his training in a seaport town.

At length one of them proposed that they should try to catch fish. Captain Corbet, in answer to their eager inquiries, informed them that there were fish everywhere about the bay; on learning which they became eager to try their skill. Some herring were on board, forming part of the stores, and these were taken for bait. Among the miscellaneous contents of the cabin a few hooks were found, which were somewhat rusty, it is true, yet still good enough for the purpose before them. Lines, of course, were easily procured, and soon a half dozen baited hooks were down in the water, while a half dozen boys, eager with suspense, watched the surface of the water.

For a half hour they held their lines suspended without any result; but at the end of that time, a cry from Phil roused them, and on looking round they saw him clinging with all his might to his line, which was tugged at tightly by something in the water. Bruce ran to help him, and soon their united efforts succeeded in landing on the deck of the vessel a codfish of very respectable size. The sight of this was greeted with cheers by the others, and served to stimulate them to their work.

After this others were caught, and before half an hour more some twenty cod-fish, of various sizes, lay about the deck, as trophies of their piscatory skill. They were now more excited than ever, and all had their hooks in the water, and were waiting eagerly for a bite, when an exclamation from Captain Corbet roused them.

On turning their heads, and looking in the direction where he was pointing, they saw a steamboat approaching them. It was coming from the head of the bay on the New Brunswick side, and had hitherto been concealed by the projecting cape.

"What's that?" said Bart. "Is it the St. John steamer?"

"No, SIR," said the captain. "She's a man-o'-war steamer--the revenoo cutter, I do believe."

"How do you know?"

"Why, by her shape."

"She seems to be coming this way."

"Yes, bound to Minas Bay, I s'pose. Wal, wal, wal! strange too,--how singoolar-ly calm an onterrified I feel in'ardly. Why, boys, I've seen the time when the sight of a approachin revenoo vessel would make me shiver an shake from stem to starn. But now how changed! Such, my friends, is the mootability of human life!"

The boys looked at the steamer for a few moments, but at length went back to their fishing. The approaching steamer had nothing in it to excite curiosity: such an object was too familiar to withdraw their thoughts from the excitement of their lines and hooks, and the hope which each had of surpassing the other in the number of catches animated them to new trials. So they soon forgot all about the approaching steamer.

But Captain Corbet had nothing else to do, and so, whether it was on account of his lack of employment, or because of the sake of old associations, he kept his eyes fixed on the steamer. Time passed on, and in the space of another half hour she had drawn very near to the Antelope.

Suddenly Captain Corbet slapped his hand against his thigh.

"Declar, if they ain't a goin to overhaul us!" he cried.

At this the boys all turned again to look at the steamer.

"Declar, if that fellow in the gold hat ain't a squintin at us through his spy-glass!" cried the captain.

As the boys looked, they saw that the Antelope had become an object of singular attention and interest to those on board of the steamer. Men were on the forecastle, others on the main deck, the officers were on the quarter-deck, and all were earnestly scrutinizing the Antelope. One of them was looking at her through his glass. The Antelope, as she lay at anchor, was now turned with her stern towards the steamer, and her sails flapping idly against the masts. In a few moments the paddles of the steamer stopped, and at the same instant a gun was fired.

"Highly honored, kind sir," said Captain Corbet, with a grin.

"What's the matter?" asked Bart.

"Matter? Why that thar steamer feels kine o' interested in us, an that thar gun means, HEAVE TO."

"Are you going to heave to?"

"Nary heave."

"Why not?"

"Can't come it no how; cos why, I'm hove to, with the anchor hard and fast, ony they can't see that we're anchored."

Suddenly a cry came over the water from a man on the quarter-deck.

"Ship aho-o-o-o-o-oy!"

"Hel-lo-o-o-o-o!"

Such was the informal reply of Captain Corbet.

"Heave to-o-o-o, till I send a boat aboard."

"Hoo-r-a-a-a-ay!"

Such was again Captain Corbet's cheerful and informal answer.

"Wal! wal wal!" he exclaimed, "it does beat my grandmother--they're goin to send a boat aboard."

"What for?"

Captain Corbet grinned, and shook his head, and chuckled very vehemently, but said nothing. He appeared to be excessively amused with his own thoughts. The boys looked at the steamer, and then at Captain Corbet, in some wonder; but as he said nothing, they were silent, and waited to see what was going to happen. Meanwhile Solomon, roused from some mysterious culinary duties by the report of the gun, had scrambled upon the deck, and stood with the others looking out over the water at the steamer.

In a few moments the steamer's boat was launched, and a half dozen sailors got in, followed by an officer. Then they put off, and rowed with vigorous strokes towards the schooner.

Captain Corbet watched the boat for some time in silence.

"Cur'ouser an cur'ouser," he said, at length. "I've knowed the time, boys, when sech an incident as this, on the briny deep, would have fairly keeled me over, an made me moot, an riz every har o' my head; but look at me now. Do I tremble? do I shake? Here, feel my pulse."

Phil, who stood nearest, put his finger on the outstretched wrist of the captain.

"Doos it beat?"

"No," said Phil.

"Course it beats; but then it ony beats nateral. You ain't feelin the right spot--the humane pulse not bein sitooated on the BACK of the hand," he added mildly, "but here;" and he removed Phil's inexperienced finger to the place where the pulse lies. "Thar, now," he added, "as that pulse beats now, even so it beat a half hour ago, before that thar steamer hev in sight. Why, boys, I've knowed the time when this humane pulse bet like all possessed. You see, I've lived a life of adventoor, in spite of my meek and quiet natoor, an hev dabbled at odd times in the smugglin business. But they don't catch me this time--I've retired from that thar, an the Antelope lets the revenoo rest in peace."

The boat drew nearer and nearer, and the officer at the stern looked scrutinizingly at the Antelope. There was an air of perplexity about his face, which was very visible to those on board, and the perplexity deepened and intensified as his eyes rested on the flag of the "B. O. W. C."

"Leave him to me," said Captain Corbet. "Leave that thar young man to me. I enjy havin to do with a revenoo officer jest now; so don't go an put in your oars, but jest leave him to me."

"All right, captain; we won't say a word," said Bruce. "We'll go on with our fishing quietly. Come, boys--look sharp, and down with your lines."

The interest which they had felt in these new proceedings had caused the boys to pull up their hooks; but now, at Bruce's word, they put them in the water once more, and resumed their fishing, only casting sidelong glances at the approaching boat.

In a few minutes the boat was alongside, and the officer leaped on board. He looked all around, at the fish lying about the deck, at the boys engaged in fishing, at Captain Corbet, at Solomon, at the mysterious flag aloft, and finally at the boys. These all took no notice of him, but appeared to be intent on their task.

"What schooner is this?" he asked, abruptly.

"The schooner Antelope, Corbet master," replied the captain.

"Are you the master?"

"I am."

"Where do you belong?"

"Grand Pre."

"Grand Pre?

"Yes."

"Hm," he replied, with a stare around--"Grand Pre--ah---hm."

"Yes, jest so."

"What's that?"

"I briefly remarked that it was jest so."

"What's the reason you didn't lie to, when you were hailed?"

"Lay to?"

"Yes."

"Couldn't do it."

"What do you mean by that?" asked the officer, who was rather ireful, and somewhat insulting in his manner.

"Wal bein as I was anchored here hard an fast, I don't exactly see how I could manage to go through that thar manoeuvre, unless you'd kindly lend me the loan of your steam ingine to do it on."

"Look here, old man; you'd better look out."

"Wal, I dew try to keep a good lookout. How much'll you take for the loan o' that spy-glass o' yourn?"

"Let me see your papers."

"Papers?"

"Yes, your papers."

"Hain't got none."

"What's that?"

"Hain't got none."

"You--haven't--any--papers?"

"Nary paper."

The officer's brow grew dark. He looked around the vessel once more, and then looked frowningly at Captain Corbet, who encountered his glance with a serene smile.

"Look here, old man," said he; "you can't come it over me. Your little game's up, old fellow. This schooner's seized."

"Seized? What for?"

"For violation of the law, by fishing within the limits."

"Limits? What limits?"

"No foreign vessel can come within three miles of the shore."

"Foreign vessel? Do you mean to call me a foreigner?"

"Of course I do. You're a Yankee fisherman."

"Am I?"

"Of course you are; and what do you mean by that confounded rag up there?" cried the officer, pointing to the flag of the "B. O. W. C." "If you think you can fish in this style, you'll find yourself mistaken. I know too much about this business."

"Do you? Well, then, kind sir, allow me to mention that you've got somethin to larn yet--spite o' your steam injines an spy-glasses."

"What's that?" cried the officer, furious. "I'll let you know. I arrest you, and this vessel is seized."

"Wait a minute, young sir," cried Captain Corbet; "not QUITE so fast, EF you please. You'll get YOURSELF arrested. What do you mean by this here? Do you know who I am? I, sir, am a subject of Queen Victory. My home is here. I'm now on my own natyve shore. A foreigner, am I? Let me tell you, sir, that I was born, brung up, nourished, married, an settled in this here province, an I've got an infant born here, an I'm not a fisherman, an this ain't a fishin vessel. You arrest me ef you dar. You'll see who'll get the wust of it in the long run. I'd like precious well to get damages--yea, swingin damages--out of one of you revenoo fellers."

The officer looked around again. It would not do to make a mistake. Captain Corbet's words were not without effect.

"Yea!" cried Captain Corbet. "Yea, naval sir! I'm a free Nova Scotian as free as a bird. I cruise about my natyve coasts whar I please. Who's to hender? Seize me if you dar, an it'll be the dearest job you ever tried. This here is my own private pleasure yacht. These are my young friends, natyves, an amatoor fishermen. Cast your eye down into yonder hold, and see if this here's a fishin craft."

The officer looked down, and saw a cooking stove, trunks, and bedding. He looked around in doubt.

But this scene had lasted long enough.

"O, nonsense!" said Bart, suddenly pulling up his line, and coming forward; "see here--it's all right," said he to the officer. "We're not fishermen. It's as he says. We're only out on a short cruise, you know, for pleasure, and that sort of thing."

As Bart turned, the others did the same. Bruce lounged up, dragging his line, followed by Arthur and the others.

"We're responsible for the schooner," said Bruce, quietly. "It's ours for the time being. We don't look like foreign fishermen--do we?"

The officer looked at the boys, and saw his mistake at once. He was afraid that he had made himself ridiculous. The faces and manners of the boys, as they stood confronting him in an easy and self-possessed manner, showed most plainly the absurdity of his position. Even the mysterious flag became intelligible, when he looked at the faces of those over whom it floated.

"I suppose it's all right," he muttered, in a vexed tone, and descended into the boat without another word.

"Sorry to have troubled you, captain," said Corbet, looking blandly after the officer; "but it wan't my fault. I didn't have charge of that thar injine."

The officer turned his back without a word, and the men pulled off to the steamer.

The captain looked after the boat in silence for some time.

"I'm sorry," said he, at length, as he heaved a gentle sigh,--"I'm sorry that you put in your oars--I do SO like to sass a revonoo officer."

III.

Solomon surpasses himself.--A Period of Joy is generally followed by a Time of Sorrow.--Gloomy Forebodings.--The Legend of Petticoat Jack.--Captain Corbet discourses of the Dangers of the Deep, and puts in Practice a new and original Mode of Navigation.

This interruption put an end to their attempts at fishing, and was succeeded by another interruption of a more pleasing character, in the shape of dinner, which was now loudly announced by Solomon. For some time a savory steam had been issuing from the lower regions, and had been wafted to their nostrils in successive puffs, until at last their impatient appetite had been roused to the keenest point, and the enticing fragrance had suggested all sorts of dishes. When at length the summons came, and they went below, they found the dinner in every way worthy of the occasion. Solomon's skill never was manifested more conspicuously than on this occasion; and whether the repast was judged of by the quantity or the quality of the dishes, it equally deserved to be considered as one of the masterpieces of the distinguished artist who had prepared it.

"Dar, chil'en," he exclaimed, as they took their places, "dar, cap'en, jes tas dem ar trout, to begin on, an see if you ever saw anythin to beat 'em in all your born days. Den try de stew, den de meat pie, den de calf's head; but dat ar pie down dar mustn't be touched, nor eben so much as looked at, till de las ob all."

And with these words Solomon stepped back, leaning both hands on his hips, and surveyed the banquet and the company with a smile of serene and ineffable complacency.

"All right, Solomon, my son," said Bart. "Your dinner is like yourself--unequalled and unapproachable."

"Bless you, bless you, my friend," murmured Bruce, in the intervals of eating;

"if there is any contrast between this present voyage and former ones, it is all due to our unequalled caterer."

"How did you get the trout, Solomon?" said Phil.

"De trout? O, I picked 'em up last night down in de village," said Solomon. "Met little boy from Gaspereaux, an got 'em from him."

"What's this?" cried Tom, opening a dish--"not lobster!"

"Lobster!" exclaimed Phil.

"So it is."

"Why, Solomon, where did you get lobster?"

"Is this the season for them?"

"Think of the words of the poet, boys," said Bart, warningly,--

"In the months without the R,
Clams and lobsters pison are."

Solomon meanwhile stood apart, grinning from ear to ear, with his little black beads of eyes twinkling with merriment.

"Halo, Solomon! What do you say to lobsters in July?"

Solomon's head wagged up and down, as though he were indulging in some quiet, unobtrusive laughter, and it was some time before he replied.

"O, neber you fear, chil'en," he said; "ef you're only goin to get sick from lobsters, you'll live a long day. You may go in for clams, an lobsters, an oysters any time ob de yeah you like,--ony dey mus be cooked up proper."

"I'm gratified to hear that," said Bruce, gravely, "but at the same time puzzled. For Mrs. Pratt says the exact opposite; and so here we have two great authorities in direct opposition. So what are we to think?"

"O, there's no difficulty," said Arthur, "for the doctors are not of equal authority. Mrs. Pratt is a quack, but Solomon is a professional--a regular, natural, artistic, and scientific cook, which at sea is the same as doctor."

The dinner was prolonged to an extent commensurate with its own inherent excellence and the capacity of the boys to appreciate it; but at length, like all things mortal, it came to a termination, and the company went up once more to the deck. On looking round it was evident to all that a change had taken place.

Four miles away lay Ile Haute, and eight or ten miles beyond this lay the long line of Nova Scotia. It was now about four o'clock, and the tide had been rising for three hours, and was flowing up rapidly, and in a full, strong current. As yet there was no wind, and the broad surface of the bay was quite smooth and unruffled. In the distance and far down the bay, where its waters joined the horizon, there was a kind of haze, that rendered the line of separation between sea and sky very indistinct. The coast of Nova Scotia was at once enlarged and obscured. It seemed now elevated to an unusual height above the sea line, as though it had been suddenly brought several miles nearer, and yet, instead of being more distinct, was actually more obscure. Even Ile Haute, though so near, did not escape. Four miles of distance were not sufficient to give it that grand indistinctness which was now flung over the Nova Scotia coast; yet much of the mysterious effect of the haze had gathered about the island; its lofty cliffs seemed to tower on high more majestically, and to lean over more frowningly; its fringe of black sea-weed below seemed blacker, while the general hue of the island had changed from a reddish color to one of a dull slaty blue.

"I don't like this," said Captain Corbet, looking down the bay and twisting up his face as he looked.

"Why not?"

Captain Corbet shook his head.

"What's the matter?"

"Bad, bad, bad!" said the captain.

"Is there going to be a storm?"

"Wuss!"

"Worse? What?"

"Fog."

"Fog?"

"Yes, hot an heavy, thick as puddin, an no mistake. I tell you what it is, boys: judgin from what I see, they've got a bran-new steam injine into that thar fog mill at Grand Manan; an the way they're goin to grind out the fog this here night is a caution to mariners."

Saying this, he took off his hat, and holding it in one hand, he scratched his venerable head long and thoughtfully with the other.

"But I don't see any fog as yet," said Bart.

"Don't see it? Wal, what d'ye call all that?" said the captain, giving a grand comprehensive sweep with his arm, so as to take in the entire scene.

"Why, it's clear enough."

"Clear? Then let me tell you that when you see a atmosphere like this here, then you may expect to see it any moment changed into deep, thick fog. Any moment--five minutes 'll be enough to snatch everything from sight, and bury us all in the middle of a unyversal fog bank."

"What'll we do?"

"Dew? That's jest the question."

"Can we go on?"

"Wal--without wind--I don't exactly see how. In a fog a wind is not without its advantages. That's one of the times when the old Antelope likes to have her sails up; but as we hain't got no wind, I don't think we'll do much."

"Will you stay here at anchor?"

"At anchor? Course not. No, sir. Moment the tide falls again, I'll drift down so as to clear that pint there,--Cape Chignecto,--then anchor; then hold on till tide rises; and then drift up. Mebbe before that the wind 'll spring up, an give us a lift somehow up the bay."

"How long before the tide will turn?"

"Wal, it'll be high tide at about a quarter to eight this evenin, I calc'late."

"You'll drift in the night, I suppose."

"Why not?"

"O, I didn't know but what the fog and the night together might be too much for you."

"Too much? Not a bit of it. Fog, and night, and snow-storms, an tide dead agin me, an a lee shore, are circumstances that the Antelope has met over an over, an fit down. As to foggy nights, when it's as calm as this, why, they're not wuth considerin."

Captain Corbet's prognostication as to the fog proved to be correct. It was only for a short time that they were allowed to stare at the magnified proportions of the Nova Scotia coast and Ile Haute. Then a change took place which attracted all their attention.

The change was first perceptible down the bay. It was first made manifest by the rapid appearance of a thin gray cloud along the horizon, which seemed to take in both sea and sky, and absorbed into itself the outlines of both. At the same time, the coast of Nova Scotia grew more obscure, though it lost none of its magnified proportions, while the slaty blue of Ile Haute changed to a grayer shade.

This change was rapid, and was followed by other changes. The thin gray cloud, along the south-west horizon, down the bay, gradually enlarged itself; till it grew to larger and loftier proportions. In a quarter of an hour it had risen to the dimensions of the Nova Scotia coast. In a half an hour it was towering to double that height. In an hour its lofty crest had ascended far up into the sky.

"It's a comin," said Captain Corbet. "I knowed it. Grind away, you old fog mill! Pile on the steam, you Grand Mananers!"

"Is there any wind down there?"

"Not a hooter."

"Is the fog coming up without any wind?"

"Course it is. What does the fog want of wind?"

"I thought it was the wind that brought it along."

"Bless your heart, the fog takes care of itself. The wind isn't a bit necessary. It kine o' pervades the hull atmosphere, an rolls itself on an on till all creation is over-spread. Why, I've seen everything changed from bright sunshine to the thickest kind of fog in fifteen minutes,--yea, more,--and in five minutes."

Even while they were speaking the fog rolled on, the vast accumulation of mist rose higher and yet higher, and appeared to draw nearer with immense rapidity. It seemed as though the whole atmosphere was gradually becoming condensed, and precipitating its invisible watery vapor so as to make it visible in far-extending fog banks. It was not wind, therefore, that brought on the clouds, for the surface of the water was smooth and unruffled, but it was the character of the atmosphere itself from which this change was wrought. And still, as they looked at the approaching mist, the sky overhead was blue, and the sun shone bright. But the gathering clouds seemed now to have gained a greater headway, and came on more rapidly. In a few minutes the whole outline of the Nova Scotia coast faded from view, and in its place there appeared a lofty wall of dim gray cloud, which rose high in the air, fading away into the faintest outline. Overhead, the blue sky became rapidly more obscured; Ile Haute changed again from its grayish blue to a lighter shade, and then became blended with the impenetrable fog that was fast enclosing all things; and finally the clouds grew nearer, till the land nearest them was snatched from view, and all around was alike shrouded under the universal veil; nothing whatever was visible. For a hundred yards, or so, around them, they could see the surface of the water; but beyond this narrow circle, nothing more could be discerned.

"It's a very pooty fog," said Captain Corbet, "an I only wonder that there ain't any wind. If it should come, it'll be all right."

"You intend, then, to go on just the same."

"Jest the same as ef the sky was clear. I will up anchor as the tide begins to fall, an git a good piece down, so as to dodge Cape Chegnecto, an there wait for the rising tide, an jest the same as ef the sun was shinin. But we can't start till eight o'clock this evenin. Anyhow, you needn't trouble yourselves a mite. You may all go to sleep, an dream that the silver moon is guidin the traveller on the briny deep."

The scene now was too monotonous to attract attention, and the boys once more sought for some mode of passing the time. Nothing appeared so enticing as their former occupation of fishing, and to this they again turned their attention. In this employment the time passed away rapidly until the summons was given for tea. Around the festive board, which was again prepared by Solomon with his usual success, they lingered long, and at length, when they arose, the tide was high. It was now about eight o'clock in the evening, and Captain Corbet was all ready to start. As the tide was now beginning to turn, and was on the ebb, the anchor was raised, and the schooner, yielding to the pressure of the current, moved away from her anchorage ground. It was still thick, and darkness also was coming on. Not a thing could be discerned, and by looking at the water, which moved with the schooner, it did not seem as though any motion was made.

"That's all your blindness," said the captain, as they mentioned it to him. "You can't see anything but the water, an as it is movin with us, it doesn't seem as though we were movin. But we air, notwithstandin, an pooty quick too. I'll take two hours' drift before stoppin, so as to make sure. I calc'late about that time to get to a place whar I can hit the current that'll take me, with the risin tide, up to old Petticoat Jack."

"By the way, captain," said Phil, "what do you seafaring men believe about the origin of that name--Petitcodiac? Is it Indian or French?"

"'Tain't neither," said Captain Corbet, decidedly. "It's good English; it's 'Petticoat Jack;' an I've hearn tell a hundred times about its original deryvation. You see, in the old French war, there was an English spy among the French, that dressed hisself up as a woman, an was familiarly known, among the British generals an others that emply'd him, as 'Petticoat Jack.' He did much to contriboot to the defeat of the French; an arter they were licked, the first settlers that went up thar called the place, in honor of their benefacture, 'Petticoat Jack;' an it's bore that name ever sence. An people that think it's French, or Injine, or Greek, or Hebrew, or any other outlandish tongue, don't know what they're talkin about. Now, I KNOW, an I assure you what I've ben a sayin's the gospel terewth, for I had it of an old seafarin man that's sailed this bay for more'n forty year, an if he ain't good authority, then I'd like to know who is--that's all."

At this explanation of the etymology of the disputed term, the boys were silent, and exchanged glances of admiration.

It was some minutes after eight when they left their anchorage, and began to drift once more. There was no moon, and the night would have been dark in any case, but now the fog rendered all things still more obscure. It had also grown much thicker than it had been. At first it was composed of light vapors, which surrounded them on all sides, it is true, but yet did not have that dampness which might have been expected. It was a light, dry fog, and for two or three hours the deck, and rigging, and the clothes of those on board remained quite dry. But now, as the darkness increased, the fog became denser, and was more surcharged with heavy vapors. Soon the deck looked as though it had received a shower of rain, and the clothes of those on board began to be penetrated with the chill damp.

"It's very dark, captain," said Bruce, at last, as the boys stood near the stern.

"Dradful dark," said the captain, thoughtfully.

"Have you really a good idea of where we are?"

"An idee? Why, if I had a chart,--which I haven't, cos I've got it all mapped out in my head,--but if I had one, I could take my finger an pint the exact spot where we are a driftin this blessed minute."

"You're going straight down the bay, I suppose."

"Right--yea, I am; I'm goin straight down; but I hope an trust, an what's more, I believe, I am taking a kine o' cant over nigher the New Brunswick shore."

"How long will we drift?"

"Wal, for about two hours--darsn't drift longer; an besides, don't want to."

"Why not?"

"Darsn't. Thar's a place down thar that every vessel on this here bay steers clear of, an every navigator feels dreadful shy of."

"What place is that?"

"Quaco Ledge," said Captain Corbet, in a solemn tone. "We'll get as near it as is safe this night, an p'aps a leetle nearer; but, then, the water's so calm and still, that it won't make any difference--in fact, it wouldn't matter a great deal if we came up close to it."

"Quaco Ledge?" said Bruce. "I've heard of that."

"Heard of it? I should rayther hope you had. Who hasn't? It's the one great, gen'ral, an standin terror of this dangerous and iron-bound bay. There's no jokin, no nonsense about Quaco Ledge; mind I tell you."

"Where does it lie?" asked Phil, after a pause.

"Wal, do you know whar Quaco settlement is?"

"Yes."

"Wal, Quaco Ledge is nigh about half way between Quaco settlement and Ile Haute, bein a'most in the middle of the bay, an in a terrible dangerous place for coasters, especially in a fog, or in a snow-storm. Many's the vessel that's gone an never heard of, that Quaco Ledge could tell all about, if it could speak. You take a good snowstorm in this Bay of Fundy, an let a schooner get lost in it, an not know whar she is, an if Quaco Ledge don't bring her up all standin, then I'm a Injine."

"Is it a large place?"

"Considerably too large for comfort," said the captain. "They've sounded it, an found the whole shoal about three an a half mile long, an a half a mile broad. It's all kivered over with water at high tide, but at half tide it begins to show its nose, an at low tide you see as pooty a shoal for shipwrecking as you may want; rayther low with pleasant jagged rocks at the nothe-east side, an about a hundred yards or so in extent. I've been nigh on to it in clear weather, but don't want to be within five miles of it in a fog or in a storm. In a thick night like this, I'll pull up before I get close."

"You've never met with any accident there, I suppose."

"Me? No, not me. I always calc'late to give Quaco Ledge the widest kine o' berth. An I hope you'll never know anythin more about that same place than what I'm tellin you now. The knowlege which one has about that place, an places gin-rally of that kine, comes better by hearsay than from actool observation."

Time passed on, and they still drifted, and at length ten o'clock came; but before that time the boys had gone below, and retired for the night. Shortly after, the rattle of the chains waked them all, and informed them that the Antelope had anchored once more.

After this they all fell asleep.

IV.

In Clouds and Darkness.--A terrible Warning.--Nearly run down.--A lively
Place.--Bart encounters an old Acquaintance.--Launched into the Deep.--
Through the Country.--The Swift Tide.--The lost Boy.

The boys had not been asleep for more than two hours, when they were
awakened by an uproar on deck, and rousing themselves from sleep, they
heard the rattle of the chains and the crank of the windlass. As their night
attire was singularly simple, and consisted largely of the dress which they
wore by day, being the same, in fact, with the exception of the hat, it was not long
before they were up on deck, and making inquiries as to the unusual noise. That the
anchor was being hoisted they already knew, but why it was they did not.

"Wal," said Captain Corbet, "thar's a good sou-wester started up, an as I had
a few winks o' sleep, I jest thought I'd try to push on up the bay, an get as far as I
could. If I'd ben in any other place than this, I wouldn't hev minded, but I'd hev
taken my snooze out; but I'm too near Quaco Ledge by a good sight, an would rayther get further off. The sou-wester'll take us up a considerable distance, an if it
holds on till arter the tide turns, I ask no more."

Soon the anchor was up, and the Antelope spread her sails, and catching the
sou-wester, dashed through the water like a thing of life.

"We're going along at a great rate, captain," said Bart.

"Beggin your pardon, young sir, we're not doin much. The tide here runs four
knots agin us--dead, an the wind can't take us more'n six, which leaves a balance
to our favor of two knots an hour, an that is our present rate of progression. You
see, at that rate we won't gain more'n four or five miles before the turn o' tide. After that, we'll go faster without any wind than we do now with a wind. O, there's
nothin like navigatin the Bay o' Fundy to make a man feel contempt for the wind.

Give me tides an anchors, I say, an I'll push along."

The wind was blowing fresh, and the sea was rising, yet the fog seemed thicker than ever. The boys thought that the wind might blow the fog away, and hinted this to the captain.

His only response was a long and emphatic whistle.

"Whe-e-e-ew! what! Blow the fog away? This wind? Why, this wind brings the fog. The sou-wester is the one wind that seafarin men dread in the Bay of Fundy. About the wust kine of a storm is that thar very identical wind blowin in these here very identical waters."

Captain Corbet's words were confirmed by the appearance of sea and sky. Outside was the very blackness of darkness. Nothing whatever was visible. Sea and sky were alike hidden from view. The waves were rising, and though they were not yet of any size, still they made noise enough to suggest the idea of a considerable storm, and the wind, as it whistled through the rigging, carried in its sound a menace which would have been altogether wanting in a bright night. The boys all felt convinced that a storm was rising, and looked forward to a dismal experience of the pangs of seasickness. To fight this off now became their chief aim, and with this intention they all hurried below once more to their beds.

But the water was not rough, the motion of the schooner was gentle, and though there was much noise above, yet they did not notice any approach of the dreaded sea-sickness, and so in a short time they all fell asleep once more.

But they were destined to have further interruptions. The interruption came this time in a loud cry from Solomon, which waked them all at once.

"Get up, chil'en! get up! It's all over!"

"What, what!" cried the boys; "what's the matter?" and springing up in the first moment of alarm, they stood listening.

As they stood, there came to their ears the roaring of the wind through the rigging, the flapping of the sails, the dashing and roaring of the waters, in the midst of which there came also a shrill, penetrating sound, which seemed almost overhead--the sound of some steam whistle.

"Dar, dar!" cried Solomon, in a tone of deadly fear. "It's a comin! I knowed it. We're all lost an gone. It's a steamer. We're all run down an drownded."

Without a word of response, the boys once more clambered on deck. All was as dark as before, the fog as thick, the scene around as impenetrable, the wind as strong. From a distance there came over the water, as they listened, the rapid beat of a steamboat's paddles, and soon there arose again the long, shrill yell of the steam whistle. They looked all around, but saw no sign of any steamer; nor could they tell exactly in which direction the sound arose. One thought it came from one side, another thought it came from the opposite quarter, while the others differed from these. As for Captain Corbet, he said nothing, while the boys were expressing their opinions loudly and confidently.

At last Bart appealed to Captain Corbet.

"Where is the steamer?"

"Down thar," said the captain, waving his hand over the stern.

"What steamer is it? the revenue steamer?"

"Not her. That revenoo steamer is up to Windsor by this time. No; this is the St. John steamer coming up the bay, an I ony wish she'd take us an give us a tow up."

"She seems to be close by."

"She is close by."

"Isn't there some danger that we'll be run down?"

As those words were spoken, another yell, louder, shriller, and nearer than before, burst upon their ears. It seemed to be close astern. The beat of the paddles was also near them.

"Pooty close!" said the captain.

"Isn't there some danger that we'll be run down?"

To this question, thus anxiously repeated, the captain answered slowly,--

"Wal, thar may be, an then again thar mayn't. Ef a man tries to dodge every possible danger in life, he'll have a precious hard time of it. Why, men air killed in walkin the streets, or knocked over by sun-strokes, as well as run down at sea. So what air we to do? Do? Why, I jest do what I've allus ben a doin; I jest keep right straight on my own course, and mind my own biz. Ten chances to one they'll never come nigh us. I've heard steamers howlin round me like all possessed, but I've never ben run down yet, an I ain't goin to be at my time o' life. I don't blieve you'll see a sign o' that thar steamer. You'll only hear her yellin--that's all."

As he spoke another yell sounded.

"She's a passin us, over thar," said the captain, waving his hand over the side. "Her whistle'll contenoo fainter till it stops. So you better go below and take your sleep out."

The boys waited a little longer, and hearing the next whistle sounding fainter, as Captain Corbet said, they followed his advice, and were soon asleep, as before.

This time there was no further interruption, and they did not wake till about eight in the morning, when they were summoned to breakfast by Solomon.

On reaching the deck and looking around, a cry of joy went forth from all. The fog was no longer to be seen, no longer did there extend around them the wall of gloomy gray, shutting out all things with its misty folds. No longer was the broad bay visible. They found themselves now in a wide river, whose muddy waters bore them slowly along. On one side was a shore, close by them, well wooded in some places, and in others well cultivated, while on the other side was another shore, equally fertile, extending far along.

"Here we air," cried Captain Corbet. "That wind served us well. We've had a fust-rate run. I calc'lated we'd be three or four days, but instead of that we've walked over in twenty-four hours. Good agin!"

"Will we be able to land at Moncton soon?"

"Wal, no; not till the next tide."

"Why not?"

"Wal, this tide won't last long enough to carry us up thar, an so we'll have to wait here. This is the best place thar is."

"What place is this?"

"Hillsborough."

"Hillsborough?"

"Yes. Do you see that thar pint?" and Captain Corbet waved his arm towards a high, well-wooded promontory that jutted out into the river.

"Yes."

"Wal, I'm goin in behind that, and I'll wait thar till the tide turns. We'll get up to Moncton some time before evenin."

In a few minutes the Antelope was heading towards the promontory; and soon she passed it, and advanced towards the shore. On passing the promontory a sight appeared which at once attracted the whole attention of the boys.

Immediately in front of them, in the sheltered place which was formed by the promontory, was a little settlement, and on the bank of the river was a ship-yard. Here there arose the stately outline of a large ship. Her lower masts were in, she was decorated with flags and streamers, and a large crowd was assembled in the yard around her.

"There's going to be a launch!" cried Bart, to whom a scene like this was familiar.

"A launch!" cried Bruce. "Hurrah! We'll be able to see it. I've never seen one in my life. Now's the time."

"Can't we get ashore?" said Arthur.

"Of course," said Phil; "and perhaps they'll let us go on board and be launched in her."

The very mention of such a thing increased the general excitement. Captain Corbet was at once appealed to.

"O, thar's lots of time," said he. "Tain't quite high tide yet. You'll have time to get ashore before she moves. Hullo, Wade! Whar's that oar?"

The boys were all full of the wildest excitement, in the midst of which Solomon appeared with the announcement that breakfast was waiting.

To which Bart replied,--

"O, bother breakfast!"

"I don't want any," said Bruce.

"I have no appetite," said Arthur.

"Nor I," said Pat.

"I want to be on board that ship," said Phil.

"We can easily eat breakfast afterwards," said Tom.

At this manifest neglect of his cooking, poor Solomon looked quite heart-broken; but Captain Corbet told him that he might bring the things ashore, and this in some measure assuaged his grief.

It did not take long to get ready. The oar was flung on board the boat, which had thus far been floating behind the schooner; and though the boat had a little too much water on board to be comfortable, yet no complaints were made, and in a few minutes they were landed.

"How much time have we yet?" asked Bart, "before high tide?"

"O, you've got fifteen or twenty minutes," said Captain Corbet.

"Hurrah, boys! Come along," said Bart; and leading the way, he went straight to the office.

As he approached it he uttered suddenly a cry of joy.

"What's the matter, Bart?"

Bart said nothing, but hurried forward, and the astonished boys saw him shaking hands very vigorously with a gentleman who seemed like the chief man on the place. He was an old acquaintance, evidently. In a few minutes all was explained. As the boys came up, Bart introduced them as his friends, and they were all warmly greeted; after which the gentleman said,--

"Why, what a crowd of you there is! Follow me, now. There's plenty of room for you, I imagine, in a ship of fifteen hundred tons; and you've just come in time."

With these words he hurried off, followed by all the boys. He led the way up an inclined plane which ran up to the bows of the ship, and on reaching this place they went along a staging, and finally, coming to a ladder, they clambered up, and found themselves on the deck of the ship.

"I must leave you now, Bart, my boy," said the gentleman; "you go to the quarter-deck and take care of yourselves. I must go down again."

"Who in the world is he, Bart?" asked the boys, as they all stood on the quarter-deck.

"Was there ever such luck!" cried Bart, joyously. "This is the ship Sylph, and that is Mr. Watson, and he has built this ship for my father. Isn't it odd that we should come to this place at this particular time?"

"Why, it's as good as a play."

"Of course it is. I've known Mr. Watson all my life, and he's one of the best men I ever met with. He was as glad to see me as I was to see him."

But now the boys stopped talking, for the scene around them began to grow exciting. In front of them was the settlement, and in the yard below was a crowd who had assembled to see the launch. Behind them was the broad expanse of the Petitcodiac River, beyond which lay the opposite shore, which went back till it terminated in wooded hills. Overhead arose the masts, adorned with a hundred flags and streamers. The deck showed a steep slope from bow to stern. But the scene around was nothing, compared with the excitement of suspense, and expectation.

In a few minutes the hammers were to sound. In a few minutes the mighty fabric on which they were standing would move, and take its plunge into the water.

The suspense made them hold their breath, and wait in perfect silence.

Around them were a few men, who were talking in a commonplace way. They were accustomed to launches, and an incident like this was as nothing in their lives, though to the boys it was sufficient to make their hearts throb violently, and deprive them of the power of speech.

A few minutes passed.

"We ought to start soon," said Bart, in a whisper; for there was something in the scene which made them feel grave and solemn.

The other boys nodded in silence.

A few minutes more passed.

Then there arose a cry.

And then suddenly there came to their excited ears the rattle of a hundred hammers. Stroke after stroke, in quick succession, was dealt upon the wedges, which thus raised the vast structure from her resting-place. For a moment she stood motionless, and then--

Then with a slow motion, at first scarce perceptible, but which every instant grew quicker, she moved down her ways, and plunged like lightning into the water. The stern sank deep, then rose, and then the ship darted through the water across the river. Then suddenly the anchor was let go, and with the loud, sharp rattle of chains, rushed to the bed of the river. With a slight jerk the ship stopped.

The launch was over.

A boat now came from the shore, bringing the builder, Mr. Watson; and at the same time a steamer appeared, rounding a point up the river, and approaching them.

"Do you want to go to St. John, Bart?"

"Not just yet, sir," said Bart.

"Because if you do you can go down in the ship. The steamer is going to take her in tow at once. But if you don't want to go, you may go ashore in the boat. I'm sorry I can't stay here to show you the country, my boy; but I have to go down in the ship, and at once, for we can't lie here in the river, unless we want to be left high and dry at low tide. So good by. Go to the house. Mrs. Watson'll make you comfortable as long as you like; and if you want to take a drive you may consider my horses your own."

With these words he shook hands with all the boys for good by, and after seeing them safely on board the boat, he waited for the steamer which was to tow the Sylph down the bay. The boys then were rowed ashore. By the time they landed, the steamer had reached the ship, a stout cable was passed on board and secured, her anchor was weighed, and then, borne on by steam, and by the tide, too, which had already turned, the Sylph, in tow of the steamer, passed down the river, and was soon out of sight.

Bart then went to see Mrs. Watson, with all the boys. That lady, like her husband, was an old acquaintance, and in the true spirit of hospitality insisted on every one of them taking up their abode with her for an indefinite period. Finding that they could not do this, she prepared for them a bounteous breakfast, and then persuaded them to go off for a drive through the country. This invitation they eagerly accepted.

Before starting, they encountered Captain Corbet.

"Don't hurry back, boys," said he, "unless you very pertik'l'ry wish to go up to Moncton by the arternoon tide. Don't mind me. I got several things to occoopy me here."

"What time could we start up river?"

"Not before four."

"O, we'll be back by that time."

"Wal. Ony don't hurry back unless you like. I got to buy some ship-bread, an I got to fix some things about the boat. It'll take some time; so jest do as you like."

Being thus left to their own devices, and feeling quite unlimited with regard to time, the boys started off in two wagons, and took a long drive through the country. The time passed quickly, and they enjoyed themselves so much that they did not get back until dusk.

"It's too late now, boys, to go up," said the captain, as he met them on their return. "We've got to wait till next tide. It's nearly high tide now."

"All right, captain; it'll do just as well to go up river to-night."

"Amen," said the captain.

But now Mrs. Watson insisted on their staying to tea, and so it happened that it was after nine o'clock before they were ready to go on board the Antelope. Going down to the shore, they found the boat ready, with some articles which Captain Corbet had procured.

"I've been fixing the gunwales," said he; "an here's a box of pilot-bread. We were gettin out of provisions, an I've got in a supply, an I've bought a bit of an old sail that'll do for a jib. I'm afeard thar won't be room for all of us. Some of you better stay ashore, an I'll come back."

"I'll wait," said Bart, taking his seat on a stick of timber.

"An I'll wait, too," said Bruce.

The other boys objected in a friendly way, but Bart and Bruce insisted on waiting, and so the boat at length started, leaving them behind.

In a short time it reached the schooner.

Captain Corbet secured the boat's painter to the stem, and threw the oar on board.

"Now, boys, one of you stay in the boat, an pass up them things to me--will you?"

"All right," said Tom. "I'll pass them up."

On this Captain Corbet got on board the schooner, followed by Arthur, and Phil, and Pat. Tom waited in the boat.

"Now," said Captain Corbet, "lift up that thar box of pilot-bread fust. 'Tain't heavy. We'll get these things out afore we go ashore for the others."

"All right," said Tom.

He stooped, and took the box of biscuit in his arms.

At that time the tide was running down very fast, and the boat, caught by the tide, was forced out from the schooner with such a pressure that the rope was stiffened out straight.

Tom made one step forward. The next instant he fell down in the bottom of the boat, and those on board of the schooner who were looking at him saw, to their horror, that the boat was sweeping away with the tide, far down the river.

V.

A Cry of Horror.--What shall we do?--Hard and fast.--Bart and Bruce.--
Gloomy Intelligence.--The Promontory.--The Bore of the Petitcodiac.--A
Night of Misery.--A mournful Waking.--Taking Counsel.

A cry of horror escaped those on board, and for some time they stood silent
in utter dismay.

"The rope wasn't tied," groaned Arthur.

"Yes, it was," said Captain Corbet; "it bruk; catch me not tyin it. It bruk;
see here!" and he held up in the dim light the end of the rope which still was fastened to the schooner. "I didn't know it was rotten," he moaned; "'tain't over ten
year old, that bit o' rope, an I've had it an used it a thousand times without its ever
thinkin o' breakin."

"What can we do?" cried Arthur. "We must do something to save him."

Captain Corbet shook his head.

"We've got no boat," said he.

"Boat! Who wants a boat?"

"What can we do without a boat?"

"Why, up anchor, and go after him with the schooner."

"The schooner's hard and fast," said Captain Corbet, mournfully.

"Hard and fast?"

"Yes; don't you notice how she leans? It's only a little, but that's a sign that her
keel's in the mud."

"I don't believe it! I won't believe it!" cried Arthur. "Come, boys, up with the
anchor."

As the boys rushed to the windlass, Captain Corbet went there, too, followed
by the mate, and they worked at it for some time, until at last the anchor rose to

the surface.

But the Antelope did not move. On the contrary, a still greater list to one side, which was now unmistakable, showed that the captain was right, and that she was actually, as he said, hard and fast. This fact had to be recognized, but Arthur would not be satisfied until he had actually seen the anchor, and then he knew that the vessel was really aground.

"Do you mean to say," he cried at last, "that there is nothing to be done?"

"I don't see," said Captain Corbet, "what thar is to be done till the schewner muves."

"When will that be?"

"Not till to-morrow mornin."

"How early?"

"Not before eight o'clock."

"Eight o'clock!" cried Arthur, in horror.

"Yes, eight o'clock. You see we had to come in pooty nigh to the shore, an it'll be eight o'clock before we're floated."

"And what'll become of poor Tom?" groaned Arthur.

"Wal," said the captain, "don't look on the wust. He may get ashore."

"He has no oar. The oar was thrown aboard of the schooner."

"Still he may be carried ashore."

"Is there any chance?"

"Wal, not much, to tell the truth. Thar's no use of buo-oyin of ourselves up with false hopes; not a mite. Thar's a better chance of his bein picked up. That thar's likely now, an not unnatooral. Let's all don't give up. If thar's no fog outside, I'd say his chances air good."

"But it may be foggy."

"Then, in that case, he'll have to drift a while--sure."

"Then there's no hope."

"Hope? Who's a sayin thar's no hope? Why, look here; he's got provisions on board, an needn't starve; so if he does float for a day or two, whar's the harm? He's sure to be picked up eventooally."

At this moment their conversation was interrupted by a loud call from the promontory. It was the voice of Bruce.

While these events had been taking place on board the schooner, Bruce and Bart had been ashore. At first they had waited patiently for the return of the boat, but finally they wondered at her delay. They had called, but the schooner was too far off to hear them. Then they waited for what seemed to them an unreasonably long time, wondering what kept the boat, until at length Bruce determined to try and get nearer. Burt was to stay behind in case the boat should come ashore in his absence. With this in view he had walked down the promontory until he had reached the extreme point, and there he found himself within easy hail of the Antelope.

"Schooner ahoy!" he cried.

"A-ho-o-o-o-y!" cried Captain Corbet.

"Why don't you come and take us off?" he cried.

After this there was silence for some time. At last Captain Corbet shouted out,--

"The boat's lost."

"What!"

"The boat's adrift."

Captain Corbet said nothing about Tom, from a desire to spare him for the present. So Bruce thought that the empty boat had drifted off, and as he had been prepared to hear of some accident, he was not much surprised.

But he was not to remain long in ignorance. In a few moments he heard Arthur's voice.

"Bruce!"

"Hallo!"

"The boat's gone."

"All right."

"TOM'S ADRIFT IN HER!"

"What!" shouted Bruce.

"TOM'S ADRIFT IN HER."

At this appalling intelligence Bruce's heart seemed to stop beating.

"How long?" he dried, after a pause.

"Half an hour," cried Arthur.

"Why don't you go after him?" cried Bruce again.

"We're aground," cried Arthur.

The whole situation was now explained, and Bruce was filled with his own share of that dismay which prevailed on board of the schooner; for a long time nothing more was said. At length Arthur's voice sounded again.

"Bruce!"

"Hallo!"

"Get a boat, and come aboard as soon as you can after the tide turns."

"All right. How early will the tide suit?"

"Eight o'clock."

"Not before?"

"No."

After this nothing more was said. Bruce could see for himself that the tide was falling, and that he would have to wait for the returning tide before a boat could be launched. He waited for some time, full of despair, and hesitating to return to Bart with his mournful intelligence. At length he turned, and walked slowly back to his friend.

"Well, Bruce?" asked Bart, who by this time was sure that some accident had happened.

"The boat's adrift."

"The boat!"

"Yes; and what's worse, poor Tom!"

"Tom!" cried Bart, in a horror of apprehension.

"Yes, Tom's adrift in her."

At this Bart said not a word, but stood for some time staring at Bruce in utter dismay.

A few words served to explain to Bart the situation of the schooner, and the need of getting a boat.

"Well," said Bart, "we'd better see about it at once. It's eleven o'clock, but we'll find some people up; if not, we'll knock them up."

And with these words the two lads walked up from the river bank.

On reaching the houses attached to the shipyard, they found that most of the people were up. There was a good deal of singing and laughter going on, which the boys interpreted to arise from a desire to celebrate the launching of the ship. They went first to Mrs. Watson's house, where they found that good lady up. She listened to their story with undisguised uneasiness, and afterwards called in a number of men, to whom she told the sad news. These men listened to it with very serious faces.

"It's no joke," said one, shaking his head. The others said nothing, but their faces spoke volumes.

"What had we better do?" asked Bruce.

"Of course ye'll be off as soon as ye can get off," said one.

"The lad might have a chance," said another. "The return tide may drift him back, but he may be carried too far down for that."

"He'll be carried below Cape Chignecto unless he gets to the land," said another.

"Isn't there a chance that he'll be picked up?" asked Bart.

The man to whom he spoke shook his head.

"There's a deal of fog in the bay this night," said he.

"Fog? Why, it's clear enough here."

"So it is; but this place and the Bay of Fundy are two different things."

"A regular sou-wester out there," said another man.

"An a pooty heavy sea by this time," said another.

And in this way they all contributed to increase the anxiety of the two boys, until at last scarce a ray of hope was left.

"You'd better prepare yourselves for the worst," said one of the men. "If he had an oar he would be all right; but, as it is--well, I don't care about sayin what I think."

"O, you're all too despondent," said Mrs. Watson. "What is the use of looking on the dark side? Come, Bart, cheer up. I'll look on the bright side. Hope for the best. Set out on the search with hope, and a good heart. I'm confident that he will be safe. You will pick him up yourselves, or else you will hear of his escape somewhere. I remember two men, a few years ago, that went adrift and were saved."

"Ay," said one of the men, "I mind that well. They were Tom Furlong and Jim Spencer. But that there boat was a good-sized fishing boat; an such a boat as that might ride out a gale."

"Nonsense," said Mrs. Watson. "You're all a set of confirmed croakers. Why,

Bart, you've read enough shipwreck books to know that little boats have floated in safety for hundreds of miles. So hope for the best; don't be down-hearted. I'll send two or three men down now to get the boat ready for you. You can't do anything till the morning, you know. Won't you stay here? You had better go to bed at once."

But Bart and Bruce could not think of bed.

"Well, come back any time, and a bed will be ready for you," said Mrs. Watson. "If you want to see about the boat now, the men are ready to go with you."

With those words she led the way out to the kitchen, where a couple of men were waiting. Bart and Bruce followed them down to a boat-house on the river bank, and saw the boat there which Mrs. Watson had offered them. This boat could be launched at any time, and as there was nothing more to be done, the boys strolled disconsolately about, and finally went to the end of the promontory, and spent a long time looking out over the water, and conversing sadly about poor Tom's chances.

There they sat late in the night, until midnight came, and so on into the morning. At last the scene before them changed from a sheet of water to a broad expanse of mud. The water had all retired, leaving the bed of the river exposed.

Of all the rivers that flow into the Bay of Fundy none is more remarkable than the Petitcodiac. At high tide it is full--a mighty stream; at low tide it is empty--a channel of mud forty miles long; and the intervening periods are marked by the furious flow of ascending or descending waters.

And now, as the boys sat there looking out upon the expanse of mud before them, they became aware of a dull, low, booming sound, that came up from a far distant point, and seemed like the voice of many waters sounding from the storm-vexed bay outside. There was no moon, but the light was sufficient to enable them to see the exposed riverbed, far over to the shadowy outline of the opposite shore. Here, where in the morning a mighty ship had floated, nothing could now float; but the noise that broke upon their ears told them of the return of the waters that now were about to pour onward with resistless might into the empty channel, and send successive waves far along into the heart of the land.

"What is that noise?" asked Bruce. "It grows louder and louder."

"That," said bart, "is the Bore of the Petitcodiac."

"Have you ever seen it?"

"Never. I've heard of it often, but have never seen it."

But their words were interrupted now by the deepening thunder of the approaching waters. Towards the quarter whence the sound arose they turned their heads involuntarily. At first they could see nothing through the gloom of night; but at length, as they strained their eyes looking down the river, they saw in the distance a faint, white, phosphorescent gleam, and as it appeared the roar grew louder, and rounder, and more all-pervading. On it came, carrying with it the hoarse cadence of some vast surf flung ashore from the workings of a distant storm, or the thunder of some mighty cataract tumbling over a rocky precipice.

And now, as they looked, the white, phosphorescent glow grew brighter, and then whiter, like snow; every minute it approached nearer, until at last, full before them and beneath them, there rolled a giant wave, extending across the bed of the river, crescent-shaped, with its convex side advancing forwards, and its ends following after within short distance from the shore. The great wave rolled on, one mass of snow-white foam, behind which gleamed a broad line of phosphorescent lustre from the agitated waters, which, in the gloom of night, had a certain baleful radiance. As it passed on its path, the roar came up more majestically from the foremost wave; and behind that came the roar of other billows that followed in its wake. By daylight the scene would have been grand and impressive; but now, amid the gloom, the grandeur became indescribable. The force of those mighty waters seemed indeed resistless, and it was with a feeling of relief that the boys reflected that the schooner was out of the reach of its sweep. Its passage was swift, and soon it had passed beyond them; and afar up the river, long after it had passed from sight, they heard the distant thunder of its mighty march.

By the time the wave had passed, the boys found themselves excessively weary with their long wakefulness.

"Bart, my boy," said Bruce, "we must get some rest, or we won't be worth anything to-morrow. What do you say? Shall we go back to Mrs. Watson's?"

"It's too late--isn't it?"

"Well, it's pretty late, no doubt. I dare say it's half past two; but that's all the more reason why we should go to bed."

"Well."

"What do you say? Do you think we had better disturb Mrs. Watson, or not?"

"O, no; let's go into the barn, and lie down in the hay."

"Very well. Hay makes a capital bed. For my part, I could sleep on stones."

"So could I."

"I'm determined to hope for the best about Tom," said Bruce, rising and walking off, followed by Bart. "Mrs. Watson was right. There's no use letting ourselves be downcast by a lot of croakers--is there?"

"No," said Bart.

The boys then walked on, and in a few minutes reached the ship-yard.

Here a man came up to them.

"We've been looking for you everywhere," said the man. "Mrs. Watson is anxious about you."

"Mrs. Watson?"

"Yes. She won't go to bed till you get back to the house. There's another man out for you, up the river."

"O, I'm sorry we have given you all so much trouble," said Bart; "but we didn't think that anybody would bother themselves about us."

"Well, you don't know Mrs. Watson that's all," said the man, walking along with them. "She's been a worrytin herself to death about you; and the sooner she sees you, the better for her and for you."

On reaching the house the boys were received by Mrs. Watson. One look at her was enough to show them that the man's account of her was true. Her face was pale, her manner was agitated, and her voice trembled as she spoke to them, and asked them where they had been.

Bart expressed sorrow at having been the cause of so much trouble, and assured her he thought that she had gone to bed.

"No," said she; "I've been too excited and agitated about your friend and about you. But I'm glad that you've been found; and as it's too late to talk now, you had better go to bed, and try to sleep."

With these words she gently urged them to their bedroom; and the boys, utterly worn out, did not attempt to withstand her. They went to bed, and scarcely had their heads touched the pillows before they were fast asleep.

Meanwhile the boys on board the Antelope had been no less anxious; and, unable to sleep, they had talked solemnly with each other over the possible fate of poor Tom. Chafing from their forced inaction, they looked impatiently upon the ebbing water, which was leaving them aground, when they were longing to be floating on its bosom after their friend, and could scarcely endure the thought of the suspense to which they would be condemned while waiting for the following morning.

Captain Corbet also was no less anxious, though much less agitated. He acknowledged, with pain, that it was all his fault, but, appealed to all the boys, one by one, asking them how he should know that the rope was rotten. He informed them that the rope was an old favorite of his, and that he would have willingly risked his life on it. He blamed himself chiefly, however, for not staying in the boat himself, instead of leaving Tom in it. To all his remarks the boys said but little, and contented themselves with putting questions to him about the coast, the tides, the wind, the currents, and the fog.

The boys on board went to sleep about one o'clock, and waked at sunrise. Then they watched the shore wistfully, and wondered why Bart and Bruce did not make their appearance. But Bart and Bruce, worn out by their long watch, did not wake till nearly eight o'clock. Then they hastily dressed themselves, and after a very hurried breakfast they bade good by to good Mrs. Watson.

"I shall be dreadfully anxious about that poor boy," said she, sadly. "Promise me to telegraph as soon as you can about the result."

Bart promised.

Then they hurried down to the beach. The tide was yet a considerable distance out; but a half dozen stout fellows, whose sympathies were fully enlisted in their favor, shoved the boat down over the mud, and launched her.

Then Bart and Bruce took the oars, and soon reached the schooner, where the boys awaited their arrival in mournful silence.

VI.

Tom adrift.--The receding Shores.--The Paddle.--The Roar of Surf--The Fog Horn.--The Thunder of the unseen Breakers.--A Horror of great Darkness.--Adrift in Fog and Night.

When the boat in which Tom was darted down the stream, he at first felt paralyzed by utter terror; but at length rousing himself, he looked around. As the boat drifted on, his first impulse was to stop it; and in order to do this it was necessary to find an oar. The oar which Captain Corbet had used to scull the boat to the schooner had been thrown on board of the latter, so that the contents of the boat might be passed up the more conveniently. Tom knew this, but he thought that there might be another oar on board. A brief examination sufficed to show him that there was nothing of the kind. A few loose articles lay at the bottom; over these was the sail which Captain Corbet had bought in the ship-yard, and on this was the box of pilot-bread. That was all. There was not a sign of an oar, or a board, or anything of the kind.

No sooner had he found out this than he tried to tear off one of the seats of the boat, in the hope of using this as a paddle. But the seats were too firmly fixed to be loosened by his hands, and, after a few frantic but ineffectual efforts, he gave up the attempt.

But he could not so quickly give up his efforts to save himself. There was the box of biscuit yet. Taking his knife from his pocket, he succeeded in detaching the cover of the box, and then, using this as a paddle, he sought with frantic efforts to force the boat nearer to the shore. But the tide was running very swiftly, and the cover was only a small bit of board, so that his efforts seemed to have but little result. He did indeed succeed in turning the boat's head around; but this act, which was not accomplished without the severest labor, did not seem to bring her nearer to the shore to any perceptible extent. What he sought to do was to achieve some definite motion to the boat, which might drag her out of the grasp of the swift current; but that was the very thing which he could not do, for so strong was that grasp, and so swift was that current, that even an oar would have scarcely accomplished what he wished. The bit of board, small, and thin, and frail, and wielded with great difficulty and at a fearful disadvantage, was almost useless.

But, though he saw that he was accomplishing little or nothing, he could not bring himself to give up this work. It seemed his only hope; and so he labored on, sometimes working with both hands at the board, sometimes plying his frail paddle with one hand, and using the other hand at a vain endeavor to paddle in the water. In his desperation he kept on, and thought that if he gained ever so little, still, by keeping hard at work, the little that he gained might finally tell upon the direction of the boat--at any rate, so long as it might be in the river. He knew that the river ran for some miles yet, and that some time still remained before he would reach the bay.

Thus Tom toiled on, half despairing, and nearly fainting with his frenzied exertion, yet still refusing to give up, but plying his frail paddle until his nerveless arms seemed like weights of lead, and could scarce carry the board through the water. But the result, which at the outset, and in the very freshness of his strength, had been but trifling, grew less and less against the advance of his own weakness and the force of that tremendous tide, until at last his feeble exertions ceased to have any appreciable effect whatever.

There was no moon, but it was light enough for him to see the shores--to see that he was in the very centre of that rapid current, and to perceive that he was being borne past those dim shores with fearful velocity. The sight filled him with despair, but his arms gained a fresh energy, from time to time, out of the very desperation of his soul. He was one of those natures which are too obstinate to give up even in the presence of despair itself; and which, even when hope is dead, still forces hope to linger, and struggles on while a particle of life or of strength remains. So, as he toiled on, and fought on, against this fate which had suddenly fixed itself upon him, he saw the shores on either side recede, and knew that every passing moment was bearing him on to a wide, a cruel, and a perilous sea. He took one hasty glance behind him, and saw what he knew to be the mouth of the river close at hand; and beyond this a waste of waters was hidden in the gloom of night. The sight lent new energy to his fainting limbs. He called aloud for help. Shriek after shriek burst from him, and rang wildly, piercingly, thrillingly upon the air of night. But those despairing shrieks came to no human ear, and met with no response. They died away upon the wind and the waters; and the fierce tide, with swifter flow, bore him onward.

The last headland swept past him; the river and the river bank were now lost to him. Around him the expanse of water grew darker, and broader, and more terrible. Above him the stars glimmered more faintly from the sky. But the very habit of exertion still remained, and his faint plunges still dipped the little board into the water; and a vague idea of saving himself was still uppermost in his mind. Deep down in that stout heart of his was a desperate resolution never to give up while strength lasted; and well he sustained that determination. Over him the mist came floating, borne along by the wind which sighed around him; and that mist gradually overspread the scene upon which his straining eyes were fastened. It shut out the overhanging sky. It extinguished the glimmering stars. It threw a veil over the receding shores. It drew its folds around him closer and closer, until at last everything was hidden from view. Closer and still closer came the mist, and thicker and ever thicker grew its dense folds, until at last even the water, into which he still thrust his frail paddle, was invisible. At length his strength failed utterly. His hands refused any longer to perform their duty. The strong, indomitable will remained, but the power of performing the dictates of that will was gone. He fell back upon the sail that lay in the bottom of the boat, and the board fell from his hands.

And now there gathered around the prostrate figure of the lost boy all the terrors of thickest darkness. The fog came, together with the night, shrouding all things from view, and he was floating over a wide sea, with an impenetrable wall of thickest darkness closing him in on all sides.

As he thus lay there helpless, he had leisure to reflect for the first time upon the full bitterness of his situation. Adrift in the fog, and in the night, and borne onward swiftly down into the Bay of Fundy--that was his position. And what could he do? That was the one question which he could not answer. Giving way now to the rush of despair, he lay for some time motionless, feeling the rocking of the waves, and the breath of the wind, and the chill damp of the fog, yet unable to do anything against these enemies. For nearly an hour he lay thus inactive, and at the end of that time his lost energies began to return. He rose and looked around. The scene had not changed at all; in fact, there was no scene to change. There was nothing but black darkness all around. Suddenly something knocked against the boat. He reached out his hand, and touched a piece of wood, which the next instant slipped from his grasp. But the disappointment was not without its alleviation, for he thought that he might come across some bits of drift wood, with which he could do something, perhaps, for his escape. And so buoyant was his soul, and so obstinate his courage, that this little incident of itself served to revive his faculties. He went to the stern of the boat, and sitting there, he tried to think upon what might be best to be done.

What could be done in such a situation? He could swim, but of what avail was that? In what direction could he swim, or what progress could he make, with such a tide? As to paddling, he thought of that no more; paddling was exhausted, and his board was useless. Nothing remained, apparently, but inaction. Inaction was indeed hard, and it was the worst condition in which he could be placed, for in such a state the mind always preys upon itself; in such a state trouble is always magnified, and the slow time passes more slowly. Yet to this inaction he found himself doomed.

He floated on now for hours, motionless and filled with despair, listening to the dash of the waves, which were the only sounds that came to his ears. And so it came to pass, in process of time, that by incessant attention to these monotonous sounds, they ceased to be altogether monotonous, but seemed to assume various cadences and intonations. His sharpened ears learned at last to distinguish between the dash of large waves and the plash of small ones, the sighing of the wind, the pressure of the waters against the boat's bows, and the ripple of eddies under its stern. Worn out by excitement and fatigue, he lay motionless, listening to sounds like these, and taking in them a mournful interest, when suddenly, in the midst of them, his ears caught a different cadence. It was a long, measured sound, not an unfamiliar one, but one which he had often heard--the gathering sound which breaks out, rising and accumulating upon the ear, as the long line of surf falls upon some rocky shore. He knew at once what this was, and understood by it that he was near some shore; but what shore it might be he could not know. The sound came up from his right, and therefore might be the New Brunswick coast, if the boat had preserved its proper position. But the position of the boat had been constantly changing as she drifted along, so that it was impossible to tell whether he was drifting stern foremost or bow foremost. The water moved as the boat moved, and there was no means by which to judge. He listened to the surf, therefore, but made no attempt to draw nearer to it. He now knew perfectly well that with his present resources no efforts of his could avail anything, and that his only course would be to wait. Besides, this shore, whatever it was, must be very different, he thought, from the banks of the Petitcodiac. It was, as he thought, an iron-bound shore. And the surf which he heard broke in thunder a mile away, at the foot of giant precipices, which could only offer death to the hapless wretch who might be thrown among them. He lay, therefore, inactive, listening to this rolling surf for hours. At first it grew gradually louder, as though he was approaching it; but afterwards it grew fainter quite as gradually, until at length it could no longer be heard.

During all these lonely hours, one thing afforded a certain consolation, and that was, the discovery that the sea did not grow rougher. The wind that blew was the sou-wester, the dreaded wind of fog and, storm; but on this occasion its strength was not put forth; it blew but moderately, and the water was not very greatly disturbed. The sea tossed the little boat, but was not high enough to dash over her, or to endanger her in any way. None of its spray ever came upon the recumbent form in the boat, nor did any moisture come near him, save that which was deposited by the fog. At first, in his terror, he had counted upon meeting a tempestuous sea; but, as the hours passed, he saw that thus far there had been nothing of the kind, and, if he were destined to be exposed to such a danger, it lay as yet in the future. As long as the wind continued moderate, so long would he toss over the little waves without being endangered in any way. And thus, with all these thoughts, sometimes depressing, at other times rather encouraging, he drifted on.

Hours passed away.

At length his fatigue overpowered him more and more, and as he sat there in the stern, his eyes closed, and his head fell heavily forward. He laid it upon the sail which was in front of him, so as to get an easier position, and was just closing his eyes again, when a sound came to his ears which in an instant drove every thought of sleep and of fatigue away, and made him start up and listen with intense eagerness.

It was the sound of a fog horn, such as is used by coasting vessels, and blown during a fog, at intervals, to give warning of their presence. The sound was a familiar one to a boy who had been brought up on the fog-encircled and fish-haunted shores of Newfoundland; and Tom's hearing, which had been almost hushed in slumber, caught it at once. It was like the voice of a friend calling to him. But for a moment he thought it was only a fancy, or a dream, and he sat listening and quivering with excitement. He waited and listened for some time, and was just about to conclude that it was a dream, when suddenly it came again. There was no mistake this time. It was a fog horn. Some schooner was sailing these waters. O for daylight, and O for clear weather, so that he might see it, and make himself seen! The sound, though clear, was faint, and the schooner was evidently at a considerable distance; but Tom, in his eagerness, did not think of that. He shouted with all his strength. He waited for an answer, and then shouted again. Once more he waited, and listened, and then again and again his screams went forth over the water. But still no response came. At last, after some interval, the fog horn again sounded. Again Tom screamed, and yelled, and uttered every sound that could possibly convey to human ears an idea of his presence, and of his distress.

The sounds of the fog horn, however, did not correspond with his cries. It was blown at regular intervals, which seemed painfully long to Tom, and did not seem to sound as if in answer to him. At first his hope was sustained by the discovery that the sounds were louder, and therefore nearer; but scarcely had he assured himself of this, when he perceived that they were growing fainter again, as though the schooner had approached him, and then sailed away. This discovery only stimulated him to more frantic exertions. He yelled more and more loudly, and was compelled, at last, to cease from pure exhaustion. But even then he did not cease till long after the last notes of the departing fog horn had faintly sounded in his ears.

It was a disappointment bitter indeed, since it came after a reviving hope. What made it all the worse was a fixed idea which he had, that the schooner was no other than the Antelope. He felt confident that she had come at once after him, and was now traversing the waters in search of him, and sounding the horn so as to send it to his ears and get his response. And his response had been given with this result! This was the end of his hopes. He could bear it no longer. The stout heart and the resolute obstinacy which had so long struggled against fate now gave way utterly.

He buried his face in his hands, and burst into a passion of tears.

He wept for a long time, and roused himself, at last, with difficulty, to a dull despair. What was the use of hoping, or thinking, or listening? Hope was useless. It was better to let himself go wherever the waters might take him. He reached out his hand and drew the sail forward, and then settling himself down in the stern of the boat, he again shut his eyes and tried to sleep. But sleep, which a short time before had been so easy, was now difficult. His ears took in once more the different sounds of the sea, and soon became aware of a deeper, drearer sound than any which had hitherto come to him. It was the hoarse roar of a great surf, far more formidable than the one which he had heard before. The tumult and the din grew rapidly louder, and at length became so terrific that he sat upright, and strained his eyes in the direction from which it came. Peering thus through the darkness, he saw the glow of phosphorescent waves wrought out of the strife of many waters; and they threw towards him, amid the darkness, a baleful gleam which fascinated his eyes. A feeling came to him now that all was over. He felt, as though he were being sucked into some vortex, where Death lay in wait for him. He trembled. A prayer started to his lips, and burst from him. Suddenly his boat seemed caught by some resistless force, and jerked to one side; the next instant it rose on some swelling wave, and was shot swiftly forward. Tom closed his eyes, and a thrill of horror passed through every nerve. All at once a rude shock was felt, and the boat shook, and Tom thought he was going down. It seemed like the blow of a rock, and he could think only of the ingulfing waters. But the waters hesitated to claim their prey; the rushing motion ceased; and soon the boat was tossing lightly, as before, over the waves, while the hoarse and thunderous roar of those dread unseen breakers, from which he had been so wondrously saved, arose wrathfully behind, as though they were howling after their escaped victim. A cry of gratitude escaped Tom, and with trembling lips he offered a heart-felt prayer to that divine Power whose mighty hand had just rescued him from a terrible doom.

Tom's agitation had been so great that it was long before he could regain his former calm. At last, however, his trembling subsided. He heard no longer the howling surf. All was calm and quiet. The wind ceased, the boat's motion was less violent, the long-resisted slumber came once more to his eyes. Still his terror kept off sleep, and as his eyes would close, they would every moment open again, and he would start in terror and look around.

At length he saw that the darkness was less profound. Light was coming, and that light was increasing. He could see the dark waters, and the gloomy folds of the enclosing mist became apparent. He gave a heavy sigh, partly of terror at the thought of all that he had gone through, and partly of relief at the approach of light.

Well might he sigh, for this light was the dawn of a new day, and showed him that he had been a whole night upon the waters.

And now he could no longer struggle against sleep. His eyes closed for the last time. His head fell forward on the wet sail.

He was sound asleep.

VII.

Lost in the Fog.--The Shoal and its Rocks.--Is it a Reef?--The Truth.--Hoisting Sail.--A forlorn Hope.--Wild Steering.--Where am I?--Land, ho!

Tom slept for many hours; and when he at length awoke, he was stiffened in every limb, and wet to the skin. It was his constrained position and the heavy fog which had done this. He sat up and looked around with a bewildered air; but it did not take a long time for him to collect his wandering faculties, and arrive at the full recollection of his situation. Gradually it all came before him--the night of horror, the long drift, the frantic struggles, the boom of the surf, the shrill, penetrating tone of the fog horn, his own wild screams for help, the thunder of the breakers, and the grasp of the giant wave; all these, and many more, came back to his mind; and he was all too soon enabled to connect his present situation with the desperate position of the preceding night.

In spite of all these gloomy thoughts, which thus rushed in one accumulated mass over his soul, his first impulse had nothing to do with these things, but was concerned with something very different from useless retrospect, and something far more essential. He found himself ravenously hungry; and his one idea was to satisfy the cravings of his appetite.

He thought at once of the box of biscuit.

The sail which he had pulled forward had very fortunately covered it up, else the contents might have been somewhat damaged. As it was, the upper edges of the biscuits, which had been exposed before being covered by the sail, were somewhat damp and soft, but otherwise they were not harmed; and Tom ate his frugal repast with extreme relish. Satisfying his appetite had the natural effect of cheering his spirits, and led him to reflect with thankfulness on the very fortunate presence of that box of biscuit in the boat. Had it not been for that, how terrible would his situation be! But with that he could afford to entertain hope, and might reasonably expect to endure the hardships of his situation. Strange to say, he was not at all thirsty; which probably arose from the fact that he was wet to the skin.

Immersing one's self in water is often resorted to by shipwrecked mariners, when they cannot get a drink, and with successful results. As for Tom, his whole night had been one long bath, in which he had been exposed to the penetrating effects of the sea air and the fog.

He had no idea whatever of the time. The sun could not be seen, and so thick was the fog that he could not even make out in what part of the sky it might be. He had a general impression, however, that it was midday; and this impression was not very much out of the way. His breakfast refreshed him, and he learned now to attach so much value to his box of biscuit, that his chief desire was to save it from further injury. So he hunted about for the cover, and finding it underneath the other end of the sail, he put it on the box, and then covered it all up. In this position the precious contents of the box were safe.

The hour of the day was a subject of uncertainty, and so was the state of the tide. Whether he was drifting up or down the bay he could not tell for certain. His recollection of the state of the tide at Petitcodiac, was but vague. He reckoned, however, from the ship launch of the preceding day, and then, allowing sufficient time for the difference in the tide, he approximated to a correct conclusion. If it were midday, he thought that the tide would be about half way down on the ebb.

These thoughts, and acts, and calculations took up some time, and he now began to look around him. Suddenly his eye caught sight of something not far away, dimly visible through the mist. It looked like a rock. A farther examination showed him that such was the case. It was a rock, and he was drifting towards it. No sooner had he ascertained this, than all his excitement once more awakened. Trembling from head to foot at this sudden prospect of escape, he started to his feet, and watched most eagerly the progress of the boat. It was drifting nearer to the rock. Soon another appeared, and then another. The rocks were black, and covered with masses of sea-weed, as though they were submerged at high tide. A little nearer, and he saw a gravelly strand lying just beyond the rocks. His excitement grew stronger and stronger, until at last it was quite uncontrollable. He began to fear that he would drift past this place, into the deep water again. He sprang into the bows, and grasping the rope in his hand, stood ready to leap ashore. He saw that he was drawing nearer, and so delayed for a while. Nearer he came and nearer. At length the boat seemed to pass along by the gravelly beach, and move by it as though it would go no nearer. This Tom could not endure. He determined to wait no longer. He sprang.

He sank into the water up to his armpits, but he did not lose his hold of the rope. Clutching this in a convulsive grasp, he regained his foothold, which he had almost lost, and struggled forward. For a few moments he made no headway, for the boat, at the pressure of the current, pulled so hard that he could not drag it nearer. A terrible fear came to him that the rope might break. Fortunately it did not, and, after a short but violent struggle, Tom conquered the resistance of the tide, and pulled the boat slowly towards the shore. He then towed it near to the rocks, dragged its bows up as far as he could, and fastened it securely.

Then he looked around.

A few rocks were near him, about six feet high, jutting out of the gravel; and beyond these were others, which rose out of the water. Most of them were covered with sea-weed. A few sticks of timber were wedged in the interstices of the nearest rocks. As to the rest, he saw only a rocky ledge of small extent, which was surrounded by water. Beyond this nothing was visible but fog.

At first he had thought that this was a beach, but now he began to doubt this. He walked all around, and went into the water on every side, but found no signs of any neighboring shore. The place seemed rather like some isolated ledge. But where was it, and how far away was the shore? If he could only tell that! He stopped, and listened intently; he walked all around, and listened more intently still, in hopes of hearing the sound of some neighboring surf. In vain. Nothing of the kind came to his ears. All was still. The water was not rough, nor was there very much wind. There was only a brisk breeze, which threw up light waves on the surface.

After a time he noticed that the tide was going down, and the area of the ledge was evidently enlarging. This inspired hope, for he thought that perhaps some long shoal might be disclosed by the retreating tide, which might communicate with the main land. For this he now watched intently, and occupied himself with measuring the distance from the rock where his boat was tied. Doing this from time to time, he found that every little while the number of paces between the rock and the water's edge increased. This occupation made the time pass rapidly; and at last Tom found his stopping-place extending over an area of about a hundred yards in length, and half as many in breadth. The rocks at one end had increased in apparent size, and in number; but the ledge itself remained unchanged in its general character.

This, he saw, was its extreme limit, beyond which it did not extend. There was no communication with any shore. There was no more indication now of land than when he had first arrived. This discovery was a gradual one. It had been heralded by many fears and suspicions, so that at last, when it forced itself on his convictions, he was not altogether unprepared. Still, the shock was terrible, and once more poor Tom had to struggle with his despair--a despair, too, that was all the more profound from the hopes that he had been entertaining. He found, at length, in addition to this, that the tide was rising, that it was advancing towards his resting-place, and that it would, no doubt, overflow it all before long. It had been half tide when he landed, and but a little was uncovered; at full tide he saw that it would all be covered up by the water,--sea weed, rocks, and all,--and concealed from human eye.

In the midst of these painful discoveries there suddenly occurred to him the true name and nature of this place.

Quaco Ledge!

That was the place which Captain Corbet had described. He recalled now the full description. Here it lay before him; upon it he stood; and he found that it corresponded in every respect with the description that the captain had given. If this were indeed so, and the description were true,--and he could not doubt this,--how desperate his situation was, and how he had been deceived in his false hopes! Far, far away was he from any shore!--in the middle of the bay; on a place avoided by all--a place which he should shun above all other places if he hoped for final escape!

And now he was as eager to quit this ill-omened place as he had once been to reach it. The tide was yet low. He tried to push the boat down, but could not. He saw that he would have to wait. So he got inside the boat, and, sitting down, he waited patiently. The time passed slowly, and Tom looked despairingly out over the water. Something attracted his attention. It was a long pole, which had struck against the edge of the shoal. He got out of the boat, and, securing it, he walked back again. It was some waif that had been drifting about till it was thus cast at his feet. He thought of taking it for a mast, and making use of the sail. The idea was an attractive one. He pulled the sail out, unfolded it, and found it to be the jib of some schooner. He cut off one end of this, and then with his knife began to make a hole in the seat for his mast. It was very slow work, but he succeeded at last in doing it, and inserted the pole. Then he fastened the sail to it. He was rather ignorant of navigation, but he had a general idea of the science, and thought he would learn by experience. By cutting off the rope from the edge of the sail he obtained a sheet, and taking off the cover of the biscuit box a second time, he put this aside to use as a rudder.

But now, in what direction ought he to steer?

This was an insoluble problem. He could tell now by the flow of the current the points of the compass, but could not tell in which direction he ought to go. The New Brunswick coast he thought was nearest, but he dreaded it. It seemed perilous and unapproachable. He did not think much better of the Nova Scotia coast. He thought rather of Cape d'Or, as a promising place of refuge, or the Petitcodiac. So, after long deliberation, he decided on steering back again, especially as the wind was blowing directly up the bay.

By the time that he had finished these preparations and deliberations the boat was afloat. Eagerly Tom pushed it away from the shoal; eagerly, and with trembling hands, he let the sail unfold, and thrust the board into the water astern. The boat followed the impulse of the wind, and the young sailor saw with delight that his experiment was successful, and before long the dark rocks of Quaco Ledge were lost to view.

Now, where there is a definite object to steer by, or a compass to guide one, and a decent rudder, even an inexperienced hand can manage to come somewhere near the point that he aims at. But take a boat like Tom's, and a rude and suddenly extemporized sail, with no other rudder than a bit of board, with no compass, and a surrounding of thick fog, and it would puzzle even an experienced sailor to guide himself aright. Tom soon suspected that his course was rather a wild one; his board in particular became quite unmanageable, and he was fatigued with trying to hold it in the water. So he threw it aside, and boldly trusted to his sail alone.

The boat seemed to him to be making very respectable progress. The wind was fresh, and the sea only moderate. The little waves beat over the bows, and there was quite a commotion astern. Tom thought he was doing very well, and heading as near as possible towards the Petitcodiac. Besides, in his excitement at being thus saved from mere blind drifting, he did not much care where he went, for he felt assured that he was now on the way out of his difficulties.

In an hour or two after leaving the ledge it grew quite dark, and Tom saw that it would be necessary to prepare for the night. His preparations were simple, consisting in eating a half dozen biscuit. He now began to feel a little thirsty, but manfully struggled against this feeling. Gradually the darkness grew deeper, until at last it assumed the intense character of the preceding night. But still Tom sat up, and the boat went on. The wind did not slacken, nor did the boat's progress cease. Hours passed by in this way. As to the tides, Tom could not tell now very well whether they were rising or falling, and, in fact, he was quite indifferent, being satisfied fully with his progress. As long as the wind distended his sail, and bore the boat onward, he cared not whether the tide favored or opposed.

Hours passed, but such was Tom's excitement that he still bore up, and thought nothing of rest or of sleep. His attention was needed, too, and so he kept wide awake, and his ears were ever on the stretch to hear the slightest sound. But at last the intense excitement and the long fatigue began to overpower him. Still he struggled against his weakness, and still he watched and listened.

Hours passed on, and the wind never ceased to fill the sail, and the boat never ceased to go onward in a course of which Tom could have no idea. It was a course totally different from the one which be intended--a course which depended on the chance of the wind; and one, too, which was varied by the sweep of the tide as it rose or fell; but the course, such as it was, continued on, and Tom watched and waited until, at last, from sheer exhaustion, he fell sound asleep.

His dreams were much disturbed, but he slept on soundly, and when he awaked it was broad day. He looked around in deep disappointment. Fog was everywhere, as before, and nothing could be seen. Whether he was near any shore or not he could not tell. Suddenly he noticed that the wind was blowing from an opposite direction. How to account for this was at first a mystery, for the fog still prevailed, and the opposite wind could not bring fog. Was it possible that the boat had turned during his sleep? He knew that it was quite possible. Indeed, he believed that this was the case. With this impression he determined to act on the theory that the boat had turned, and not that the wind had changed. The latter idea seemed impossible. The wind was the chill, damp fog wind--the sou-wester. Convinced of this, Tom turned the boat, and felt satisfied that he had resumed his true course.

After a time the wind went down, and the sail flapped idly against the mast. Tom was in a fever of impatience, but could do nothing. He felt himself to be once more at the mercy of the tides. The wind had failed him, and nothing was left but to drift. All that day he drifted, and night came on. Still it continued calm. Tom was weary and worn out, but so intense was his excitement that he could not think of sleep. At midnight the wind sprung up a little; and now Tom determined to keep awake, so that the boat might not again double on her track. He blamed himself for sleeping on the previous night, and losing so much progress. Now he was determined to keep awake.

His resolution was carried out. His intense eagerness to reach some shore, no matter where, and his fear of again losing what he had gained, kept sleep from his eyes. All that night he watched his boat. The wind blew fitfully, sometimes carrying the boat on rapidly, again dying down.

So the next morning came.

It was Thursday.

It was Monday night when he had drifted out, and all that time he had been on the deep, lost in the fog.

And now, wearied, dejected, and utterly worn out, he looked around in despair, and wondered where this would end. Fog was everywhere, as before, and, as before, not a thing could be seen.

Hours passed on; the wind had sprang up fresh, and the boat went on rapidly.

Suddenly Tom sprang upright, and uttered a loud cry.

There full before him he saw a giant cliff, towering far overhead, towards which the boat was sailing. At its base the waves were dashing. Over its brow trees were bending. In the air far above he heard the hoarse cries of sea-gulls.

In his madness he let the boat drive straight on, and was close to it before he thought of his danger. He could not avoid it now, however, for he did not know how to turn the boat. On it went, and in a few moments struck the beach at the base of the cliff.

The tide was high; the breeze was moderate, and there was but little sun. The boat was not injured by running ashore there. Tom jumped out, and, taking the rope in his hands, walked along the rough and stony beach for about a hundred yards, pulling the boat after him. There the cliff was succeeded by a steep slope, beyond which was a gentle, grass-grown declivity. Towards this he bent his now feeble steps, still tugging at the boat, and drawing it after him.

At length he reached the grassy slope, and found here a rough beach. He fastened the boat securely to the trunk of a tree that grew near.

Then he lifted out the box of biscuit, and over this he threw the sail.

He stood for a few moments on the bank, and looked all around for signs of some human habitation; but no signs appeared. Tom was too exhausted to go in search of one. He had not slept for more than thirty hours. The country that he saw was cleared. Hills were at a little distance, but the fog which hung all around concealed everything from view. One look was enough.

Overwhelmed with gratitude, he fell upon his knees, and offered up a fervent prayer of thankfulness for his astonishing escape.

Then fatigue overpowered him, and, rolling himself up in the sail, he went to sleep.

VIII.

Off in Search.--Eager Outlook.--Nothing but Fog.--Speaking a Schooner.--
Pleasant Anecdotes.--Cheer up.--The Heart of Corbet.

After the arrival of Bruce and Bart, Captain Corbet did not delay his departure much longer. The vessel was already afloat, and though the tide was still rising, yet the wind was sufficiently favorable to enable her to go on her way. The sails were soon set, and, with the new boat in tow, the Antelope weighed anchor, and took her departure. For about two hours but little progress was made against the strong opposing current; yet they had the satisfaction of reaching the mouth of the river, and by ten o'clock, when the tide turned and began to fall, they were fairly in the bay. The wind here was ahead, but the strong tide was now in their favor, and they hoped for some hours to make respectable progress.

During this time they had all kept an anxious lookout, but without any result. No floating craft of any kind appeared upon the surface of the water. Coming down the river, the sky was unclouded, and all the surrounding scene was fully visible; but on reaching the bay, they saw before them, a few miles down, a lofty wall of light-gray cloud. Captain Corbet waved his hand towards this.

"We're in for it," said he, "or we precious soon will be."

"What's that?" asked Phil.

"Our old friend--a fog bank. You'd ought to know it by this time, sure."

There it lay, a few miles off, and every minute brought them nearer. The appearance of the fog threw an additional gloom over the minds of all, for they saw the hopeless character of their search. Of what avail would it be to traverse the seas if they were all covered by such thick mists? Still nothing else was to be done, and they tried to hope for the best.

"Any how," said Captain Corbet, "thar's one comfort. That thar fog may go as quick as it come. It ony needs a change of wind. Why, I've knowed it all vanish in half an hour, an the fog as thick as it is now."

"But sometimes it lasts long--don't it?"

"I should think it did. I've knowed it hang on for weeks."

At this gloomy statement the boys said not a word.

Soon after the schooner approached the fog bank, and in a little while it had plunged into the midst of its misty folds. The chill of the damp clouds, as they enveloped them, struck additional chill to their hearts. It was into the midst of this that poor Tom had drifted, they thought, and over these seas, amidst this impenetrable atmosphere, he might even now be drifting. In the midst of the deep dejection consequent upon such thoughts, it was difficult for them to find any solid ground for hope.

The wind was moderate, yet adverse, and the schooner had to beat against it. As she went on each tack, they came in sight of the shores; but as time passed, the bay widened, and Captain Corbet kept away from the land as much as possible. All the time the boys never ceased to maintain their forlorn lookout, and watched over the sides, and peered anxiously through the mist, in the hope that the gloomy waters might suddenly disclose to their longing eyes the form of the drifting boat and their lost companion.

"I tell you what it is, boys," said Captain Corbet, after a long and thoughtful silence; "the best plan of acting in a biz of this kind is to pluck up sperrit an go on. Why, look at me. You mind the time when that boat, that thar i-dentical, individdle boat, drifted away onst afore, with youns in it. You remember all about that,--course. Well, look at me. Did I mourn? Did I fret? Was I cast down? Nary down; not me. I cheered up. I cheered up Mr. Long. I kep everybody in good sperrits. An what was the result? Result was, you all turned up in prime order and condition, a enjyin of yourselves like all possessed, along with old O'Rafferty.

"Again, my friends," he continued, as the boys made no remark, "consider this life air short an full of vycissitoods. Ups an downs air the lot of pore fallen hoomanity. But if at the fust blast of misforten we give up an throw up the game, what's the good of us? The question now, an the chief pint, is this--Who air we, an whar air

we goin, an what air we purposin to do? Fust, we air hooman beins; secondly, we
air a traversin the vast an briny main; and thirdly, we hope to find a certain friend
of ourn, who was borne away from us by the swellin tide. Thar's a aim for us--a
high an holy aim; an now I ask you, as feller-critters, how had we ought to go about
it? Had we ought to peek, an pine, an fret, an whine? Had we ought to snivel, and
give it up at the fust? Or had we ought, rayther, to be up an doin,--pluck up our
sperrits like men, and go about our important work with energy? Which of these
two, my friends? I pause for a reply."

This was quite a speech for Captain Corbet, and the effort seemed quite an exhaustive one. He paused some time for a reply; but as no reply was forthcoming, he
continued his remarks.

"Now, see here," said he; "this here whole business reminds me of a story I once
read in a noospaper, about a man up in this here identical river, the Petticoat Jack,
who, like a fool, pulled up his boat on the bank, and wont off to sleep in her. Wal,
as a matter of course, he floated off,--for the tide happened to be risin,--an when he
woke up out of his cool an refreshin slumbers, he found himself afar on the briny
deep, a boundin like 'a thing of life,' o'er the deep heavin sea. Besides, it was precious foggy,--jest as it is now,--an the man couldn't see any more'n we can. Wal, the
story went on to say, how that thar man, in that thar boat, went a driftin in that thar
fashion, in that thar fog; an he drifted, an drifted, an derifted, for days an days, up
an down, on one side an t'other side, an round every way,--an, mind you, he hadn't
a bit to eat, or to drink either, for that matter,--'t any rate, the paper didn't mention
no such thing; an so, you know, he drifted, an d-e-e-e-rifted,--until at last he druv
ashore. An now, whar d'ye think he druv?"

The boys couldn't think.

"Guess, now."

The boys couldn't guess.

"D'ye guv it up?"

They did.

"Wal, the paper said, he druv ashore at Grand Manan; but I've my doubts about
it."

The captain paused, looked all around through the fog, and stood for a moment
as though listening to some sound.

"I kine o' thought," said he, "that I detected the dash of water on the shore. I rayther think it's time to bring her round."

The vessel was brought round on another tack, and the captain resumed his conversation.

"What I was jest sayin," he continued, "reminds me of a story I onst heard, or read, I forget which (all the same, though), about two boys which went adrift on a raft. It took place up in Scott's Bay, I think, at a ship-yard in that thar locality.

"These two unfortunate children, it seems, had made a raft in a playful mude, an embarkin on it they had been amoosin theirselves with paddlin about by pushin it with poles. At length they came to a pint where poles were useless; the tide got holt of the raft, an the ferrail structoor was speedily swept onward by the foorus current. Very well. Time rolled on, an that thar raft rolled on too,--far over the deep bellew sea,--beaten by the howlin storm, an acted upon by the remorseless tides. I leave you to pictoor to yourselves the sorrow of them thar two infant unfortunits, thus severed from their hum an parients, an borne afar, an scarce enough close on to keep 'em from the inclemency of the weather. So they drifted, an drifted, an de-e-rifted, until at last they druv ashore; an now, whar do you think it was that they druv?"

The boys couldn't say.

"Guess now."

The boys declined.

"Try."

They couldn't.

"Name some place."

They couldn't think of any.

"D'ye guv it up?" asked the captain, excitedly.

They did.

"Well, then," said he, in a triumphant tone, "they druv ashore on Brier Island; an ef that thar ain't pooty tall driftin, then I'm a Injine."

To this the boys had no reply to make.

"From all this," continued the captain, "you must perceive that this here driftin is very much more commoner than you hev ben inclined to bleeve it to be. You also must see that thar's every reason for hope. So up with your gizzards! Pluck up your sperrits! Rise and look fortin an the footoor squar in the face. Squar off at fortin, an hav it out with her on the spot. I don't want to hev you go mopin an whinin about this way. Hello!"

Captain Corbet suddenly interrupted his remarks by an exclamation. The exclamation was caused by the sudden appearance of a sail immediately to windward. She was coming up the bay before the wind, and came swiftly through the fog towards them. In passing on her way, she came astern of the Antelope.

"Schooner, ahoy!" cried Captain Corbet; and some conversation took place, in which they learned that the stranger was the schooner Wave, from St. John, and that she had not seen any signs whatever of any drifting boat.

This news was received sadly by the boys, and Captain Corbet had to exert his utmost to rouse them from their depression, but without much effect.

"I don't know how it is," said he, plaintively, "but somehow your blues air contiguous, an I feel as ef I was descendin into a depression as deep as yourn. I don't remember when I felt so depressed, cept last May--time I had to go off in the Antelope with taters, arter I thought I'd done with seafarin for the rest of my life. But that thar vessel war wonderously resussutated, an the speouse of my buzzum druv me away to traverse the sea. An I had to tar myself away from the clingin gerasp of my weepin infant,--the tender bud an bulossum of an old man's life--tar myself away, an feel myself a outcast. Over me hovered contennooly the image of the pinin infant, an my heart quivered with responsive sympathy. An I yearned-- an I pined--an I groaned--an I felt that life would be intoll'ble till I got back to the babby. An so it was that I passed away, an had scace the heart to acknowledge your youthful cheers. Wal, time rolled on, an what's the result? Here I air. Do I pine now? Do I peek? Not a pine! Not a peek! As tender a heart as ever bet still beats in this aged frame; but I am no longer a purray to sich tender reminiscinsuz of the babby as onst used to consume my vitals."

Thus it was that the venerable captain talked with the boys, and it was thus that he sought, by every possible means, to cheer them up. In this way the day passed on, and after five or six hours they began to look for a turn of tide. During this time the schooner had been beating; and as the fog was as thick as ever, it was impossible for the boys to tell where they were. Indeed, it did not seem as though they had been making any progress.

"We'll have to anchor soon," said the captain, closing his eyes and turning his face meditatively to the quarter whence the wind came.

"Anchor?"

"Yes."

"What for?"

"Wal, you see it'll soon be dead low tide, an we can't go on any further when it turns. We'll have wind an tide both agin us."

"How far have we come now?"

"Wal, we've come a pooty considerable of a lick now--mind I tell you. 'Tain't, of course, as good as ef the wind had ben favorable, but arter all, that thar tide was a pooty considerable of a tide, now."

"How long will you anchor?"

"Why, till the next tarn of tide,--course."

"When will that be?"

"Wal, somewhar about eleven o'clock."

"Eleven o'clock?"

"Yes."

"Why, that's almost midnight."

"Course it is."

"Wouldn't it be better to cruise off in the bay? It seems to me anything is better than keeping still."

"No, young sir; it seems to me that jest now anythin is better than tryin to cruise in the bay, with a flood tide a comin up. Why, whar d'ye think we'd be? It would ony take an hour or two to put us on Cape Chignecto, or Cape d'Or, onto a place that we wouldn't git away from in a hurry,--mind I tell you."

To this, of course, the boys had nothing to say. So, after a half hour's further sail, the anchor was dropped, and the Antelope stopped her wanderings for a time.

Tedious as the day had been, it was now worse. The fog was as thick as ever, the scene was monotonous, and there was nothing to do. Even Solomon's repasts had, in a great measure, lost their attractions. He had spread a dinner for them, which at other times, and under happier circumstances, would have been greeted with uproarious enthusiasm; but at the present time it was viewed with comparative indifference. It was the fog that threw this gloom over them. Had the sky been clear, and the sun shining, they would have viewed the situation with comparative equanimity; but the fog threw terror all its own around Tom's position; and by shutting them in on every side, it forced them to think of him who was imprisoned in the same way--their lost companion, who now was drifting in the dark. Besides, as long as they were in motion, they had the consciousness that they were doing something, and that of itself was a comfort; but now, even that consolation was taken away from them, and in their forced inaction they fell back again into the same despondency which they had felt at Petitcodiac.

"It's all this fog, I do believe," said Captain Corbet. "If it want for this you'd all cheer up, an be as merry as crickets."

"Is there any prospect of its going away?"

"Wal, not jest yet. You can't reckon on it. When it chooses to go away, it does so. It may hang on for weeks, an p'aps months. Thar's no tellin. I don't mind it, bein as I've passed my hull life in the middle of fog banks; but I dare say it's a leetle tryin to youns."

The repast that Solomon spread for them on that evening was scarce tasted, and to all his coaxings and remonstrances the boys made no reply. After the tea was over, they went on deck, and stared silently into the surrounding gloom. The sight gave them no relief, and gave no hope. In that dense fog twilight came on soon, and with the twilight came the shadows of the night more rapidly. At last it grew quite dark, and finally there arose all around them the very blackness of darkness.

"The best thing to do," said Captain Corbet, "is to go to sleep. In all kinds of darkness, whether intunnel or extunnel, I've allus found the best plan to be to sleep it off. An I've knowed great men who war of my opinion. Sleep, then, young sirs, while yet you may, while yer young blood is warm, an life is fresh an fair, an don't put it off to old age, like me, for you mayn't be able to do it. Look at me! How much d'ye think I've slep sence I left Mud Creek? Precious little. I don't know how it is, but bein alone with you, an havin the respons'bility of you all, I kine o' don't feel altogether able to sleep as I used to do; an sence our late loss--I--wal, I feel as though I'd never sleep agin. I'm talkin an talkin, boys, but it's a solemn time with me. On me, boys, rests the fate of that lad, an I'll scour these here seas till he turns up, ef I hev to do it till I die. Anxious? Yes, I am. I'm that anxious that the diskivery of the lost boy is now the one idee of my life, for which I forget all else; but allow me to say, at the same time, that I fully, furmly, an conshuentiously bleve an affum, that my conviction is, that that thar lad is bound to turn up all right in the end--right side up--with care--sound in every respect, in good order an condition, jest as when fust shipped on board the good schooner Antelope, Corbet master, for Petticoat Jack, as per bill ladin."

The captain's tones were mournful. He heaved a deep sigh as he concluded, and relapsed into a profound and melancholy silence.

The boys waited on deck for some time longer, and finally followed his advice, and sought refuge below. They were young and strong, and the fatigue which they felt brought on drowsiness, which, in spite of their anxiety, soon deepened into sleep. All slept, and at length Captain Corbet only was awake. It was true enough, as he had said, the fate of the lost boy rested upon him, and he felt it. His exhortations to the boys about keeping up their courage, and his stories about lost men who had drifted to a final rescue, were all spoken more with reference to himself than to them. He sought to keep up his own courage by these words. Yet, in spite of his efforts, a profound depression came over him, and well nigh subdued him. No one knew better than he the many perils which beset the drifting boat in these dangerous waters--the perils of storm, the perils of fog, the perils of thick darkness, the perils of furious tides, the perils of sunken rocks, of shoals, and of iron-bound coasts. The boys had gone to sleep, but there was no sleep for him. He wandered restlessly about, and heavy sighs escaped him. Thus the time passed with him until near midnight. Then he roused the mate, and they raised the anchor and hoisted the sails. It was now the turn of tide, and the waters were falling again, and the current once more ran down the bay. To this current he trusted the vessel again, beating, as before, against the head wind, which was still blowing; and thus the Antelope worked her way onward through all that dark and dismal night, until at last the faint streaks of light in the east proclaimed the dawn of another day.

Through all that night the boys slept soundly. The wind blew, the waves dashed, but they did not awake. The anchor was hoisted, and the sails were set, but the noise failed to rouse them. Weariness of body and anxiety of mind both conspired to make their sleep profound. Yet in that profound sleep the anxiety of their minds made itself manifest; and in their dreams their thoughts turned to their lost companion. They saw him drifting over the stormy waters, enveloped in midnight darkness, chilled through with the damp night air, pierced to the bone by the cold night wind; drifting on amid a thousand dangers, now swept on by furious tides towards rocky shores, and again drawn back by refluent currents over vast sunken sea-ledges, white with foam. Thus through all the night they slept, and as they slept the Antelope dashed on through the waters, whose foaming waves, as they tumbled against her sides and over her bows, sent forth sounds that mingled with their dreams, and became intermingled with poor Tom's mournful cries.

IX.

Awake once more.--Where are we?--The giant cliff.--Out to Sea.--Anchoring and Drifting.--The Harbor.--The Search.--No Answer.--Where's Solomon?

Scarce had the streaks of light greeted Captain Corbet's eyes, and given him the grateful prospect of another day, when the boys awaked and hurried up on deck. Their first act was to take a hurried look all around. The same gloomy and dismal prospect appeared--black water and thick, impenetrable fog.

"Where are we now, Captain?" asked Bruce.

"Wal, a con-siderable distance down the bay."

"What are you going to do?"

"Wal--I've about made up my mind whar to go."

"Where?"

"I'm thinkin of puttin into Quaco."

"Quaco?"

"Yes."

"How far is it from here?"

"Not very fur, 'cordin to my calc'lations. My idee is, that the boat may have drifted down along here and got ashore. Ef so, he may have made for Quaco, an its jest possible that we may hear about him."

"Is this the most likely place for a boat to go ashore?"

"Wal, all things considered, a boat is more likely to go ashore on the New Brunswick side, driftin from Petticoat Jack; but at the same time 'tain't at all certain. Thar's ony a ghost of a chance, mind. I don't feel over certain about it."

"Will we get to Quaco this tide?"

"Scacely."

"Do you intend to anchor again?"

"Wal, I rayther think I'll hev to do it. But we'd ought to get to Quaco by noon, I calc'late. I'm a thinkin--Hello! Good gracious!"

The captain's sudden exclamation interrupted his words, and made all turn to look at the object that had called it forth. One glance showed an object which might well have elicited even a stronger expression of amazement and alarm.

Immediately in front of them arose a vast cliff,--black, rocky, frowning,--that ascended straight up from the deep water, its summit lost in the thick fog, its base white with the foaming waves that thundered there. A hoarse roar came up from those breaking waves, which blended fearfully with the whistle of the wind through the rigging, and seemed like the warning sound of some dark, drear fate. The cliff was close by, and the schooner had been steering straight towards it. So near was it that it seemed as though one could have easily tossed a biscuit ashore.

But though surprised, Captain Corbet was not in the least confused, and did not lose his presence of mind for a moment. Putting the helm hard up, he issued the necessary commands in a cool, quiet manner; the vessel went round, and in a few moments the danger was passed. Yet so close were they, that in wearing round it seemed as though one could almost have jumped from the stern upon the rocky shelves which appeared in the face of the lofty cliff.

Captain Corbet drew a long breath.

"That's about the nighest scratch I remember ever havin had," was his remark, as the Antelope went away from the land. "Cur'ous, too; I don't see how it happened. I lost my reckonin a little. I'm a mile further down than I calc'lated on bein."

"Do you know that place?" asked Bart.

"Course I know it."

"It's lucky for us we didn't go there at night."

"Yes, it is rayther lucky; but then there wan't any danger o' that, cos, you see, I kep the vessel off by night, an the danger couldn't hev riz. I thought we were a mile further up the bay; we've been a doin better than I thought for."

"Shall we be able to get into Quaco any sooner?"

"Wal, not much."

"I thought from what you said that we were a mile nearer."

"So we air, but that don't make any very great difference."

"Why, we ought to get in all the sooner, I should think."

"No; not much."

"Why not? I don't understand that."

"Wal, you see it's low tide now."

"The tides again!"

"Yes; it's allus the tides that you must consider here. Wal, it's low tide now, an the tide's already on the turn, an risin. We've got to anchor."

"Anchor!"

"Yes."

"What, again?"

"Yes, agin. Even so. Ef we didn't anchor we'd only be drifted up again, ever so far, an lose all that we've ben a gainin. We're not more'n a mile above Quaco Harbor, but we can't fetch it with wind an tide agin us; so we've got to put out some distance an anchor. It's my firm belief that we'll be in Quaco by noon. The next fallin tide will carry us thar as slick as a whistle, an then we can pursue our investigations."

The schooner now held on her course for about a mile away from the shore, and then came to anchor. The boys had for a moment lost sight of this unpleasant necessity, and had forgotten that they had been using up the hours of the ebb tide while asleep. There was no help for it, however, and they found, to their disgust, another day of fog, and of inaction.

Time passed, and breakfast came. Solomon now had the satisfaction of seeing them eat more, and gave manifest signs of that satisfaction by the twinkle of his eye and the lustre of his ebony brow. After this the time passed on slowly and heavily; but at length eleven o'clock came, and passed, and in a short time they were once more under way.

"We're going to Quaco now--arn't we?" asked Phil.

"Yes; right straight on into Quaco Harbor, fair an squar."

"I don't see how it's possible for you to know so perfectly where you are."

"Young sir, there ain't a nook, nor a corner, nor a hole, nor a stun, in all the outlinin an configoortion of this here bay but what's mapped out an laid down all c'rect in this here brain. I'd undertake to navigate these waters from year's end to year's end, ef I was never to see the sun at all, an even ef I was to be perpetooly surrounded by all the fogs that ever riz. Yea, verily, and moreover, not only this here bay, but the hull coast all along to Bosting. Why, I'm at home here on the rollin biller. I'm the man for Mount Desert, an Quoddy Head, an Grand Manan, an all other places that air ticklish to the ginrality of seafarin men. Why, young sir, you see before you, in the humble an unassumin person of the aged Corbet, a livin, muvin, and sea-goin edition of Blunt's Coast Pilot, revised and improved to a precious sight better condition than it's ever possible for them fellers in Bosting to get out. By Blunt's Coast Pilot, young sir, I allude to a celebrated book, as big as a pork bar'l, that every skipper has in his locker, to guide him on his wanderin way--ony me. I don't have no call to use sech, being myself a edition of useful information techin all coastin matters."

The Antelope now proceeded quickly on her way. Several miles were traversed.

"Now, boys, look sharp," said the captain; "you'll soon see the settlement."

They looked sharp.

For a few moments they went onward through the water, and at length there was visible just before them what seemed like a dark cloud extending all along. A few minutes further progress made the dark cloud still darker, and, advancing further, the dark cloud finally disclosed itself as a line of coast. It was close by them, and, even while they were recognizing it as land, they saw before them the outline of a wharf.

"Good agin!" cried the captain. "I didn't come to the wharf I wanted, but this here'll do as well as any other, an I don't know but what it'll do better. Here we air, boys. Stand by thar, mate, to let fall the jib."

On they went, and in a few minutes more the Antelope wore round, and her side just grazed the wharf. The mate jumped ashore, lines were secured, and the Antelope lay in safety.

"An now, boys, we may all go ashore, an see if we can hear anything about the boat."

With these words Captain Corbet stepped upon the wharf, followed by all the boys, and they all went up together, till they found themselves on a road. There they saw a shop, and into this they entered. No time was to be lost; the captain at once told his story, and asked his question.

The answer was soon made.

Nothing whatever was known there about any boat. Two or three schooners had arrived within two days, and the shopkeeper had seen the skippers, but they had not mentioned any boat. No boat had drifted ashore anywhere near, nor had any strange lad arrived at the settlement.

This intelligence depressed them all.

"Wal, wal," said the captain, "I didn't have much hopes; it's jest as I feared; but, at the same time, I'll ask further. An first and foremost I'll go an see them schooners."

He then went off with the boys in search of the schooners just mentioned. These were found without difficulty. One had come from up the bay, another from St. John, and a third from Eastport. None of them had encountered anything like a drilling boat. The one from up the bay afforded them the greatest puzzle. She must have come down the very night of Tom's accident. If he did drift down the bay in his boat, he must have been not very far from the schooner. In clear weather he could not have escaped notice; but the skipper had seen nothing, and heard nothing. He had to beat down against the wind, and anchor when the tide was rising; but, though he thus traversed so great an extent of water, nothing whatever attracted his attention.

"This sets me thinkin," said the captain, "that, perhaps, he mayn't have drifted down at all. He may have run ashore up thar. Thar's a chance of it, an we must all try to think of that, and cheer up, as long as we can."

Leaving the schooners, the captain now went through the settlement, and made a few inquiries, with no further result. Nothing had been heard by any one about any drifting boat, and they were at last compelled to see that in Quaco there was no further hope of gaining any information whatever about Tom.

After this, the captain informed the boys that he was going back to the schooner to sleep.

"I haven't slep a wink," said he, "sence we left Grand Pre, and that's more'n human natur can ginrally stand; so now I'm bound to have my sleep out, an prepare for the next trip. You boys had better emply yourselves in inspectin this here village."

"When shall we leave Quaco?"

"Wal, I'll think that over. I haven't yet made up my mind as to what's best to be done next. One thing seems certain. There ain't no use goin out in this fog, an I've half a mind to wait here till to-morrow."

"To-morrow!"

"Yes,--an then go down to St. John."

"But what'll poor Tom be doing?"

"It's my firm belief that he's all right," said Captain Corbet, confidently. "At any rate, you'd better walk about now, an I'll try an git some sleep."

As there was nothing better to be done, the boys did as he proposed, and wandered about the village. It was about two miles long, with houses scattered at intervals along the single street of which it was composed, with here, and there a shipyard. At one end was a long, projecting ledge, with a light-house; at the other there was a romantic valley, through which a stream ran into the bay. On the other side of this stream were cliffs of sandstone rocks, in which were deep, cavernous hollows, worn by the waves; beyond this, again, was a long line of a precipitous shore, in whose sides were curious shelves, along which it was possible to walk for a great distance, with the sea thundering on the rocks beneath. At any other time they would have taken an intense enjoyment in a place like this, where there were so many varied scenes; but now their sense of enjoyment was blunted, for they carried in their minds a perpetual anxiety. None the less, however, did they wander about, penetrating up the valley, exploring the caverns, and traversing the cliffs.

They did not return to the schooner till dusk. It would not be high tide till midnight, and so they prolonged their excursion purposely, so as to use up the time. On reaching the schooner they were welcomed by Captain Corbet.

"I declar, boys," said he, "I'm getting to be a leetle the biggest old fool that ever lived. It's all this accident. It's onmanned me. I had a nap for two or three hours, but waked at six, an ever sence I've been a worretin an a frettin about youns. Sence that thar accident, I can't bar to have you out of my sight, for I fear all the time that you ar gettin into mischief. An now I've been skeart for two mortal hours, a fancyin you all tumblin down from the cliffs, or a strugglin in the waters."

"O, we can take care of ourselves, captain," said Bart

"No, you can't--not you. I wouldn't trust one of you. I'm getting to be a feeble creetur too,--so don't go away agin."

"Well, I don't think we'll have a chance in Quaco. Arn't we going to leave to-night?"

"Wal, that thar is jest the pint that I've been moosin on. You see it's thick; the fog's as bad as ever. What's the use of going out to-night? Now, ef we wait till to-morrow, it may be clear, an then we can decide what to do."

At this proposal, the boys were silent for a time. The experience which they had formed of the bay and its fogs showed them how useless would be any search by night, and the prospect of a clear day, and, possibly, a more favorable wind on the morrow, was very attractive. The question was debated by all, and considered in all its bearings, and the discussion went on until late, when it was finally decided that it would be, on the whole, the wisest course to wait until the following day. Not the least influential of the many considerations that occurred was their regard for Captain Corbet. They saw that he was utterly worn out for want of sleep, and perceived how much he needed one night's rest. This finally decided them.

Early on the following morning they were all up, and eager to see if there was any change in the weather. The first glance around elicited a cry of admiration from all of them. Above, all was clear and bright. The sun was shining with dazzling lustre; the sky was of a deep blue, and without a cloud on its whole expanse; while the wide extent of the bay spread out before them, blue like the sky above, which it mirrored, and throwing up its waves to catch the sunlight. A fresh north wind was blowing, and all the air and all the sea was full of light and joy.

The scene around was in every respect magnificent. The tide was low, and the broad beach, which now was uncovered by the waters, spread afar to the right and left in a long crescent that extended for miles. On its lower extremity it was terminated by a ledge of black rocks, with the light-house before spoken of, while its upper end was bounded by cavernous cliffs of red sandstone, which were crowned with tufted trees. Behind them were the white houses of the village, straggling irregularly on the borders of the long road, with here and there the unfinished fabric of some huge ship; while in the background were wooded hills and green sloping fields. Out on the bay a grander scene appeared. Far down arose a white wall, which marked the place where the fog clouds were sullenly retreating; immediately opposite, and forty miles away over the water, arose the long line of the Nova Scotia coast, which bounded the horizon; while far up arose Cape Chignecto, and beside it towered up the dark form of a lonely island, which they knew, in spite of the evident distortion of its shape, to be no other than Ile Haute.

The wondrous effects which can be produced by the atmosphere were never more visible to their eyes than now. The coast of Nova Scotia rose high in the air, dark in color, apparently only half its actual distance away, while the summit of that coast seemed as level as a table. It seemed like some vast structure which had been raised out of the water during the night by some magic power. Ile Haute arose to an extraordinary height, its summit perfectly level, its sides perfectly perpendicular, and its color a dark purple hue. Nor was Cape Chignecto less changed. The rugged cliff arose with magnified proportions to a majestic height, and took upon itself the same sombre color, which pervaded the whole of the opposite coast.

Another discussion was now begun as to their best plan of action. After talking it all over, it was finally decided to go to St. John. There they would have a better opportunity of hearing about Tom; and there, too, if they did hear, they could send messages to him, or receive them from him. So it was decided to leave at about eleven o'clock, without waiting for high tide; for, as the wind was fair, they could go on without difficulty. After coming to this conclusion, and learning that the tide would not be high enough to float the schooner until eleven, they all took break-fast, and stimulated by the exhilarating atmosphere and the bright sunshine, they dispersed down the village towards the light-house.

By ten o'clock they were back again. The tide was not yet up, and they waited patiently.

"By the way, captain," asked Bart, "what's become of Solomon?"

"Solomon? O, he took a basket an went off on a kine o' foragin tower."

"Foraging?"

"Yes. He said he'd go along the shore, and hunt for lobsters."

"The shore? What shore?"

"Why, away up thar," said the captain, pointing towards the headland at the upper end of the village.

"How long since?"

"Wal, jest arter breakfast. It must hev ben afore seven."

"It's strange that he hasn't got back."

"Yes; he'd ought to be back by this time."

"He can't get any lobsters now; the tide is too high."

"That's a fact."

They waited half an hour. The rising tide already touched the Antelope's keel.

"Solomon ought to be back," cried Bart, starting up.

"That's so," said Captain Corbet.

"I'm afraid something's happened. He's been gone too long. Two hours were enough."

The boys all looked at one another with anxious faces.

"If he went up that shore," said Bart, "he may have got caught by the tide. It's a very dangerous place for anybody--let alone an old man like him."

"Wal, he did go up thar; he said partic'lar that he wanted to find somethin of a relish, an would hunt up thar. He said, too, he'd be back by nine."

"I'm certain something's happened," cried Bart, more anxiously than before. "If he's gone up there, he's been caught by the tide."

Captain Corbet stared, and looked uneasy.

"Wal, I must say, that thar's not onlikely. It's a bad place, a dreadful bad place,--an him an old man,--a dreadful bad place. He'd be down here by this time, ef he was alive."

"I won't wait any longer," cried Bart. "I must go and see. Come along, boys. Don't let's leave poor old Solomon in danger. Depend upon it, he's caught up there somewhere."

"Wal, I think you're right," said Captain Corbet, "an I'll go too. But ef we do go, we'd better go with some preparations."

"Preparations? What kind of preparations?"

"O, ony a rope or two," said Captain Corbet; and taking a coil of rope over his arm, he stepped ashore, and all the boys hurried after him.

"I feel kine o' safer with a kile o' rope,--bein a seafarin man," he remarked. "Give a seafarin man a rope, an he'll go anywhar an do anythin. He's like a spider onto a web."

X.

Tom ashore.--Storm at Night.--Up in the Morning.--The Cliffs and the Beach.--A startling Discovery.--A desert Island.--A desperate Effort.-- Afloat again.

Tom slept soundly for a long time in the spot where he had flung himself. The sense of security came to the assistance of his wearied limbs, and lulled him into profounder slumbers. There was nothing here that might rudely awaken him--no sudden boat shocks, no tossings and heavings of waves, no hoarse, menacing thunders of wrathful surges from rocky shores; nor were there distressing dreams to harass him, or any anxieties carried from his waking hours into the land of slumbers to annoy and to arouse. From Monday night until this time on Thursday, he had known but little sleep, and much fatigue and sorrow. Now the fatigue and the sorrow were all forgotten, and the sleep was all his own. Not a thought had he given to the land which he had reached so strangely. It was enough for him that he felt the solid ground beneath his feet.

For hours he slept there, lying there like a log, wrapped in the old sail, moving not a limb, but given up altogether to his refreshing slumber. At length he waked, and, uncovering his head, looked around. At first he thought that he was in the boat, then he grew bewildered, and it was only after a persistent effort of memory that he could recollect his position.

He looked all around, but nothing was visible. There was nothing around him but darkness, intense and utter. It was like the impenetrable veil that had enshrouded him during the night of his memorable voyage. He could not see where his boat was. A vague idea which he had of examining its fastening was dismissed. He felt hungry, and found the biscuit box lying under one corner of the sail. A few of these were sufficient to gratify his hunger. Nothing more could be done, and he saw plainly that it would be necessary for him to wait there patiently until morning. Once more, therefore, he rolled himself up in the sail, and tried to go to sleep. But at first his efforts were vain. The first fatigue had passed away, and now that he had been refreshed by sleep, his mind was too much occupied by thoughts of his past voyage to be readily lulled to sleep again. He could not help wondering what Captain Corbet and the boys were doing. That they were searching for him everywhere he well knew, but which direction they had chosen he could not tell. And what was the place whither he had drifted? He felt confident that it was the mouth of the Petitcodiac, and could not help wondering at the accuracy of his course; yet, while wondering, he modestly refrained from taking the credit of it to himself, and rather chose to attribute it to the wind and tide. It was by committing himself so completely to their guidance, he thought, that he had done so well.

In the midst of such thoughts as these, Tom became aware of the howling of the wind and the dash of the waters. Putting forth his head, he found that there was quite a storm arising; and this only added to his contentment. No fear had he now, on this solid ground, of rising wind or swelling wave. Even the fog had lost its terrors. It was with feelings like these that he once more covered up his head from the night blast; and not long after he was once more asleep.

When he next awaked, it was day. Starting to his feet, he looked around him, and shouted for joy. The sky was clear. The sun was rising, and its rays, coming from over the distant hills, were glittering over the surface of the water. The wind had changed. The fog had dispersed.

No sooner had he seen this than he was filled with curiosity to know where he was. This did not look much like the mouth of the Petitcodiac. He stared around with a very strange sensation.

Immediately beside him, where he was standing, the easy slope went back for a hundred yards or so, covered with short, wild grass, with here and there a stunted tree. Turning round, he saw the land rising by a steep acclivity towards the heights which bordered on the sea in such tremendous cliffs. Over the heights, and along the crest of those cliffs, were flying great flocks of sea-gulls, which kept up one incessant chorus of harsh, discordant screams. In front of him spread out a broad sheet of water, on the opposite side of which arose a lofty line of coast. Into this there penetrated a long strait, beyond which he could see broad waters and distant shores--a bay within a bay, approached by this strait. On each side of the strait were lofty, towering cliffs; and on one side, in particular, the cliffs were perpendicular, and ran on in a long and unbroken wall. The extremity of the cliff nearest him was marked by a gigantic mass of broken rock, detached from the main land, and standing alone in awful grandeur.

What place was this? Was this the mouth of the Petitcodiac? Was that broad bay a river? Was he still dreaming, or what did it all mean? And that gigantic fragment severed from a cliff, which thus stood guard at the entrance of a long strait, what was that? Could it be possible? Was there indeed any other broken cape, or could it be possible that this was Cape Split?

He hurried up the slope, and on reaching the top, saw that it descended on the other side towards the water. This water was a broad sheet, which extended for seven or eight miles, and was terminated by a lofty coast that extended down the bay as far as the eye could reach. One comprehensive glance was sufficient. He saw it all, and understood it all. It was not the mouth of the Petitcodiac River. It was the entrance to the Basin of Minas that lay before him. There lay the great landmarks, seen under new aspects, it is true, yet now sufficiently distinguishable. There was the Nova Scotia coast. In yonder hollow was Scott's Bay. That giant rock was Cape Split. The long channel was the Strait of Minas, and the cliffs opposite were Cape d'Or and Cape Chignecto.

And now the recognition of all these places brought to him a great and sudden shock.

For what was this place on which he stood? Was it any part of the main land?

It was not.

He looked around.

It was an island.

He saw its lofty cliffs, its wooded crest, its flocks of sea-gulls, its sloping east end, where he stood, running down to a low point. He had seen them all at a distance before; and now that he stood here, he recognized all.

He was on Ile Haute!

The moment that he recognized this startling fact, he thought of his boat. He hurried to the beach. The tide was very low. To his immense relief he found the fastening of the boat secure, and he turned away at once, without any further examination, to think over his situation, and consider the best plan for reaching the main land. Making a comfortable seat for himself on the sail, he sat down, and drawing out the box, he took some biscuit. Then feeling thirsty, he went off in search of fresh water. Before he had walked many paces he found a brook.

The brook was a small one, which ran from the lofty west end of the island to the low land of the east, and thence into the bay. The water was good, and Tom satisfied his thirst by a long draught.

Judging by the position of the sun, it was now about seven o'clock in the morning; and Tom seated himself once more, and began to try to think how it was that he should have come in a direction so entirely different from the one which he had believed himself to be taking. He had fully expected to land at Petitcodiac, and he found himself far away on the other side of the bay. Yet a little reflection showed him how useless it was to try to recall his past voyage, and how impossible it was for him to account for it, ignorant as he was of the true direction of the wind and of the tide. He contented himself with marking a rude outline of his course on his memorandum book, making allowance for the time when he turned on that course; and having summed it all up to his own satisfaction in a crooked line which looked like a slip-knot, he turned his attention to more important matters.

There was one matter of first-rate importance which now pressed itself upon his thoughts, and that was, how to escape from his present situation. As far as he could see, there was no inhabitant on the island, no house, no cultivation, and no domestic animal. If there had been anything of that kind, they would be visible, he knew, from the point where he was standing. But all was deserted; and beyond the open ground in his neighborhood arose the east end, wooded all over its lofty summit. From Captain Corbet's words, and from his own observation, he knew that it was a desert island, and that if he wished to escape he would have to rely altogether upon his own resources.

With this conclusion he once more turned his attention to his surroundings.

Nearest to him was Cape d'Or, about four miles away, and Cape Split, which was some distance farther. Then there was the Nova Scotia shore, which appeared to be seven or eight miles distant. On the beach and within sight was the boat which offered a sure and easy mode of passing over to the main land. But no sooner did he recognize this fact than a difficulty arose. How was he to make the passage?

The boat had come ashore at high tide, and was close up to the grassy bank. The tide was far down, and between the boat and the water was a broad beach, covered with cobblestones, and interspersed with granite boulders. It was too heavy a weight for him to move any distance, and to force it down to the water over such a beach was plainly impossible. On the other hand, he might wait until the boat floated at high tide, and then embark. But this, again, would be attended with serious difficulties. The tide, he saw, would turn as soon as he should get fairly afloat, and then he would have to contend with the downward current. True, he might use his sail, and in that case he might gain the Nova Scotia shore; but his experience of the tides had been so terrible a one, that he dreaded the tremendous drift which he would have to encounter, and had no confidence in his power of navigating under such circumstances. Besides, he knew well that although the wind was now from the north, it was liable to change at any moment; so that even if he should be able to guide his boat, he might yet be suddenly enveloped by a fog when but half way over, and exposed once more to all those perils from which he had just escaped. The more he thought of all these dangers, the more deterred he felt from making any such attempt. Rather would he wait, and hope for escape in some other way.

But, as yet, he did not feel himself forced to anything so desperate as that. There was another alternative. At high tide the boat would be afloat, and then, as the tide fell, he could keep her afloat until it was at its lowest. He could then embark, and be carried by the returning water straight on to the Straits of Minas, and up into the basin. He now made a calculation, and concluded that it would be high tide about midday, and low tide about six in the evening. If he were to embark at that time, he would have two hours of daylight in which to run up with the tide. He saw now that his whole plan was perfectly feasible, and it only remained to make preparations for the voyage. As the whole afternoon would be taken up in floating the boat down to low-water mark, the morning would have to be employed in making whatever arrangements might be necessary.

Certain things were needed which required all that time. His hastily extemporized mast and sail had done wonderfully well, but he needed something to steer with. If he could only procure something that would serve the purpose of a rudder, he would feel well prepared for his voyage.

On the search for this he now started. He walked all about the open ground, looking around in all directions, to see if he could find anything, but without any success. Then he ascended the declivity towards the woods, but nothing appeared which was at all adapted to meet his wants. He saw a young tree, which he thought might do, and tried to cut it down with his pocket-knife. After about an hour's hard work he succeeded in bringing it down, and another hour was spent in trimming the branches. The result of all this labor at length lay at his feet in the shape of a rough pole, with jagged splinters sticking out all over it, which promised to be of about as much utility as a spruce bush. In utter disgust he turned away, leaving the pole on the ground, and making up his mind to sail, as he did before, without any rudder. In this mood he descended the declivity, and walked disconsolately towards the shore which was on the side of the island directly opposite to where the boat lay. He had not yet been near enough to see the beach; but now, as he came nearer, a cry of delight escaped him involuntarily; for there, all along the beach, and close up to the bank, lay an immense quantity of drift-wood, which had been brought here by the tide from all the upper waters of the bay. It was a most heterogeneous mixture that lay before him--chips from timber ponds, logs from ship-yards, boards from saw-mills, deals, battens, fence posts, telegraph poles, deal ends, edgings, laths, palings, railway sleepers, treenails, shingles, clapboards, and all the various forms which wood assumes in a country which makes use of it as the chief material of its manufactures. Along the countless streams that flow into the bay, and along its far-winding shores, and along the borders of all its subsidiary bays, and inlets, and basins, the manufacture of wood is carried on--in saw-mills, in ship-yards, and in timber ponds; and the currents that move to and fro are always loaded with the fragments that are snatched away from these places, most of which are borne afar out to sea, but many of which are thrown all along the shores for hundreds of miles. Ile Haute, being directly in the way of some of the swiftest currents, and close by the entrance to a basin which is surrounded by mills and ship-yards, naturally received upon its shores an immense quantity of these scattered and floating fragments. Such was the sight that now met the eyes of Tom, and presented him with a countless number of fragments of wood adapted to his wants, at the very time when he had worked fruitlessly for two hours at fashioning one for himself.

Looking over the heaps of drift-wood, he found many pieces which suited him; and out of these he chose one which was shaped a little like an oar. Securing this prize, he walked over to where the sail was, and deposited it there.

Then he ate some biscuit, and, after taking a draught from the cool brook, he rested, and waited, full of hope, for the rising of the tide.

It was now rapidly approaching the boat. Tom watched it for some time, and felt new happiness as he viewed the roll of every little surf. There was not much wind, and nothing but a gentle ripple on the water. All this was in his favor; for, if he wished for anything now, it was a moderate breeze and a light sea. From time to time he turned his attention to the Straits of Minas, and arranged various plans in his mind. At one time he resolved to try and reach Pereau; again he thought that he would be content if he could only get to Parrsboro'; and yet again, he came to the wise conclusion that if he got to any settlement at all he would be content. At another time he half decided to take another course, and try to reach Scott's Bay, where he felt sure of a warm welcome and a plenteous repast. Aiming thus at so many different points, it mattered but little to him in what particular direction the tide might sweep him, so long as it carried him up the bay.

The tide now came nearer, and Tom went down to the beach for a few moments. He paced the distance between the boat and the water. He noticed a few things lying in the boat. In the bow was a coil of rope which Captain Corbet had probably obtained when he was ashore at Petitcodiac. There was also a tin pan, used for baling.

As the tide drew nearer, Tom began to feel more and more impatient. Again and again he paced the intervening space between the boat and the water, and chafed and fretted because it did not lessen more rapidly. If the boat were once fairly afloat, he felt that the time would pass much more rapidly; for then he would be working at some definite task, and not standing idly waiting.

But everything has an end; and so, at length, the end came here. The water rose higher and higher, until, at length, it touched the keel. Tom gave a shout of joy.

He now untied the rope, and tried to shorten his suspense by pushing the boat towards the water; but his strength was insufficient. He could not move it. He would have to wait longer.

Thus far the things which he had taken out had been lying on the grass. It was now time to put them on board. So he carried down the sail, folded it up, and stowed it away neatly at the bottom of the boat. On this he stood the box of biscuit, taking care to put the cover over it, and to spread over that again one fold of the sail.

This took up some time, and he had the gratification of seeing that the water had come up a few feet farther. He now tried once more to force the boat down, using his piece of board as a lever; but the board bent, and almost broke, without moving the boat. He stood for a moment waiting, and suddenly thought of the pole which he had left up in the woods. He determined to get this, and perhaps, with its help, he would be able to accomplish his wishes. So off he started at a run, and in a few minutes reached the place. Hurrying back again, he inserted one end of the pole under the bow, and exerted all his force to press the boat downward into the water. At first it did not move; but shortly after, when the water had risen still higher, he made a new effort. This time he succeeded; the boat moved slightly.

Again.

The boat moved farther.

Once more.

Still farther.

And now he made a final trial. Thrusting the pole again underneath, he exerted all his force for the last time, and pushed the boat down for about a yard.

It was at last afloat.

The tide had not yet fully attained its height, but was close to it. The wind was blowing from the north, as before, and quite moderately. The sea sparkled and glittered in the rays of the sun. The little wavelets tossed their heads on high, and danced far away ever the sea. The air was bright, and stimulating, and exhilarating. All the scene filled Tom's heart with gladness; and the approach of his deliverance deepened and intensified this feeling.

XI.

Afloat again.--The rushing Water.--Down to the Bottom.--Desperate
Circumstances.--Can they be remedied?--New Hopes and Plans.

The boat was at last afloat before Tom's eyes.

At first he had thought of holding it by the painter, and patiently standing on the beach, but the sight of it now changed his purposes. He thought that it would be a far more sensible plan to get on board, and keep the boat near the beach in that way. His bit of stick, which he had found among the drift-wood, could be used as an oar, and was good enough to enable him to move the boat as much as would be necessary. As he would have to wait for six hours at least, it was a matter of great importance that he should be as little fatigued as possible, especially as he had to look forward to a voyage, after the tide had fallen, attended with the possibility of increased labor and exertion. All these thoughts came rapidly to his mind, but passed in much less time than it takes to tell it, so that Tom had scarcely seen the boat afloat than he rushed through the water, and clambered into it. Then, taking his stick, he stood up and looked around.

The scene around has already been described. Tom kept his stick in the water, so as to have it ready for use. He purposed keeping the boat at a convenient distance from the shore by pushing and paddling. By keeping it within a distance of from three to six yards, he thought he would, for the present at least, be able to keep afloat, and yet avoid the sweep of the tides. He did not expect to remain in this particular spot all the time, but expected to find some place which would be out of the way of the tide, where he could float comfortably without being forced to keep in too close to the land.

But suddenly Tom's thoughts and speculations were rudely interrupted.

It appeared to him that there was a very unusual feeling about the boat. She did not seem as high out of the water as she ought to have been, and her bows seemed to be lower than they had been. There was also a slight vibration in her, which he had never noticed before, and which struck him now as very peculiar. In the midst of this there came to his ears a low, faint, and scarcely perceptible sound, made up of peculiar bubbling and gurgling noises, which sounded from the boat.

One brief examination showed him that the boat was certainly very much deeper in the water than she had been.

Five seconds later her bows had sunk farther.

Two seconds more, and Tom's feet were surrounded by water up to his ankles.

The boat was filling!

Scarce had he made this discovery than the water rose swiftly up, the boat sank quickly down, the sea rolled over her sides, and the boat went to the bottom.

Very fortunate was it for Tom, at that moment, that he had not pushed out farther from the shore. When the boat went down he was not more than three or four yards off, and he did not sink lower than up to his neck. But the shock was a sudden one, and for a moment almost paralyzed him. The next instant, however, he recovered from it; and looking round, he saw the box of biscuit floating within his reach. Making a wild dash at this, he secured it, and waded ashore with it in safety. He then turned mournfully to look after the boat, and found that it was visible, floating on the surface. As he left it, it had floated up, his weight being the only thing that had sent it below. The tide was still coming in, so that it did not float away. Tom flung off his coat and waistcoat, and hurrying into the water, soon caught and dragged it as near as he could to the beach. Then he secured it once more, and waited. Standing there, he looked gloomily at the vessel, wherein such precious hopes had been freighted only to be lost. What had happened? Why could not the boat float? What was the matter with her? These were the wondering questions which occurred to him without his being able to give any answer.

One thing he saw plainly, and that was, that he had lost this tide. The next high tide would be after midnight, and the next would be between one and two on the following day. If he could find out what was the matter with the boat, and fix it, he would have to wait till the next day, unless he chose to watch for his chance after midnight, and make the journey then.

He was not a boy who could be long inactive; so now, after a brief period, in which he gave up to the natural despondency of his soul, he stirred himself up once more, and sought comfort in occupation. The box of biscuit did not seem much injured, it had not floated long enough for the sea-water to penetrate it. Assuring himself of this, he next turned to the boat and took out its contents. These were the old sail, the coil of rope, and the baling dipper.

By this time the tide had reached its height, and after the usual time of delay, began to fall once more. The boat was secured to the shore, and after a time the water began to leave her. Tom sat at a little distance, wondering what could be the matter with her, and deferring his examination until the boat should be left aground. It was a mystery to him how this sudden change had occurred, and why the boat, which had floated so well during his long drift, should now, all of a sudden, begin to leak with such astonishing rapidity. Something must have happened--something serious, too; but what it was, or how it had happened, he could not, for the life of him, conjecture.

As Tom sat there, the tide gradually left the boat; and as the tide left, the water ran out, keeping at just the same level inside as the water outside. This showed, even to his inexperienced eyes, that the leak must be a very large one, since it admitted of such a ready flow of water in and out. The water descended lower and lower as he sat, until, at last, the boat was left by the retreating waves. The water had all run out.

Tom now advanced, and proceeded to examine her. When he was arranging her cargo before, the coil of rope had been in the bows. This had prevented him from detecting anything wrong in the boat. But now, since everything had been taken out, one glance only was quite sufficient to make known to him instantly the whole difficulty. There, in the bows, underneath the very place where the coil of rope had lain, was a huge aperture. The planks had been beaten in, and one side of the bow was destroyed beyond hope of remedy.

The sight of such an irremediable calamity as this renewed for a time the despondency which he had felt at the first sinking of the boat. Full of depression, he turned away, and tried to account for it all. It was on the previous day that he had landed--about twenty-four hours ago. How had he passed the time since then, and what had happened? This he tried to remember.

In the first place, up to the moment of landing the boat was perfectly sound, and far from all injury. It had not been hurt during the drift. It had struck at one place, but the long voyage that had followed showed that no damage had resulted. Finally, it had not been harmed by landing on Quaco Ledge. Since that time he had drifted in safety far across the bay, without meeting with any accident. All this proved clearly that the damage must have been done to the boat since his landing on the island.

He found it very difficult to recall anything that had happened since then. On his first arrival he was worn out and exhausted. He remembered vaguely how he came in sight of the giant cliff, how he dragged the boat along, how he secured it to a tree, and then how he flung himself down on the grass and fell asleep. After that all was obscure to his memory; but he could recall his waking at midnight and listening to the roar of the wind and the dash of the surf. Evidently there must have been a heavier sea on the beach at that time than when he landed, and this was sufficient to account for the accident to the boat. She had been beating on the rough rocks at high tide, exposed to the full sweep of the surf, and her bows had been stove in.

The melancholy spectacle of the ruined boat made Tom see that his stay on the island might be prolonged even beyond the following day. No sooner had this thought occurred to him than he went over to the articles which he had taken out of the boat, and passed them all in review before him, as though he were anxious to know the full extent of his resources. He spread out the wet sail in the sun. He spread out his coat and waistcoat. In the pocket of the latter he found a card of matches, which were a little damp. These he seized eagerly and laid on the top of a stone, exposed to the rays of the sun, so as to dry them. The clothes which he kept on were wet through, of course, but he allowed them to dry on him.

He had been working now pretty industriously all the morning, first at searching after a piece of wood, then in cutting down the pole, then in searching among the drift-wood, and finally at the boat. He felt, at length, hungry; and as he could not yet decide upon what was to be done next, he determined to satisfy his desires, and kill the time by taking his dinner. The repast was a frugal one, consisting as before, of biscuit, which were washed down by cold water; but Tom did not complain. The presence of food of any sort was a cause for thankfulness to one in his position, and it was with a feeling of this sort, in spite of his general depression of spirits, that he ate his meal.

After this he felt much more refreshed, and began to consider what he had better do next. Of course, the centre of interest to him was the boat, and he could not give up that hope of escape without a struggle. As long as there was a hope of making his way from the island by means of that, so long might he keep up his heart; but if the damage that had been done should prove irreparable, how would he be able to endure his situation? Whatever it was, it would be best to know the worst once for all. Perhaps he might stop the leak. He had material around which seemed to be the right sort of thing to stop a leak with. He had the piece of sail, which could be cut up into small pieces, and used to stop the leak. If he had possessed a hatchet and some nails, he would have made an effort to repair the fracture in the planks of the boat; but as he had nothing of that sort, he tried to devise some method by which the water might be kept out. As he thought, there gradually grew up in his mind the rude outline of a plan which promised something, and seemed to him to be certainly worth trying. At any rate, he thought, it will serve to give me an occupation; and any occupation, even if it proves to be of no practical value, is better than sitting here doing nothing at all.

Having something to do once more quickened Tom's energies anew, and starting to his feet, he prepared to put his plan into execution. First of all, in order to carry out that plan, it was necessary for him to get a number of blocks and boards of different sizes. These, he knew, could easily be found among the driftwood on the beach. Over there he hurried, and after a moderate search he succeeded, at length, in finding bits of wood that seemed suited to the purpose which he had in view. With these he came back to the boat; but as there was a large number of them, he had to make several journeys before the whole collection was brought over.

Then he took his pole, and, putting a block under it, used it as a lever to raise up the boat. By dexterous management he succeeded in doing this, and at the same time he ran a board underneath the bow of the boat as it was slightly raised. This manoeuvre he repeated several times, each time raising his lever higher, by means of a higher fulcrum, and thus constantly raising the bow of the boat; while after each elevation the bow was secured in its new position by running an additional board underneath it, over the other preceding boards. By carefully and perseveringly pursuing this course, he at length succeeded in raising the bow of the boat about a foot in the air. This gave him an opportunity to examine it thoroughly outside as well as inside, and to see the whole extent of the damage that had been done.

It has already been said that the damage was serious. Tom's examination now convinced him that it was in every respect as serious as he had supposed, if not still more so. Even if he did possess a hatchet and nails, or a whole box full of tools, he doubted whether it would be in his power to do anything whatever in the way of repairing it. No less than three of the lower planks of the bows, down to the very keel, were beaten in and broken so badly that they seemed actually crushed and mangled. It must have been a fearful beating, and pounding, and grinding on the rocks which had caused this. The planks, though thus broken, still held together; but it seemed to Tom that with a blow of his fist he could easily beat it all in; and as he looked at it he could not help wondering how it had happened that the work which the rocks had thus so nearly effected had not been completely finished. However, the planks did hold together yet; and now the question was, Could any thing be done?

In answer to this question, Tom thought of the old sail and the coil of rope. Already he had conceived the rude outline of a plan whereby the entrance of the water might be checked. The plan was worth trying, and he determined to set about it at once, and use up the hours before him as long as he could, without any further delay. If by any possibility he could stop that leak, he determined to start off at the next high tide, that very night, and run the risk. It was a daring, even a foolhardy thought; but Tom was desperate, and the only idea which he had was, to escape as soon as possible.

He now made some measurements, after which he went to the old sail, and cut a piece from the end of it. This he divided into smaller pieces, each about a yard square. Each of these pieces he folded up in three folds, so as to make them about a foot wide and eighteen inches long. Others he folded into six folds, making them about half the size of the larger pieces. All this took up much time, for he measured and planned very carefully, and his calculations and measurements had to be done slowly and cautiously. Returning to the boat with these bits of folded canvas, he put one of the larger pieces on the inside, against the bow, right over the broken place.

Another large piece was placed carefully over this, and then the smaller pieces were laid against these. In this way he adjusted all the pieces of canvas in such a way as to cover up the whole place where the leak was.

Then he went over to the drift-wood, and spent a long time searching after some bits of wood. He at length found a half dozen pieces of board, about a foot long, and from six to eight inches in width. He also found some bits of scantling, and palings, which were only a foot or so in length. All these he brought back, and laid them down on the beach near the boat.

He now proceeded to place these bits of wood in the bows, in such a way as to keep the canvas in a firm position. His idea was, that the canvas, by being pressed against the opening, might keep out the water, and the wood, by being properly arranged, might keep the canvas secure in its place. The arrangement of the wood required the greatest care. First of all, he took the smallest bits, and stood these up against the canvas, so that they might correspond as nearly as possible with the curve of the bows. A few more pieces were placed in the hollow part of this curve, and outside these the larger pieces were placed. Between the outside pieces and the inner ones he thrust some of the smallest pieces which he could find. After thus arranging all his boards, he found that there lay between the outside board and the first seat of the boat a space of about one foot. Selecting a piece of wood of about that length, he put one end against the board, and the other against the seat, and pressed it into a position where it served to keep the board tight in its place. Then he took other pieces of about the same length, and arranged them in the same way, so that, by being fixed between the board and the seat, they might keep the whole mass of boards and canvas pressed tight against the opening in the bows. After placing as many blocks in position as he conveniently could, his next work was to secure them all. In order to effect this, another journey to the drift-wood was necessary, and another search. This time he selected carefully a number of sticks, not more than half an inch in thickness, some of them being much thinner. He found pieces of paling, and laths, and shingles which suited his ideas. Returning with these to the boat, he proceeded to thrust them, one by one, into the interstices of the boards, using a stone to drive them into their places.

At last the work was finished as far as he could accomplish it, and there remained nothing more to be done. As far as he could see, by shaking, and pulling, and pushing at the collection of sticks and canvas, it was very firm and secure. Every stick seemed to be tight, and the pressure which they maintained against the aperture was so strong that the wood-work now was forced out a little distance beyond the outline of the boat. He examined most carefully all about the bows on the outside, but saw no place which did not seem to be fully protected. It seemed to him now as though that piled-up canvas ought to resist the entrance of the water, or, if not, at least that it ought not to allow it to enter so rapidly but that he could easily keep the boat baled out.

He was not altogether confident, yet he was hopeful, and as determined as ever to make a trial.

XII.

Waiting for high Water.--A Trial.--A new Discovery.--Total Failure.--
Down again.--Overboard.--A Struggle for Life.

Tom's work was thus, at length, accomplished, and it remained now to get the boat in readiness and wait. Slowly and carefully he raised the bow by means of the lever, and one by one he withdrew the boards which held it up. At last the boat lay on the beach, ready to receive the uplifting arms of the returning tide whenever it should make its appearance again. Tom saw with satisfaction that the boat was about three yards down below high-water mark, on the spot to which he had dragged it after the failure of his last experiment. This, of course, would be so much in his favor, for it would thus be able to float before the water should reach its height.

He had worked hard all the afternoon, and it was already dark. The tide, which had been falling, had some time ago reached its lowest point, and was now returning. Between him and the lowest point was a great distance, for the tides here rise to a perpendicular height of over forty feet; but Tom knew that the time required to traverse the long space that here intervened between high and low-water mark was precisely the same as if it had only to rise a few feet.

He was very hungry, but some things had yet to be done. He had to put on board the boat the articles that he had taken ashore. His matches were now quite dry, and he put them in his pocket with a deep sense of their value to him in his present position. His clothes also were dry, and these he put on. The sail, the coil of rope, and the box of biscuit were put on board the boat. Tom had still to make his frugal repast; but this was soon accomplished, and he felt again a sense of exceeding thankfulness at the possession of the box of biscuit. At length his evening meal was over, and by the time that he had finished it, it had grown quite dark. He now went to the boat, and tied up the sail around the mast. There was nothing to which he could fasten the boat; but it was not necessary, as he was on the watch. The water continued smooth, the wind was from the north, as before, and there was no sign of fog. Overhead the sky was free from clouds, and the stars twinkled pleasantly to his upturned eyes, as if to encourage him. There was no moon, however, and though it was not very dark, yet it was sufficiently so to veil the nearest shores in gloom, and finally to withdraw them altogether from his view. Still it was not a matter of necessity that he should see the opposite shores, for he knew that his chief, and indeed his only reliance must be upon the tide; and this would bear him in its upward course on the morrow. The night was only needed to float the boat down as far as low-water mark. The process of floating her would serve to test the security of the fastenings, and show whether he could venture to make the attempt.

For hours Tom waited, sometimes seated in the boat, at other times walking along the beach down to the water. He found it difficult to keep himself awake, and therefore did not venture to sit down long. Wearied with his long work through the day, the necessity of constant exertion wearied him still more, until at length he could scarce draw his legs after him. But all things have an end, and so it was with Tom's dreary watch; for at length the waters came up, and touched the boat, and surrounded it, until at last, to his great joy, Tom found himself afloat. He seized his stick, and pushed the boat into deeper water, a few yards off, with the intention of keeping her at about that distance from the shore.

The one thought that was now in his mind referred exclusively to his work in the boat. Was it firm? Would it hold? Did it leak? The boat was floating, certainly. How long would if continue to do so? For a few minutes he waited anxiously, as he floated there in deep water, with his eyes fixed on the work in the bow, and his ears listening intently to detect any sign of that warning, gurgling sound, which had struck terror to his heart on his last embarkation. But no sign came of any sound of that sort, and he heard nothing but the gentle dash of the water against the sides of the boat. Thus about five minutes passed. At the end of that time, he raised the sail, which he had laid along the bottom of the boat, and examined underneath it. The first touch of his fingers at the bottom lessened very largely the hope that was in him, and at once chased away the feeling of exultation that was rising. For there, in the bottom of the boat, he felt as much as an inch of water. After the first shock, he tried to believe that it was only the water that was in the boat before; and so, taking comfort in this thought, he waited for further developments, but at the same time took the dipper, so as to be ready to bale out the water, and have a struggle for it in case the worst should happen.

Another minute assured him that this was not the water which had been in the boat before. A new supply was entering, and in the space of that short time of waiting it had risen to the height of another inch. Tom felt a sudden pang of dismay, but his stout heart did not quail, nor did his obstinate resolution falter. Since it was the sea water that was coming in, he determined to have a fight with it for the possession of the boat. So he set to work bravely, and began to bale. He pulled up the sail, so as to have plenty of elbow-room, and worked away, dipping out the water; but, as he dipped, he perceived that it was gradually getting deeper. He dipped faster, but without any visible improvement, indeed, his efforts seemed to have but very little effect in retarding the entrance of the water. It grew deeper and deeper. One inch of water soon deepened to two inches, and thence to three. Soon after four inches were felt.

And now the water came in more rapidly. It seemed to Tom as though it had been delayed at first, for a little time, in finding an entrance, but that now, after the entrance was found, it came pouring in with ever-accelerated speed. Tom struggled on, hoping against hope, and keeping up his efforts long after they were proved to be useless. But the water came in faster and faster, until at length Tom began to see that he must seek his safety in another way. Flinging down his dipper, then, with a cry of vexation, he started up, and, seizing his bit of board, he looked around for the shore.

He had been caught by some side current, and had been carried along in such a way that he was about a hundred yards from the island, and seemed to be drifting up the bay. The dark, shadowy shores were much farther away than he had suspected. While struggling to bale out the boat, he had forgotten how necessary it was to keep near to the shore. He now saw his mistake, and strove to paddle the boat back again. With such a clumsy oar it is not likely that he could have achieved his desire at all, had the flood tide been stronger; but now it was about at its height, and would soon turn, if it was not turning already. The current, therefore, was but a weak one, and Tom found himself able to move slowly back; but his progress was very slow, and working at such a disadvantage was excessively fatiguing. At last he saw that if he trusted to paddling he could never reach the shore. In a moment another idea suggested itself; there was no time to lose, and he at once acted on it. Darting forward, he loosed the sail. The wind was still blowing from the north; at once the sail was filled, and, yielding to this new power, the boat began to move more rapidly. Tom tied the sheet astern, and, seizing his paddle, tried to scull the boat. For some minutes he kept up this work, and the boat moved steadily forward, nearer and still nearer, until the land was at length not more than thirty or forty yards off.

But by this time the danger had come nearer, and the boat was already half full of water. Tom began to see that it could not float as far as the shore. What was he to do? He waited a little longer. He looked around. The boat was drawing nearer, yet soon it must go down. To ease it, it would be necessary to relieve it of his own weight. He did not lose his presence of mind for a moment, but determined at once to jump overboard. In his perfect coolness he thought of one or two things which were of importance to him, and performed them swiftly and promptly. First he took the box of biscuit, and placed it on the heap of boards and canvas in the bows, so that it might remain as long as possible out of reach of the water. Then he took the card of matches out of his waistcoat pocket, and put them in his hat, which he replaced on his head. To secure thus from damage the two necessaries of food and fire was but the work of a few seconds. To throw off his coat, waistcoat, and trousers, and hang them over the top of the short mast, was the work of a few seconds more. By the time this had been done, the water was nearly up to the gunwales. In five seconds more the boat would have gone down; but, so well had Tom's work been done, and so promptly, that these five seconds were saved. Having done what he wished, he let himself down into the water; and, holding on by the stern of the boat, he allowed himself to float after it, kicking out at the same time, so as to assist, rather than retard, its progress.

By this time the land was not more than twenty yards away. The boat did not sink so rapidly now, but kept afloat much better; still the water rose to a level with the gunwales, and Tom was too much rejoiced to find that it kept afloat at all to find fault with this. The wind still blew, and the sail was still up; so that the waterlogged vessel went on at a very respectable rate, until at length half the distance which Tom had noticed on going overboard was traversed. The boat seemed to float now, though full of water, and Tom saw that his precious biscuit, at any rate, would not be very much harmed. Nearer and nearer now he came until at last, letting himself down, his feet touched bottom. A cry of delight escaped him; and now, bracing himself firmly against the solid land below, he urged the boat on faster, until at length her deep-sunk bows grated against the gravel of the beach.

He hurried up to the box of biscuit, and put this ashore in a safe place; after which he secured the boat to a jagged rock on the bank. He found now that he had come to a different part of the beach altogether, for his boat was lying at the spot where the little brook ran into the sea. Well was it for him, in that rash and hazardous experiment, that he had floated off before the tide was high. It had led to his drifting up the bay, instead of down, and by a weak current, instead of a strong one. The wind had thus brought him back. Had it been full tide, he would have drifted out from the shore, and then have been carried down the bay by the falling water to swift and sure destruction.

Tom now took off his wet shirt, and put on the dry clothes which he had so prudently hung on the top of the mast. He perceived that he had not a very pleasant lookout for the night, for the sail which he had formerly used to envelop himself with was now completely saturated. It was also too dark to go to the woods in search of ferns or mosses on which to sleep. However, the night was a pleasant one, and the grass around would not be so bad a resting-place as he had been forced to use while drifting in the boat. He had now become accustomed to hardship by bitter experience, and so he looked forward to the night without care.

The day had been an eventful one, indeed, for him, and his last adventure had been full of peril, from which he had been most wonderfully rescued.

These thoughts were in his mind, and he did not fail to offer up prayers of heartfelt gratitude to that good and merciful Being who had thus far so wonderfully preserved him. With such feelings in his heart, he sought out a sleeping-place, and after some search he found a mossy knoll. Seating himself here, he reclined his back against it, and in a few minutes the worn-out boy was buried in a deep sleep.

He slept until late on the following day, and on waking looked around to see if there were any sails in view. None were visible. The tide was about half way up, and the wide waters spread before him without any vessel in sight. He then began his preparations for the day. He hung his shirt upon a bush, and spread out the wet sail on the grass. An examination of the biscuit showed him that they had scarcely been injured at all, the water having penetrated only the lower part of the box. He removed the lower layer of biscuit, and spread them out on a rock in the sun to dry. After this he breakfasted, and wandered about for a time. He then took a swim, and felt much refreshed. By the time that his swim was over, he found that the hot sun had dried his shirt, so that he could once more assume that very important article of clothing.

The sun climbed high towards the zenith, and the tide came up higher, as Tom sat there alone on his desert island, looking out upon the sea. The boat from which he had hoped so much had proved false to those hopes, and all the labors of the previous day had proved useless. His attempt to escape had nearly resulted in his destruction. He had learned from that experiment that no efforts of his could now effect his rescue. He had done the very best he could, and it would not be possible for him, with his present resources, to contrive anything better than that which had so miserably failed. If he could only procure some tar, he might then stop up the interstices; but as it was, nothing of his construction would avail to keep back the treacherous entrance of the water. It seemed now to him that his stay on the island was destined to be prolonged to a much greater extent than he had first thought of, and there did not seem any longer a hope of saving himself by his own exertions.

Alone on a desert island!

It was a dreadful fact which now forced itself more and more upon Tom's mind, until at length he could think of nothing else. Hitherto he had fought off the idea whenever it presented itself, and so long as he had been able to indulge in any hope of freeing himself by his own exertions, he prevented himself from sinking into the gloom of utter despair. But now he could no longer save himself from that gloom, and the thought grew darker and drearier before him--the one fact of his present situation.

Alone on a desert island!

A very interesting thing to read about, no doubt; and Tom, like all boys, had revelled in the portrayals of such a situation which he had encountered in his reading. No one had entered with more zest than he into the pages of Robinson Crusoe, and no one had enjoyed more than he the talks which boys love to have about their possible doings under such circumstances. But now, to be here, and find himself in such a place,--to be brought face to face with the hard, stern, dismal fact,--was another thing altogether. What oppressed him most was not the hardships of his position. These he could have withstood if there had been nothing worse. The worst part of his present life was its solitude. If Bart had been here with him, or Bruce, or Arthur, or Phil, or Pat, how different it would have been! Even old Solomon would have enabled him to pass the time contentedly. But to be alone,--all alone,--without a soul to speak to,--that was terrible.

Tom soon found that the very way to deepen his misery was to sit still and brood over it. He was not inclined to give way to trouble. It has already been seen that he was a boy of obstinate courage, resolute will, and invincible determination. He was capable of struggling to the last against any adversity; and even if he had to lose, he knew how to lose without sinking into complete despair. These moods of depression, or even of despair, which now and then did come, were not permanent. In time he shook them off, and looked about for some new way of carrying on the struggle with evil fortune.

So now he shook off this fit of depression, and starting up he determined not to sit idle any longer.

"I won't stand it," he muttered. "There's lots of things to be seen, and to be done. And first of all I've got to explore this island. Come, Tom, my boy; cheer up, old fellow. You've pretended to admire Robinson Crusoe; act up to your profession. And first of all, my boy, you've got to explore Juan Fernandez."

The sound of his own voice had the effect of encouraging and inspiriting him, while the purpose which he thus assigned to himself was sufficient to awaken his prostrated energies. There was something in the plan which roused all his curiosity, and turned his thoughts and feelings into a totally new direction. No sooner, then, had this thought occurred to him, than he at once set out to put it into execution.

First of all he took one parting look at the scene around him. The sun had now passed its meridian, and it seemed to be one o'clock or after. The tide was high. The boat, which had at first floated, was now nearly full of water. Tom threw a melancholy glance at this fresh proof of the utter futility of all his labor, and then examined the fastenings, so that it might not drift away during his absence. Then he searched among the drift-wood until he found a stout stick to assist him in climbing, and to serve as a companion in his walk, after which he started.

The sun was bright, but over the sky some clouds were gathering, and the opposite shores seemed to have grown darker than they were a few hours ago, having assumed a hue like olive green. The wind had also died away, and the water was as smooth as glass.

XIII.

Where's Solomon?--An anxious Search.--The Beach.--The cavernous Cliffs.--Up the Precipice.--Along the Shore.--Back for Boats.

The loss of Solomon had filled the boys with anxiety, and even Captain Corbet shared in the common feeling. He had preferred to set out, as he said, with a coil of rope; but the sight of this seemed to make Solomon's fate appear darker, and looked as though he might have fallen over a precipice, or into a deep pool of water. They all knew that a serious accident was not at all improbable. They had seen the lofty and rugged cliffs that lined the bay shore, and knew that the rising waters, as they dashed over them, might form the grave of a man far younger and more active than the aged Solomon. He was weak and rheumatic; he was also timid and easily confused. If the water had overtaken him anywhere, he might easily fall a prey. In his efforts to escape, he would soon become so terrified that his limbs would be paralyzed. He might then stumble over the rocks, and break some of his bones, or he might be intrapped in some recess of the cliffs, from which escape might be impossible without external help.

Full of thoughts like these, the boys went on, with Captain Corbet, up through the village, looking carefully around as they went on, and making inquiries of every one whom they met. No one, however, could give them any information. At last they reached the end of the village. Here, on the left, there arose a high hill. The road wound round this, and descended into a valley, through which a stream ran to the bay. In this valley there was a ship-yard, where the half-finished fabric of a large ship stood before them, and from which the rattle of a hundred axes rose into the air. The valley itself was a beautiful place, running up among steep hills, till it was lost to view among a mass of evergreen trees and rich foliage. Below the shipyard was a cove of no very great depth, but of extreme beauty. Beyond this was a broad beach, which, at the farthest end, was bounded by the projecting headland before alluded to. The headland was a precipitous cliff of red sandstone, crowned at the summit with a fringe of forest trees, white at its base were two or three hollow caverns, worn into the solid rock by the action of the surf. One of these was about thirty feet in height at its mouth, and ran back for sixty or seventy feet, narrowing all the way, like a funnel, from its entrance to its farthest extremity.

The tide was now nearly at its height, and progress down the beach and along the cliff was impossible. The caves were cut off also, and the water penetrated them for some distance. At low tide one could easily walk down to the extreme point of the headland, and rounding this, he would find it possible to go along in front of the cliffs for an immense distance, either by walking along the rough beach at their foot, or, if the water should rise again, by going along rocky shelves, which projected for miles from the surface of the cliff.

Reaching the head of the beach, Captain Corbet paused, and looked around.

"Before goin any further," said he, "we'd better ask the folks at this ship-yard. It ain't possible to tell whether he's gone by the beach or not. He may have gone up the valley."

"O," said Bart, dolefully, "he must have gone by the beach."

"I rayther think I'll ask, at any rate," said the captain.

So saying, he walked up towards a house that was not far off, and accosted some men who were standing there. On hearing his question, they were silent for a few moments; and at last one of them recollected seeing an aged colored man passing by early in the morning. He had a basket on his arm, and in every way corresponded to the description of Solomon. He was on his way up the shore.

"Did he go down to the pint," asked Captain Corbet, "or up to the top of the cliff?"

The man couldn't say for certain; but as far as he could recollect, it seemed to him that he went down to the pint.

"About what time?"

"Between eight and nine o'clock--in fact, about eight--not much later."

"Did he speak to any one here?"

"No; he walked past without stoppin. An do you say he ain't got back?"

"Not yet."

"Wal," said the man, "for an old feller, an a feller what don't know the country hereabouts, he's gone on a dangerous journey; an ef he's tried to get back, he's found it a pooty hard road to travel."

"Isn't there any chance of his gettin back by the cliff?"

"Not with the water risin onto his path."

"Is there any way of gettin up to the top of the cliff?"

"Wal, fur a active young feller it wouldn't be hard, but for a pore old critter like that thar, it couldn't be done--no how."

"Wal, boys," said Captain Corbet, sorrowfully, "I guess we'd better get on, an not lose any more time."

They walked away in silence for some time, until at last they reached the foot of the cliff. A path here ran up in a winding direction so as to reach the top.

"It seems too bad," said Captain Corbet, "not to be able to get to the beach. I wish I'd come in the boat. What a fool I was not to think of it!"

"O, I dare say the top of the cliff will do," said Bruce.

"Wal, it'll have to do. At any rate I've got the kile of rope."

"We shall be able to see him from the top just as well, and perhaps better."

"Wal, I hope so; but we'll be a leetle too far above him for my fancy,--ony we can use the rope, I s'pose. Can any of you youngsters climb?"

"O, yes," said Bart, "all of us."

"What kind of heads have you got--stiddy?"

"Yes, good enough," said Bruce. "I'll engage to go anywhere that I can find a foothold; and here's Bart, that'll go certainly as far, and perhaps farther. And here's Phil, that can do his share. As for Pat, he can beat us all; he can travel like a fly, upside down, or in any direction."

"Wal, I'm glad to hear that, boys, for it's likely you'll be wanted to do some climbin afore we get back. I used to do somethin in that way; but since I've growed old, an rheumatic, I've got kine o' out o' the way of it, an don't scacely feel sech confidence in myself as I used to onst. But come, we mustn't be waitin here all day."

At this they started up the path, and soon reached the top of the cliff.

Arriving here, they found themselves in a cultivated meadow, passing through which they reached a pasture field. After a walk of about a quarter of a mile, they came to the cliff that ran along the shore of the bay, and on reaching this, the whole bay burst upon their view.

It was still a beautiful day; the sun was shining brilliantly, and his rays were reflected in a path of dazzling lustre from the face of the sea. The wind was fresh, and the little waves tossed up their heads across where the sunlight fell, flashing back the rays of the sun in perpetually changing light, and presenting to the eye the appearance of innumerable dazzling stars. Far away rose the Nova Scotia shore as they had seen it in the morning, while up the bay, in the distance, abrupt, dark, and precipitous, arose the solitary Ile Haute.

Beneath them the waters of the bay foamed and splashed; and though there was not much surf, yet the waters came rolling among the rocks, seething and boiling, and extending as far as the eye could reach, up and down, in a long line of foam.

Reaching the edge, they all looked down. At the bottom there were visible the heads of black rocks, which arose above the waves at times, but which, however, at intervals, were covered with the rolling waters that tossed around them in foam and spray. Nearer and higher up there were rocks which projected like shelves from the face of the cliff, and seemed capable of affording a foothold to any climber; but their projection served also to conceal from view what lay immediately beneath.

Along the whole beach, however, up and down, there appeared no sign of human life. Anxiously they looked, hoping to see some human form, in some part of that long line of rock; but none was visible, and they looked at one another in silence.

"Wal, he don't turn up yet; that's clar," said Captain Corbet.

"We can see a great deal from here, too," said Bart, in a despondent tone.

"Ay, an that's jest what makes the wust of it. I thought that one look from a commandin pint would reveal the wanderer to our eyes."

"Perhaps he is crouching in among the rocks down there."

"Wal, I rayther think he'd manage to git up a leetle further out of the reach of the surf than all that."

"He may be farther on."

"True; an I dare say he is, too."

"There don't seem to be any place below these rocks, where he would be likely to be."

"No; I think that jest here he could climb up, as fur as that thar shelf, certain. He may be old an rheumatic, but he's able enough to climb that fur."

"I don't think anything could have happened to him here, or we should see some signs of him."

"Course we would--we'd see his remains--we'd see his basket, or his hat, floatin and driftin about. But thar's not a basket or a hat anywhar to be seen."

"The cliff is long here, and runs in so from that point, that if he went up any distance, it would be easy for him to be caught by the rising tide."

"Course it would. O, yes, course. That's the very thing that struck me. It's very dangerous for an ole inexperienced man. But come, we mustn't stand talkin, we must hurry on, or we may as well go back agin, at onst."

Starting forward, they walked on for some time in silence. For about a hundred yards they were able to keep close to the edge of the cliff, so as to look over; but after that they encountered a dense alder thicket. In order to traverse this, they had to go farther inland, where there was some sort of an opening. There they came to a wood where the underbrush was thick, and the walking difficult. This they traversed, and at length worked their way once more to the edge of the cliff. Looking down here, they found the scene very much like what it had been farther back. The waves were dashing beneath them among rocks whose black crests were at times visible among the foam, while from the cliffs there were the same projecting shelves which they had noticed before.

"See there!" cried Bart, pointing to a place behind them. "Do you see how the cliff seems to go in there--just where the alder bushes grow? That looks like a place where a man might be caught. I wonder if he isn't there."

"Can't we go and see?"

"I don't think you can git thar."

"O, it isn't far," said Bart. "I'll run back and look down. The rest of you had better go on; I'll join you soon."

"I'll go with you," said Bruce.

"Very well."

Bruce and Bart then set out, and forced their way through the dense alder bushes, until at length they found themselves near the place. Here there was a chasm in the line of cliff, reaching from the top to the bottom. The sides were precipitous, and they could see perfectly well all the way down. At the bottom the water was rolling and tossing; and this, together with the precipitous cliffs, showed them plainly that no one could have found shelter here.

Sadly and silently they returned, and rejoined the others, who had been walking along in advance.

"Wal?" said Captain Corbet, interrogatively.

Bart shook his head.

They then walked on for some time in silence. "Come," said Captain Corbet; "we've been makin one mistake ever sence we started."

"What's that?"

"We've kep altogether too still. How do we know but we've passed him somewhar along down thar. We can't see behind all them corners."

"Let's shout now--the rest of the way."

"Yes; that's it; yell like all possessed."

The cries of the boys now burst forth in shrill screams and yells, which were echoed among the woods and rocks around.

"Now," cried Captain Corbet, "all together!"

The boys shouted all together.

"That'll fetch him," said the captain, "ef anythin doos. It's a pity we didn't think of this afore. What an ole fool I must ha ben to forgit that!"

The boys now walked on shouting, and screaming, and yelling incessantly, and waiting, from time to time, to listen for an answer.

But no answer came.

At times Captain Corbet's voice sounded forth. His cry was a very peculiar one. It was high pitched, shrill, and penetrating, and seemed as though it ought to be heard for miles. But the united voices of the boys, and the far-piercing yell of the captain, all sounded equally in vain. No response came, and at last, after standing still and listening for a longer time than usual, they all looked despondingly at one another, as though each were waiting for the other to suggest some new plan of action.

Captain Corbet stood and looked musingly out upon the sea, as though the sight of the rolling waters assisted his meditations. It was some time before he spoke.

"I tell you what it is, boys," said he at last. "We've ben makin another mistake."

"How so?"

"We've gone to work wrong."

"Well, what can we do now?"

"Wal, fust an foremost, I muve we go back on our tracks."

"Go back?"

"Yas."

"Why?"

"Wal, you see, one thing,--Solomon can't hev come further than this by no possibility, onless he started straight off to walk all the way up the bay agin, back to Petticoat Jack by the shore route,--an as that's too rough a route for an ole man, why, I calc'late it's not to be thought of. Ef, on the contrairy, he only kem out to hunt for fish, 'tain't likely he come as fur as this, an in my pinion he didn't come nigh as fur. You see we're a good piece on, and Solomon wouldn't hev come so fur if he'd cal'lated to get back to the schewner. What d'ye say to that?"

"I've thought of that already," said Bruce, sadly. "We've certainly gone as far as he could possibly have gone."

"Terrew," said Captain Corbet, solemnly.

"But what can we do now?" asked Bart.

"Fust of all, go back."

"What! give him up?"

"I didn't say that. I said to go back, an keep a good lookout along the shore."

"But we've done that already."

"Yes, I know; but then we didn't begin to yell till quite lately, whereas we'd ought to hev yelled from the time of fust startin. Now, I think ef we went back yellin all the way, we'd have a chance of turnin him up somewhar back thar whar we fust came in sight of the cliff. Very likely, if he ain't already drownded, he's a twisted himself up in some holler in the cliff back thar. He couldn't hev got this fur, certain,--unless he'd ben a runnin away."

All this seemed so certain to the boys that they had nothing to say in opposition to it. In fact, as Bruce said, they had already gone as far as Solomon could possibly have gone, and this thought had occurred to them all. Captain Corbet's proposition, therefore, seemed to them the only course to follow. So they all turned and went back again.

"What I was a goin to say," remarked Captain Corbet, after walking a few paces,--"what I was a goin to say was this. The mistake I made was in not gettin a boat."

"A boat? Why we've traced the coast from the cliff well enough--haven't we?"

"No, not well enough. We'd ought to have planned this here expedition more kerfully. It wan't enough to go along the top of the cliff this here way. You see, we've not been able to take in the lower part of the cliff underneath. We'd ought to hev got a boat. Some of us could hev gone along the cliff, jest as we hev ben doin, and the others could have pulled along the shore an kep up a sharp lookout that way. We've lost any quantity o' time that way, but that's no reason why we should lose any more; so I muve that some of us go back, right straight off, an get a boat at the ship-yard, an come back. I'll go, unless some o' youns think yourselfes smarter, which ain't onlikely."

"O, you can't run, captain," said Bart. "Bruce and I will go, and we'll run all the way."

"Wal, that's the very best thing that you could do. You're both young, an ac-tyve. As for me, my days of youth an actyvity air over, an I'm in the sere an yaller leaf, with spells o' rheumatics. So you start off as quick as your legs can carry you, an ef you run all the way, so much the better."

The boys started off at this, and going on the full run, they hurried, as fast as possible, back over the path they had traversed, and through the woods, and over the fields, and down the cliff towards the ship-yard.

Phil and Pat, however, remained with Captain Corbet; and these three walked back along the edge of the cliff; still looking down carefully for signs of Solomon, and keeping up constantly their loud, shrill cries.

Thus they walked back, till, at length, they reached the place where the alders were growing. Here they were compelled to make a detour as before, after which they returned to the cliff, and walked along, shouting and yelling as when they came.

XIV.

Back again.--Calls and Cries.--Captain Corbet's Yell.--A significant Sign.--
The old Hat.--The return Cry.--The Boat rounds the Point.

Captain Corbet, with Phil and Pat, walked along the top of the cliff in this way, narrowly scrutinizing the rocks below, and calling and shouting, until, at length, they reached the place at which they had first come out upon the shore.

"Now, boys," said the captain, "from here to the pint down thar is all new ground. We must go along here, an keep a good lookout. If we hev any chance left of findin anythin, it's thar. I'm ony sorry we didn't examine this here fust an foremost, before wanderin away off up thar, whar 'tain't at all likely that Solomon ever dreamed of goin. I hope the boys won't be long gettin off that thar boat."

"Perhaps they can't get one."

"O, yes, they can. I saw two or three down thar."

They now walked on a little farther.

At this place the cliff was as steep as it had been behind; but the rocky shelves were more numerous, and down near the shore they projected, one beyond another, so that they looked like natural steps.

"If Solomon was caught by the tide anywhar hereabouts," said Captain Corbet, "thar's no uthly reason why he shouldn't save himself. He could walk up them rocks jest like goin up stairs, an git out of the way of the heaviest surf an the highest tide that these shores ever saw."

"It all depends," said Phil, "on whether he staid about here, or went farther up."

"Course--an it's my opinion that he did stay about here. He was never such an old fool as to go so far up as we did. Why, ef he'd a done so over them rocks, he'd never have got the use of his legs agin."

"Strange we don't see any signs of him."

"O, wal, thar's places yet we hevn't tried."

"One thing is certain--we haven't found any signs of him. If anything had happened, we'd have seen his basket floating."

"Yes, or his old hat."

"I should think, if he were anywhere hereabouts, he'd hear the noise; we are shouting loud enough, I'm sure. As for your voice, why, he ought to hear it a mile away; and the point down there doesn't seem to be a quarter that distance."

"O, it's further than that; besides, my voice can't penetrate so easily down thar. It gits kine o' lost among the rocks. It can go very easy in a straight line; but when it's got to turn corners an go kine o' round the edges o' sharp rocks, it don't get on so well by a long chalk. But I think I'll try an divarsify these here proceedins by yellin a leetle lower down."

So saying, Captain Corbet knelt down, and putting his head over the cliff, he uttered the loudest, and sharpest, and shrillest yell that he could give. Then he listened in silence, and the boys also listened in breathless expectation for some time. But there was no response whatever.

Captain Corbet arose with a sigh.

"Wal, boys," said he, in a mournful tone, "we must git on to the pint. We'd ought to know the wust pooty soon. But, at any rate, I'm bound to hope for the best till hope air over."

The little party now resumed their progress, and walked on towards the point, shouting at intervals, as before.

From this place on as far as the point, the ground was clear, and there was nothing to bar their way. They could go along without being compelled to make any further detour, and could keep near enough to the edge to command a view of the rocks below. They walked on, and shouted without ceasing, and thus traversed a portion of the way.

Suddenly Captain Corbet's eye caught sight of something in the water. It was round in shape, and was floating within a few feet of the shore, on the top of a wave. As Captain Corbet looked, the wave rolled from underneath it, and dashed itself upon the rocks, while the floating object seemed to be thrown farther out. The tide had turned already, and was now on the ebb, so that floating articles, such as this, were carried away from the shore, rather than towards it.

Upon this Captain Corbet fastened his gaze, and stood in silence looking at it. At length he put his hand on Phil's shoulder, and directed the attention of the boys to the floating object.

"Do you see that?" said he.

"What?"

"That thing."

"What--that round thing?"

"Yes, that round thing. Look sharp at it now. What doos it look like to your young eyes?"

Phil and Pat looked at it very carefully, and in silence. Then Phil looked up into Captain Corbet's face without saying a word.

"Wal?"

"What is it, do you think?" asked Phil, in a low voice.

"What do YOU think?"

"Sure an it's a hat--a sthraw hat," said Pat.

Captain Corbet exchanged a meaning glance with Phil.

"Do you think it's HIS hat?" asked Phil.

"Whose else can it be?"

Phil was silent, and his gaze was once more directed to the floating object. As it rose and fell on the waves, it showed the unmistakable outline of a straw hat, and was quite near enough for them to recognize its general character and color. It was dark, with the edges rather ragged, a broad brim, and a roomy crown, not by any means of a fashionable or graceful shape, but coarse, and big, and roomy, and shabby--just such a hat as Solomon had put on his head when he left Grand Pre with them on this memorable and ill-fated voyage.

They looked at it for a long time in silence, and none of them moved.

Captain Corbet heaved a deep sigh.

"This here," said he, "has been a eventfool vyge. I felt a derred persentment afore I started. Long ago I told you how the finger of destiny seemed to warn me away from the ocean main. I kem to the conclusion, you remember, that henceforth

I was to dwell under my own vine an fig tree, engaged in the tender emplymint of nussin the infant. But from this I was forced agin my own inclynations. An what's the result? Why, this--that thar hat! See here, boys;" and the venerable seaman's tone grew deeper, and more solemn, and more impressive; "see here, boys," he repeated; "for mor'n forty year hev I follered the seas, an traversed the briny deep; but, though I've hed my share of storms an accydints, though I've ben shipwrecked onst or twiste, yet never has it ben my lot to experience any loss of human life. But now, but now, boys, call to mind the startlin events of this here vyge! Think of your companion an playmate a driftin off in that startlin manner from Petticoat Jack! An now look here--gaze upon that thar! Words air footil!"

"Do you give him up, then?" cried Phil. "Poor, poor old Solomon!"

Captain Corbet shook his head.

"'Deed, thin, an I don't!" cried Pat. "What's a hat? 'Tain't a man, so it isn't. Many's the man that's lost his hat, an ain't lost his life. It's a windy place here, an ole Solomon's hat's a mile too big for him, so it is--'deed an it is."

Captain Corbet shook his head more gloomily than ever.

"Ow, sure an ye needn't be shakin yer head that way. Sure an haven't ye lost hats av yer own, over an over?"

"Never," said the captain. "I never lost a hat."

"Niver got one blowed off? 'Deed an ye must have."

"I never got one blowed off. When the wind blowed hard I allus kep 'em tied on."

"Well, Solomon hadn't any tie to his, an it cud tumble off his old pate asy enough, so it cud. Sure he's lost it jumpin over the rocks. Besides, where's his basket?"

"At the bottom, no doubt."

"Sure an it cud float."

"No; I dar say it was full of lobsters."

"Any how, I'll not believe he's gone till I see him," cried Pat, earnestly. "Seein's believin."

"Ef he's gone," said Captain Corbet, more solemnly than ever, "ye'll never see him. These waters take too good care of a man for that."

"Well, yer all givin up too soon," said Pat. "Come along now; there's lots of places yet to examin. Give one of yer loudest yells."

Captain Corbet did so. In spite of his despondency as to poor old Solomon's fate, he was not at all unwilling to try any further chances. On this occasion he seemed to gain unusual energy out of his very despair; and the yell that burst from him was so high, so shrill, so piercing, and so far penetrating, that the former cries were nothing compared to it.

"Well done!" cried Pat. "Sure an you bet yerself that time, out an out."

"Stop!" cried Phil. "Listen. What's that?"

Far away, as they listened, they heard a faint cry, that seemed like a response.

"Is that the echo?" asked Phil, anxiously.

"Niver an echo!" cried Pat, excitedly. "Shout agin, captain, darlin."

Captain Corbet gave another shout as loud and as shrill as the preceding one.

They listened anxiously.

Again they heard the cry. It was faint and far off; yet it was unmistakably a human cry. Their excitement now grew intense.

"Where did it come from?" cried Phil.

"Wal, it kine o' seemed to me that it came back thar," said the captain, pointing to the woods.

"'Deed an it didn't," cried Pat; "not a bit of it. It was from the shore, jest ahead; from the pint, so it was, or I'm a nagur."

"I think it came from the shore, too," said Phil; "but it seemed to be behind us."

"Niver a bit," cried Pat; "not back there. We've been there, an whoever it was wud have shouted afore, so he wud. No, it's ahead at the pint. He's jest heard us, an he's shoutin afther us. Hooray! Hurry up, an we'll be there in time to save him."

Pat's confidence was not without its effect on the others. Without waiting any longer, they at once set off at a run, stopping at intervals to yell, and then listening for a response. To their delight, that response came over and over again; and to their still greater joy, the sound each time was evidently louder.

Beyond a doubt, they were drawing nearer to the place from which the sounds came.

This stimulated them all the more, so that they hurried on faster.

The edge of the cliff was not covered by any trees, but the ground at its summit had been cleared, so that progress was not at all difficult. They therefore did not take much time in traversing the space that intervened between the spot where they had first heard the cry, and the point where the cliff terminated. The cry grew steadily louder, all the way, until at last, when they approached the point, it seemed to come directly from beneath.

The cliff here was perpendicular for about forty feet down, and below this it seemed to retreat, so that nothing could be seen. The tide was on the ebb; but it was still so high that its waves beat below them, and seemed to strike the base of the rock. Beyond, on the right, there was a sloping ledge, which descended from the cliffs into the sea, over which the waves were now playing.

It was from the hollow and unseen recess down at the foot of the cliff that the cry seemed to arise, which had come in response to the calls of those on the summit. On reaching the place above, they knelt down, and looked over, but were not able to distinguish any human being, or any sign of the presence of one. But as they looked anxiously over, the cry arose, not very loud, but quite distinct now, and assured them that this was the place which sheltered the one who had uttered that cry.

Captain Corbet now thrust his head over as far as he could, and gave a call in his loudest voice.

"Hal-lo-o-o-o-o-o-o-o-o-o-o-o!"

To which there came up in answer a cry that sounded like--

"Hi-i-i-i-i-i-i-i-i!"

"Solomo-o-o-o-o-o-o-o-on!"

"He-e-e-e-e-e-e-e-ey!"

"Is that yo-o-o-o-o-o-o-o-o-ou?"

"It's me-e-e-e-e-e-e-e-e!"

"Where are y-o-o-o-o-o-o-o-o-ou?"

"He-e-e-e-e-e-e-e-e-re!"

"Come u-u-u-u-u-u-u-up!"

"Ca-a-a-a-a-a-a-a-a-n't!"

"Why no-o-o-o-o-o-o-o-o-ot?"

"Too hi-i-i-i-i-i-i-i-i-gh!"

"Go round the pi-i-i-i-i-i-nt!"

"Too high ti-i-i-i-i-i-i-de!"

"Wa-a-a-a-a-a-a-a-a-it!"

"All ri-i-i-i-i-i-i-ght!"

Captain Corbet now sprang up as nimbly as a young lad, and looked at Phil and Pat with an expression of such exceeding triumph, that his face seemed fairly to shine.

"It IS Solomon!" he cried. But it was of no use for him to convey that piece of information to the boys, who already knew that fact quite as well as he did.

"It IS Solomon," he repeated; "an now the pint is, how air we to git him up?"

"Let me go down," said Pat.

"How?"

"Sure an I can git down wid that bit o' rope you have."

"Mebbe you can, an then agin mebbe you can't; but s'posin you was to git down, how upon airth would that help the matter?"

"Sure an we cud give him a pull up."

"I don't think we could manage that," said Captain Corbet, "and you couldn't, at any rate, if you were down thar with him. As far as I see, we'll hev to wait till the tide falls."

"Wouldn't it be better," said Phil, "for us to go around, so as to come nearer?"

"How? Whar?"

"Why, down to the beach, and then we could walk around the point."

"Walk? Why, it's high water."

"So it is--I forgot that."

"The fact is, we can't git any nearer than we air now. Then, agin, the boys'll be along in a boat soon. They ought to be here by this time; so let's sit down here, an wait till they heave in sight."

With a call of encouragement to Solomon which elicited a reply of satisfaction, Captain Corbet sat down upon the grass, and the boys followed his example. In this position they waited quietly for the boat to come.

Meanwhile, Bart and Bruce had hurried on as rapidly as their legs could carry them, and at length reached the path which went down to the beach. Down this they scrambled, and not long afterwards they reached the ship-yard. Here they obtained a boat without any difficulty, which the workmen launched for them; and then they pushed off, and pulled for the point, with the intention of rowing along opposite the shore, and narrowly inspecting it.

Scarcely had they reached the point, however, when a loud and well-known voice sounded from on high. They both turned and looked up, still pulling. There they saw Captain Corbet, and Phil, and Pat, all of whom were shouting and making furious gestures at them.

"We've found him! Come in closer!" cried Captain Corbet.

"Whe-e-e-re?" cried Bruce.

But before any answer could come, a loud, shrill scream, followed by a yell of delight, burst forth from some place still nearer.

Burt and Bruce both started, and looked towards the place from which this last cry came.

There a very singular and pleasing sight met their eyes.

About six feet above the water was a shelf of rock, that ran down sloping to the beach, and over this there projected a great mass of the cliff. In this recess there crouched a familiar figure. He had no hat, but between his legs, as he sat there, he held a basket, to which he clung with his knees and his hands. As he sat there his eyes were fixed upon them, and their whites seemed enlarged to twice their ordinary dimensions, while yell after yell came from him.

"Help, he-e-e-e-e-lp! Mas'r Ba-a-a-a-a-a-a-art! O, Mas'r Ba-a-a-a-a-a-a-a-a-art! He-e-e-e-e-e-e-e-e-lp! Sa-a-a-a-a-a-a-a-a-a-a-a-a-a-ave me!"

"Hurrah! hurrah!" cried Bart and Bruce, in a burst of heartfelt joy.

"He-e-e-e-e-e-e-e-e-lp!" came forth once more from Solomon.

"All right," cried Bart; and at once the boat pointed towards the place where Solomon was sitting. The water nearer the shore was somewhat rough, but fortunately there were no rocks just there, and they were able to bring the boat in close to the place where Solomon was confined. At their approach Solomon moved slowly down the incline of the rock, on his hands and knees, for there was not room for him to stand upright; and as he moved he pushed the basket before him, as though there was something inside of uncommon value. Reaching, at length, a spot where the rock was about the level of the boat, he waited for them to approach. Soon the boat touched the rock.

"Come, old Sol," cried Bart, "jump in!"

"Hyah, take hole ob dis yar," said Solomon, even in that moment of rescue refusing to move till his precious basket should be safe.

Bart grasped it, and put it into the boat, noticing, as he did so, that it was full of lobsters.

"Come, Solomon, hurry up. I don't like the boat to be knocking here this way."

"All right, sah," said Solomon, crawling along rather stiffly; "ben tied up in a knot all day, an feel so stiff dat I don't know as I'll git untied agin fur ebber mo. Was jest makin my will, any way, as you came along."

By this time Solomon had tumbled into the boat, and worked his way aft, though not without many groans.

"It's de cold rocks, an de wet," he groaned. "Sech an attack o' rheumaticses as dis ole nigga's gwine to hab beats all! Any how, I ben an sabed de lobsta. Loss me ole hat, but didn't car a mite fer dat so long as I sabed de lobsta."

"All right," cried Bart; and at this the two boys pulled away from the rocks and rounded the point. As they came into the sight of those who were waiting on the top of the cliff, a shout of joy arose.

XV.

Exploring Juan Fernandez.--The Cliffs.--The tangled Underbrush.--The Fog Bank.--Is it coming or going?--The Steamer.--Vain Appeals.--New Plans.

Starting off, as we have seen, to explore the island, Tom first directed his steps towards the elevated land which has before been mentioned. At first his path was easy, and the descent very gradual; but at length it became more difficult, and he had to ascend a steep hill, which was over-strewn with stones and interspersed with trees and mounds. Up among these he worked his way, and at length the ascent ceased. He was on the summit of the island. Here he walked to the edge of the area on which he stood, and found himself on the edge of a precipice that went sheer down to a beach, which was apparently two hundred feet beneath him. The precipice seemed actually to lean forward out of the perpendicular, and so tremendous was the view beneath, that Tom, although not by any means inclined to be nervous, found his head grow giddy as he looked down. Looking forth thus from his dizzy elevation, he could see across the bay to the New Brunswick shore, and could mark the general course which his drifting boat must have taken over those deep, dark, and treacherous waters.

The sea was broad, and blue, and tranquil, and desolate, for even from this commanding height not a sail was visible. There was nothing here which could attract Tom's attention for any long period; so he prepared to continue his progress. In front of him lay a wood, before plunging in which he turned to see if there were any vessels coming through the Straits of Minas. None were visible; so, turning back once more, he resumed his journey, and went forward among the trees.

His path now became a difficult one. It was necessary to keep away from the edge of the cliff, but still not to go out of sight of it. The trees were principally spruce and fir, but there were also birch and maple. He also noticed mountain ash and willow. Beneath him all the ground was covered with soft moss, in which he sank to his ankles, while on every side were luxuriant ferns and evergreen trailers. Tom recognized all these with great satisfaction, for they showed him the means of furnishing for himself a soft couch, that might be envied by many a man in better circumstances. Progress soon grew more difficult, for there were numerous mounds, and dense underbrush, through which he could only force his way by extreme effort. Windfalls also lay around in all directions, and no sooner would he have fairly surmounted one of them, than another would appear. Thus his progress was exceedingly slow and laborious.

After about a half an hour of strenuous exertion, Tom found himself in the midst of an almost impassable jungle of tangled, stunted fir trees. He tried to avoid these by making a detour, but found that they extended so far that he could only pass them by going along close to the edge of the cliff. This last path he chose, and clinging to the branches, he passed for more than a hundred yards along the crest of a frightful precipice, where far down there yawned an abyss, at whose bottom was the sea; while abreast of him in the air there floated great flocks of gulls, uttering their hoarse yells, and fluttering fiercely about, as though trying to drive back this intruder upon their domains. Once or twice Tom was compelled to stop, and turn away his face from the abyss, and thrust himself in among the trees; but each time he regained his courage, after a little rest, and went on as before.

At length he passed the thick spruce underbrush, and found the woods less dense. He could now work his way among them without being compelled to go so close to the edge of the cliff; and the dizzy height and the shrieks of the gulls no longer disturbed his senses. The trees here were not so high as those at the other end of the island, but were of much smaller size, and seemed stunted. There were no maples or other forest trees, but only scraggy fir, that seemed too exposed to the winds from the sea to have much health or verdure. The underbrush was wanting to a great extent, but moss was here in large quantities, and thick clusters of alder bushes. Wild shrubs also--such as raspberries and blueberries--were frequently met with; while ledges of weather-beaten rock jutted out from amid thick coverings of moss.

Walking here was not at all difficult, and he went on without any interruption, until, at last, he found any farther progress barred by a precipice. He was at the lower or western end of the island.

He looked down, and found beneath him a great precipice, while rocks jutted out from the sea, and ledges projected beyond. The gulls were present here, as elsewhere, in great flocks, and still kept up their noisy screams.

Tom looked out over the sea, and saw its waters spread far away till it was lost in the horizon. On the line of that horizon he saw a faint gray cloud, that looked like a fog bank. It had, to his eyes, a certain gloomy menace, and seemed to say to him that he had not seen the last of it yet. On the left of the broad sea, the Nova Scotia Coast ran along till it was lost in the distance; and on the right was the long line of the New Brunswick shore, both of which had now that dark hue of olive green which he had noticed on the land opposite before he had started.

Suddenly, while he was looking, his eyes caught sight of something white that glistened brightly from the blue water. It was about midway between the two coasts, and he knew it at once to be some sailing vessel. He could not make out more than one sail, and that showed that the vessel was either coming up the bay or going down; for if it had been crossing, she would, of course, have lain broadside on to his present locality, and would have thus displayed two sails to his view. The sight of this vessel agitated him exceedingly; and the question about her probable course now entered his mind, and drove away all other thoughts. Whether that vessel were going up or down became of exclusive importance to him now, if she were coming up, she might approach him, and hear his hail, or catch sight of his signals. Suddenly he reflected that he had no way of attracting attention, and a wild desire of running back and setting up the longest pole or board that he could find came into his mind; but such was the intensity of his curiosity, and the weight of his suspense, that he could not move from the spot where he was until he had satisfied himself as to the vessel's course.

He sat down not far from the edge of the precipice, and, leaning forward with his hands supporting his chin, he strained his eyes over the intervening distance, as he tried to make out in which way the vessel was going. It seemed fully ten miles away, and her hull was not visible. It was only the white of her sails that he saw; and as the sunlight played on these from time to time, or fell off from the angle of reflection, the vessel was alternately more or less visible, and thus seemed by turns to draw nearer and depart farther from his sight.

Thus for a long time he sat, alternately hoping and desponding, at every play of those sails in the sunlight. The calm of the water showed him that, even if the vessel were coming up, he could not expect any very rapid progress. There was now no wind, and the surface of the water was perfectly unruffled. Besides, he knew that the tide was falling rapidly. How, then, could he expect that the vessel could come any nearer, even if she were trying to? Thoughts like these at last made him only anxious to keep the vessel in sight. If her destination lay up the bay, she would probably anchor; if it lay down the bay, she would drift with the tide. He thought, then, that if she only would remain in sight, it would be a sufficient proof of her course.

Thus he sat, watching and waiting, with all his soul intent upon those flashing sails, and all his thoughts taken up with the question as to the course of that solitary bark. It seemed a long time to him, in his suspense; but suspense always makes time seem long. At last, however, even though he hoped so persistently for the best, his hope began to die within him. Fainter and fainter grew those sails; at intervals rarer and rarer did their flash come to his eyes, until at length the sight of them was lost altogether, and nothing met his eyes but the gloomy gray of the fog cloud on the far horizon.

Even after he had lost hope, and become convinced that she was gone, Tom sat there for a long time, in a fixed attitude, looking at that one spot. He would have sat there longer, but suddenly there came to his ears a peculiar sound, which made him start to his feet in a moment, and filled him with a new excitement.

He listened.

The sound came again.

A flush of joy spread over his face, his heart beat faster and faster, and he listened as though he could scarce believe his senses.

As he listened, the sounds came again, and this time much louder.

There was now no mistake about it. It was a regular boat, which Tom knew well to be the peculiar sound made by the floats of a steamer's paddles. He had often heard it. He had but recently heard it, when the revenue steamer was approaching the Antelope, and again during the foggy night, when the whistle roused them, and the same beat of the paddles came over the midnight waters.

And now, too, he heard it.

He gave a shout of joy, and started off to catch sight of her.

For a few paces only he ran, and then stopped.

He was puzzled. He did not know in which direction it was best to go. He was at the west end of the island, but could not make out very well the direction of the sounds. He tried to think whether the steamer would pass the island on the north side or the south. He did not know, but it seemed to him that she would certainly go to the north of it. There was no time to be lost, and standing there to listen did not seem to be of any use, even if his impatience had allowed him to do so. Accordingly he hurried back by the way that he had come along the north side of the island.

For some time he ran along through the trees, and at length, in about fifteen or twenty minutes, he reached the place where the dense underbrush was, by the edge of the cliff. From this point a wide view was commanded. On reaching it he looked out, and then up the bay, towards the Straits of Minas. He could see almost up to the straits, but no steamer appeared. For a moment he stood bewildered, and then the thought came to him, that he had mistaken altogether the steamer's course. She could not be coming down on the north side of the island, but on the south side. With a cry of grief he started back again, mourning over his error, and the time that he had lost. On reaching the more open wood, he thought that it would be better to hurry across the island to the south side, and proceeded at once to do so. The way was rough and tedious. Once or twice he had to burst through thickets of alder, and several times he had to climb over windfalls. At length, in his confusion, he lost his way altogether; he had to stop and think. The shadows of the trees showed him where the south lay, and he resumed his journey. At length, after most exhaustive efforts, he reached a part of the cliff, where a fringe of alders grew so thick, that he was scarce aware that he was at his destination, until the precipice opened beneath him. Here he stood, and, pressing apart the dense branches, he looked out.

There was the steamer, about two miles off, already below where he was standing, and going rapidly down the bay with the falling tide.

Another cry of grief burst from Tom. Where he was standing he could see the vessel, but he himself was completely concealed by the clustering bushes. He now lamented that he had left his first position, and saw that his only chance was to have remained there.

To stay where he was could not be thought of. There was scarce a chance now of doing anything, since the steamer was so far away; but what chance there was certainly depended on his being in some conspicuous position. He started off, therefore, to the west point, where he had watched the schooner for so long a time. He hurried on with undiminished energy, and bounded over windfalls, and burst through thickets, as before. But in spite of his efforts, his progress could not be more rapid than it had formerly been. His route was necessarily circuitous, and before he could find the desired point, many more minutes had elapsed.

But he reached it at last, and there, on the bare rock, springing forward, he waved his hat in the air, and sent forth a piercing cry for help. But the steamer was now as much as four or five miles away--too far altogether for his loudest cry to go. His screams and his gestures did not appear to attract the slightest attention. She moved on her way right under the eyes of the frantic and despairing boy, nor did she change her course in the slightest degree, nor did her paddles cease to revolve, but went rolling round, tossing up the foam, and bearing far, far away that boat on which poor Tom had rested his last hope.

As for Tom, he kept up his screams as long as he could utter a sound. He tore off his coat, and shook it up and down, and waved it backward and forward. But none of these things were heard or seen. The steamboat passed on, until, at length, even Tom became convinced that further efforts were useless.

This last blow was too much. Tom sank under it, and, falling on his face, he burst into a flood of tears.

Struggling up at length from this last affliction, Tom roused himself, and his buoyancy of soul began once more to assert itself.

"Come now, Thomas, my son," said he, as he dried his eyes, "this sort of thing will never do, you know. You're not a baby, my boy; you've never been given to blubbering, I think. Cheer up, then, like a man, and don't make me feel ashamed of you."

This little address to himself had, as before, the effect of restoring his equanimity, and he thought with calmness upon his recent disappointments.

He saw, by the passage of these vessels, what he had for a time lost sight of, namely, that this island, though uninhabited, was still in the middle of a bay which was constantly traversed by sailing vessels and steamboats. The latter ran regularly up to the Basin of Minas from St. John. As to the former, they were constantly passing to and fro, from the large ship down to the small fishing vessel. Inhabited countries surrounded him on every side, between the coasts of which there was a constant communication. If he only kept patient, the time must come, and that, too, before very long, when he would be delivered.

In order to secure this delivery, however, he saw that it would be necessary to arrange some way by which he might attract the notice of passing vessels. On this subject he meditated for a long time. It would be necessary, he thought, to have some sort of a signal in some conspicuous place. Among the drift-wood he might, perhaps, be able to find some sort of a pole or staff which he could set up. One might not be enough, but in that case he could put up two, or three, or half a dozen.

The next thing to decide about was the choice of a place. There was the east end, and the west end--which was the better? The west end, where he was stand-ing, was high; but then it was surrounded by trees, and unless he could set up a very tall staff, it could scarcely be noticed. The east end, on the contrary, was lower; but then it was bare, and any kind of a signal which might be set up there could hardly fail to attract attention. He could also pile up a heap of drift-wood, and set fire to it, and, by this means, if a vessel were passing by, he could be certain of securing at-tention. It did not make much difference which end the signals were placed upon, as far as referred to the passing of vessels; for all that passed by would go along the island, so that both ends would be visible to them.

As to the signals, he felt confident that he could find a staff, or, if one would not be long enough, several could be fastened together. The coil of rope in the boat would enable him to do this. The sail would afford material for a flag.

All these plans came to his mind as he stood there; and the prospect of once more doing something which was to help him to escape from his prison drove away the last vestige of his grief. His courage again arose, hope revived, and he burst forth into a light and joyous song. Very different was he now from the despairing lad who, but a short time before, had been pouring forth his tears of sorrow; and yet but a few minutes had passed since then. The steamer was yet in sight down the bay, but Tom, who had lately been so frantic in his efforts to attract her attention, now cast a glance after her of perfect indifference.

And now it was necessary for him to return to the east end of the island, and look about for the means of putting into execution his plan for making a signal.

He started off on his return without any further delay. The path back was as rough and toilsome as the way down had been; but Tom was now full of hope, and his elastic spirits had revived so thoroughly that he cared but little for the fatigue of the journey. It was traversed at last, and he descended the slope to the place from which he had started.

His exploration of the island had been quite complete. It seemed to him to be about a mile and a half in length, and a half a mile or so in width. The east end, where he had first arrived, was the only place where it was at all desirable to stay.

Immediately on his arrival he examined the boat, and found it secure. To his surprise it was now about sunset. He had forgotten the lapse of time. He was hungry; so he sat down, ate his biscuit, drank his water, and rested from the toils of the day.

XVI.

A Sign for the outer World.--A Shelter for the Outcast's Head.--Tom's Camp and Camp-bed.--A Search after Something to vary a too monotonous Diet.--Brilliant Success.

Tom sat down after his eventful day, and took his evening meal, as has been said. He rested then for some time. His excessive labors had fatigued him less than the great excitement which he had undergone, and now he felt disinclined to exert himself. But the sun had set, and darkness was coming on rapidly; so he rose, at last, and went over to the drift-wood. Here, after a search of about half an hour, he found something which was very well suited to his purpose. It was a piece of scantling about twenty feet long, and not very thick; and to this he saw that he could fasten the pole that he had made up in the woods. These two pieces would make, when joined, a very good flag-staff. These he brought up to the bank. Then he collected an armful of dry chips and sticks, which he carried over to a spot near where the boat lay. A rock was there, and against one side of this he built a pile of the chips. He then tried a match, and found that it was quite dry, and lighted it without any difficulty. With this he kindled the fire, and soon saw, with great satisfaction, a bright and cheerful blaze.

He was so delighted with the fire that he brought up a dozen more loads of wood, which he laid near. Then he drew up the bit of scantling, and bringing the coil of rope, he cut a piece off, and proceeded to fasten to the scantling the pole which he had procured in the woods. He did this by winding the rope around in a close and even wind; and, finally, on concluding his task, he found that it was bound firmly enough to stand any breeze. It took a long time to finish this; but Tom had slept late in the morning, and, though fatigued, he was not sleepy. After this he sat down in front of the fire, and enjoyed its friendly light and its genial glow. He kept heaping on the fuel, and the bright flames danced up, giving to him the first approach to anything like the feeling of comfort that he had known since he had drifted away from the Antelope. Nor was it comfort only that he was mindful of while he watched and fed the fire. He saw in this fire, as it shone out over the water, the best kind of a signal, and had some hope of being seen and hailed by some passing vessel. In this hope he sat up till midnight, looking out from time to time over the water, and expecting every instant to see the shadow of some approaching vessel.

But midnight came, and Tom at length thought of sleep. The sail had dried thoroughly through the day; so now he used it once more as a coverlet, and, folding himself in it, he reclined, as before, against the mossy bank, and slept.

On awaking the next day, he arose and looked around. To his deep disappointment, he could see nothing. There was a fog over all the scene. The wind had changed, and his old enemy was once more besieging him. It was not so thick, indeed, as it had been, being light and dry, so that the ground was not at all moistened; but still the view was obscured, so that no vessel could be seen unless it came within half a mile; and that was rather closer than most vessels would care to come to his island.

This day was Sunday, and all Tom's plans had to be deferred until the following day. However, it was not at all disagreeable to him to get rid of the necessity of work; and, indeed, never before did he fully appreciate the nature of the Day of Rest. The rest was sweet indeed to his exhausted and overworn frame, and he did not go far away from his fire. He had found some embers still glowing in the morning, and had kindled the fire anew from these, without drawing any more upon his precious store of matches. He resolved now to keep the coals alive all the time, by feeding the fire during the day, and covering it up with ashes by night.

It was Sunday,--the Day of Rest,--and Tom felt all the blessedness of rest. On the whole, it turned out to be the pleasantest day which he had known since he left the schooner. Left now to quiet reflection, he recalled the events of the last week, and had more leisure to feel thankful over the wonderful safety which he had met with. Even now on the island he was not without his comforts. He had food and warmth. So, on the whole, though he had his moments of sadness, yet the sadness was driven out by cheerfulness. It was not all dismal. The words of that poem which is familiar to every school-boy rang in his ears:--

"O, Solitude, where are the charms
    That sages have seen in thy face?
Better dwell in the midst of alarms
    Than reign in this horrible place."

Yet these words were accompanied and counterbalanced by the more pleasing and consoling sentiments of others, which on this day accorded better with Tom's mood:--

"There's mercy in every place;
    And mercy--encouraging thought!--
Gives even affliction a grace,
    And reconciles man to his lot."

Nothing occurred during the day to disturb the quiet of the island, and Tom went to bed early that night, so as to have a long sleep, and fortify himself for the labors of the morrow. The ashes were raked carefully round the coals, which, when Tom waked in the morning, were easily kindled again.

He was up early on that Monday morning. He saw, with deep disappointment, that the fog still covered every thing, and that the wind was blowing quite brisk from the south-west, and raising rather a heavy sea. But he had a great deal to do now, and to this he turned his attention.

First of all, he had to finish his signal-staff and set it up. He was very much troubled about the proper material for a flag. The canvas was rather too heavy; but as he had nothing else, he had to take this. He fastened a bit of the rope to the head of the staff, so as to form a loop, and through this he ran a piece which was long enough to serve for halyards. Thus far he had not used up more than a quarter of the coil of rope; but he needed all that was left for other purposes. The next thing was to set up his staff. To do this required much labor. He had already selected the place which seemed most suitable. It was at the extreme point of a tongue of land which projected beside the brook, and only a little distance from his resting-place.

Here the ground was soft; and choosing a sharp stone, he worked diligently for about a couple of hours, until at length he succeeded in digging a hole which was about eighteen inches in depth. Then he fastened ropes to the staff, where the pole joined it, so that four lines came down far enough to serve as stays. Having done this, he inserted the end of the staff in the hole, and thrust in the earth all around it, trampling it in, and beating it down as tight as he could with a stone. After this he procured some sticks from the drift-wood, and, sharpening the ends, he secured the stays by fastening them to these sticks, which he drove into the ground. The staff then seemed to be as secure as was necessary. It only remained now to hoist up his flag; and this he did without any difficulty, securing it at half mast, so that it might serve unmistakably as a signal of distress.

Upon completing this, Tom rested on the mound, and from that distance he contemplated the signal with a great deal of calm and quiet satisfaction. It was his own device, and his own handiwork, and he was very proud of it. But he did not allow himself a long rest. There yet remained much to be done, and to this he now directed his attention.

He had been thinking, during his last employment, upon the necessity which he had of some shelter. A plan had suggested itself which he felt confident that he could carry into execution without any very great trouble. The fog that now prevailed, and which was far different from the light mist of the previous day, accompanied also, as it was, by the damp south-west wind, made some sort of a shelter imperatively necessary, and that, too, before another night. To pass this night in the fog would be bad enough; but if it should happen to rain also, his situation would be miserable indeed.

He now set out for the beach, and found, without much difficulty, some pieces of wood which were necessary to his purpose. Bringing these back, he next looked about for a good situation. There was a rock not far from the fire, and in front of this was a smooth spot, where the land was flat, and covered with short grass. On the left it sloped to the brook. This seemed to him to be the best place on the island. It was sufficiently sheltered. It was dry, and in case of rain the water would not be likely to flood it. With all these it also possessed the advantage of being sufficiently conspicuous to any passing vessel which might be attracted by the signal-staff. Here, then, Tom determined to erect his place of residence.

His first work was to select two long and slender pieces of wood, and sharpen the ends of them. Then he drove each of them into the ground in such a way that their tops crossed one another. These he bound fast together. Two other stakes were driven into the ground, and secured in the same way, about six or seven feet off. Another long piece of scantling was then placed so as to pass from one to the other of the two crossed sticks, so that it rested upon them. This last was bound tight to the crossed sticks, and thus the whole structure formed a camp-shaped frame.

Over this Tom now threw the sail, and brought it down to the ground on either side, securing it there with pegs. At the back of the camp a piece of the sail was folded over and secured so as to cover it in; while in front another piece of the sail hung down until it nearly reached the ground. This could hang down at night, and be folded over the top by day. Tom now tore up some sods, and laid them over the edge of the canvas on each side, where it touched the ground, and placed on these heavy stones, until at length it seemed sufficiently protected from the entrance of any rain that might flow down the roof. His last task consisted in collecting a large quantity of moss and ferns from the woods, which he strewed over the ground inside, and heaped up at one end, so as to form a soft and fragrant bed. When this was accomplished the camp was finished.

It had taken a long time, and when at last the work was done, it began to grow dark. Tom noticed this with surprise. He had been working so incessantly that he was not mindful of the flight of time, and now the day was done, and the evening was upon him before he was aware. But there were other things still for him to do before he could rest from his labors. His fire was just flickering around its last embers, and if he wished to have a pleasant light to cheer the solitude and the darkness of his evening hours, it would be necessary to prepare a supply of fuel. To this he attended at once, and brought up several armfuls of drift-wood from the beach. Placing these near the fire, he kindled it up afresh, and flung upon the rising flames a generous supply of fuel. The fires caught at it, and crackled as they spread through the dry wood, and tossed up their forked tongues on high, till in the dusk of evening they illuminated the surrounding scene with a pleasant light. A few more armfuls were added, and then the work for the day was over. That work had been very extensive and very important. It had secured a means of communication with the outer world, and had also formed a shelter from the chill night air, the fog, and the storm. It was with a very natural pride that Tom cast his eyes around, and surveyed the results of his ingenuity and his industry.

The camp opened towards the fire, from which it was not so far distant but that Tom could attend to it without any very great inconvenience. The fire shone pleasantly before him as he sat down at his evening repast. As the darkness increased, it threw a ruddier glow upon all the scene around, lighting up field and hill, and sending long streams of radiance into the fog that overhung the sea. Tom had prepared an unusually large supply of fuel, this evening, for the express purpose of burning it all up; partly for his own amusement, and partly in the hope that it might meet the eyes of some passing navigator. It was his only hope. To keep his signals going by night and day was the surest plan of effecting a speedy escape. Who could tell what might be out on the neighboring sea? How did he know but that the Antelope might be somewhere near at hand, with his companions on board, cruising anxiously about in search after the missing boat? He never ceased to think that they were following after him somewhere, and to believe that, in the course of their wanderings, they might come somewhere within sight of him. He knew that they would never give him up till they assuredly knew his fate, but would follow after him, and set other vessels on the search, till the whole bay, with all its shores and islands, should be thoroughly ransacked.

Fortunate was it for him, he thought, that there was so large a supply of driftwood at hand on the beach, dry, portable, and in every way convenient for use. Thanks to this, he might now disperse the gloom of dark and foggy nights, and keep up a better signal in the dark than he could do in the light. Thus the fuel was heaped on, and the fire flamed up, and Tom sat near, looking complacently upon the brilliant glow.

Thus far, for nearly a week, he had fed on biscuit only; but now, as he ate his repast, he began to think that it was a very monotonous fare, and to wonder whether it might not be possible to find something which could give a zest to his repasts. The biscuit were holding out well, but still he felt a desire to husband his resources, and if any additional food could in any way be procured, it would not only be a relish, but would also lessen his demand upon his one sole source of supply. He thought earnestly upon the subject of fish. He turned his thoughts very seriously to the subject of fish-hooks, and tried to think of some way by which he could capture some of the fish with which these waters abounded. But this idea did not seem to promise much. In the first place, he could think of no possible way in which he could procure any serviceable hook; in the second place, even if he had a hook and line all ready and baited, he did not see how he would be able to cast it within reach of any fish. His boat would not float him even for the little distance that was required to get into the places where fish might be. He could only stand upon the beach out of their reach.

But, in the course of his thoughts, he soon perceived that other sources of food were possible to him besides the fish that were caught by hook and line. His mind reverted to the populous realm of shell-fish. These were all before him. Round the rocks and amid the sea-weed there certainly must be mussels. At low tide, amid the ledges and the sand, there surely must be some lobsters. Before him there was an extensive mud flat, where there ought to be clams. Here was his fire, always ready, by night and by day. Why should he not be able to make use of that fire, not only for cheering his mind, and giving him warmth, and signaling to passers-by, but also for cooking his meals?

This was the question that he asked himself as he ate his biscuit. He could not see why he should not be able to accomplish this. As far as he could see, there ought to be plenty of shell-fish of various kinds on these shores. The more he thought of it, the more probable it seemed. He determined to solve the difficulty as soon as possible. On former occasions he had arranged his work on the evening for the succeeding day. On this evening he marked out this work for the morrow, and arranged in his mind a comprehensive and most diligent search for shell-fish, which should embrace the whole circuit of the island.

With this in his mind, he arranged the fire as usual, so as to keep it alive, and then retired to his camp for the night. The presence of a roof over his head was grateful in the extreme. He let down the canvas folds over the entrance, and felt a peculiar sense of security and comfort. The moss and ferns which he had heaped up were luxuriously soft and deliciously fragrant. Over these he stretched his wearied limbs with a sigh of relief, and soon was asleep.

So comfortable was his bed, and so secure his shelter, that he slept longer than usual. It was late when he awaked. He hurried forth and looked around. The fog still rested over everything. If possible it was thicker and more dismal than even on the preceding day. To his surprise, he soon noticed that it had been raining quite heavily through the night. Around, in many places, he saw pools of water, and in the hollows of the rocks he saw the same. This could only have been done by the rain. Going back to his camp, he saw that the canvas was quite wet. And yet the rain had all rolled off. Not a drop had entered. The moss and the fern inside were perfectly dry, and he had not the slightest feeling of dampness about him. His camp was a complete success.

He now went off to search for clams. The tide had been high at about six in the morning. It was now, as he judged, about ten or eleven, and the water was quite low. Selecting a piece of shingle from his wood-pile, he walked down over the mud flat that extended from the point, and, after going a little distance, he noticed the holes that give indications of the presence of clams beneath. Turning up the sand, he soon threw out some of them. He now dug in several different places, and obtained sufficient for the day. These he carried back to the bank in triumph. Then he stirred up his fire, heaped on plenty of wood, and arranged his clams in front so as to roast them.

In spite of Mrs. Pratt's theories, the clams were found by Tom to be delicious, and gave such relish to the biscuit, that he began to think whether he could not make use of the baling dipper, and make a clam chowder.

This breakfast was a great success, and Tom now confidently expected to find other shell-fish, by means of which his resources might be enlarged and improved.

XVII.

Solomon's solemn Tale.--A costly Lobster.--Off again.--Steam Whistles of all Sizes.--A noisy Harbor.--Arrival Home.--No News.

The shout of joy uttered by those on the top of the cliff at seeing old Solomon safe was responded to by those in the boat; and then, as the latter went on her way, Captain Corbet set out to return to the beach, followed by Phil and Pat. Soon they were all reunited, and, the boat being landed, they returned in triumph to the Antelope.

On their way back, Solomon told them the story of his adventures.

"Went out," said he, "on a splorin scursion, cos I was termined to try an skewer somethin to make a dinnah to keep up de sperrit ob dis yah party. Ben trouble nuff, an dat's no reason why we should all starb. I tought by de looks ob tings dar was lobstas somewhar long dis yah sho, an if I got a chance, I knowed I could get 'em. Dar was lots ob time too, ef it hadn't ben fur dat ar pint; dat's what knocked me. Lots o' lobstas--could hab picked up a barl full, ony hadn't any barl to pick up."

"Well, but how did you happen to get caught?"

"Dat ar's jes what I'm a comin to. You see, I didn't tink ob dat ar pint when I went up de sho,--but knowed I had lots ob time; so I jes tought I'd make sure ob de best ob de lobstas. Wan't goin to take back any common lobstas,--bet you dat,--notin for me but de best,--de bery best ones dar. Dat ar's what kep me. It takes a heap ob time an car to get de best ones, when dar's a crowd lyin about ob all sizes, an de water comin in too."

"But didn't you see that the tide was coming up to the point?"

"Nebber see a see,--not a see; lookin ober de lobstas all de time, an mos stracted wid plexity cos I couldn't cide bout de best ones. Dar was lots an lots up dar at one place, dough I didn't go fur,--but ef I'd gone fur, I'd hab got better ones."

"How far did you go?"

"Not fur,--ony short distance,--didn't want to go too fur away for feah ob not gittin back in time. An so I started to come back pooty soon, an walked, an walked. Las, jes as I got to de pint, I rose my ole head, an looked straight afore me, an thar, clar ef I didn't fine myself shut in,--reglar prison,--mind I tell you,--an all round me a reglar cumferince ob water an rock, widout any way ob scape. Tell you what, if dar ebber was a ole rat in a trap, I was at dat ar casion."

"Couldn't you have waded through it before it got too high?"

"Waded? Not a wade; de water was rough an deep, an de bottom was stones dat I'd slipped oba an almost broke my ole head, sides bein drownded as dead as a herrin. Why, what you tink dis ole nigga's made ob? I'm not a steam injine, nor a mowin machine, nor a life boat. I'm ony a ole man, an shaky in de legs too,--mind I tell you."

"Well, how did you manage it?"

"Manage! Why, I didn't manage at all."

"How did you find that place where you were sitting?"

"Wasn't settin. I was tied up in a knot, or rolled up into a ball. Any way, I wasn't settin."

"Well, how did you find the place?"

"Wal, I jes got up dar. I stood on de sho till de water drobe me, an I kep out ob its way till at las I found myself tied up de way you saw me."

"Why didn't you halloo?"

"Hollar? Didn't I hollar like all possessed?"

"We didn't hear you."

"Wal, dat ar's dredful sterious. An me a hollarin an a yellin like mad. Tell you what, I felt as ef I'd bust my ole head open, I did yell that hard."

"Couldn't you manage to climb up that cliff?"

"Dat cliff? Climb up? Me? What! me climb up a cliff? an dat cliff? Why, I couldn't no more climb up dat ar cliff dan I could fly to de moon. No, sah. Much as I could do to keep whar I was, out ob de water. Dat was enough."

"Don't you know that we walked two miles up the shore?"

"Two miles! Two! De sakes, now, chil'en! did you, railly? Ef I'd a ony knowed you war a comin so near, wouldn't I a yelled? I bet I would."

"Why, you didn't think we'd have left you."

"Lef me? Nebber. But den I didn't tink you'd magine anyting was wrong till too late. What I wanted was help, den an dar. De trouble was, when you did come, you all made dat ar circumbendibus, an trabelled clean an clar away from me."

"We thought at first you could not be so near the point."

"But de pint was de whole difficulty. Dat's de pint."

"Well, at any rate, you've saved the lobsters."

"Yah! yah! yah! Yes. Bound to sabe dem dar. Loss my ole hat, an nearly loss my ole self; but still I hung on to dem dar lobstas. Tell you what it is now, dey come nigh onto bein de dearest lobstas you ebber eat. I'be done a good deal in de way ob puttin myself out to get a dinna at odd times for you, chil'en; but dis time I almost put myself out ob dis mortial life. So when you get your dinnas to-day, you may tink on what dat ar dinna come nigh to costin."

"I wonder that you held on to them so tight, when they brought you into such danger."

"Hole on? Why, dat ar's de berry reason why I did hole on. What, let go ob dem arter all my trouble on dat count? No. I was bound to hab somethin to show whenebber I got back, if I ebber did get back; and so here I am, all alibe, an a bringin my lobstas wid me."

"Well, Solomon," said Bart, in a kindly tone, "old man, the lobsters have come near costing us pretty dear, and we felt bad enough, I can tell you, when we went up there along the shore calling for you and getting no answer."

"What, you did car for de ole man, Mas'r Bart--did you?" said Solomon, in a tremulous voice. Tears started to his eyes as he said it, and all power of saying anything more seemed to depart from him. He fell back behind the others, and walked on for the rest of the way in silence, but at times casting upon Bart glances that spoke volumes, and talking to himself in inaudible tones.

In this way they soon reached the wharf where the schooner was lying.

The first thing that they noticed was, that the schooner was aground. The tide had gone out too far for her to float away, and consequently there was no hope of resuming their voyage for that day.

"We're in for it, captain," said Bruce

"Yes; I felt afeard of it," said the captain. "We've got to wait here till the next tide."

"We'll leave to-night, of course."

"O, yes. We must get off at the night's tide, and drop down the bay."

"How far had we better go?"

"Wal, I ben a thinkin it all over, an it's my opinion that we'd better go to St. John next. We may hear of him there, an ef he don't turn up we can send out some more vessels, an give warnin that he's astray on the briny biller."

"At what time will we be able to leave?"

"Wal, it'll not be high tide till near one o'clock, but we can git off ef thar's a wind a leetle before midnight."

"Do you think the wind will hold on?"

The captain raised his head, and looked at the sky; then he looked out to sea, and then he remained silent for a few minutes.

"Wal," said he, at last, slowly and thoughtfully, "it'll take a man with a head as long as a hoss to answer that thar. It mought hold on, an then agin it moughtn't."

"At any rate, I suppose we can drift."

"O, yes; an of the wind doosn't come round too strong, we can git nigh down pooty close to St. John by mornin."

"We'll run down with the tide."

"Percisely."

"Well, I suppose we'll have to put the time through the best way we can, and try to be patient. Only it seems hard to be delayed so much. First there was the fog, which made our search useless; and now, when there comes a bright day, when we can see where we're going, here we are tied up in Quaco all day and all night."

"It doos seem hard," said Captain Corbet, gravely, "terrible hard; an ef I owned a balloon that could rise this here vessel off the ground, an convey her through the air to her nat'ral element, I'd hev it done in five minutes, an we'd all proceed to walk the waters like things of life. But I don't happen to own a balloon, an so thar you air.

"But, boys," continued the captain, in a solemn voice, elevating his venerable chin, and regarding them with a patriarchal smile,--"boys, don't begin to go on in that thar old despondent strain. Methinks I hear some on you a repinin, an a frettin, cos we're stuck here hard an fast. Don't do it, boys; take my advice, an don't do it. Bear in mind the stirrin an memiorable events of this here mornin. See what a calamity was a threatenin us. Why, I declare to you all, thar was a time when I expected to see our aged friend Solomon no more in the flesh. You could not tell it by my manner, for I presarved a calm an collected dumeanour; but yet, I tell you, underneath all that icy calm an startlin good-natur of my attitood, I concealed a heart that bet with dark despair. At that moment, when we in our wanderins had reached the furthest extremity that we attained onto, I tell you my blood friz, an my har riz in horror! Methought it were all up with Solomon; and when I see his hat, it seemed to me jest as though I was a regardin with despairin eye his tumestun whereon war graven by no mortial hand the solemn an despairin epigram, 'Hic jacet!'

"So now, my friends," continued the captain, as he brushed a tear-drop from his eye, "let us conterrol our feelins. Let us be calm, and hope for the best. When Solomon took his departoor, an was among the missin, I thought that an evil fortin was a berroodin over us, and about to consume us. But that derream air past. Solomon is onst more among the eatables. He cooks agin the mortial repast. He lives! So it will be with our young friend who has so mysteriously drifted away from our midst. Cheer up, I say! Them's my sentiment. He'll come to, an turn up, all alive- -right side up--with care,--C. O. D.,--O. K.,--to be shaken before taken,--marked and numbered as per margin,--jest as when shipped, in good order an condition, on board the schooner Antelope, Corbet master, of Grand Pre."

These words of Captain Corbet had a very good effect upon the boys. They had already felt very much cheered by the escape of Solomon, and it seemed to them to be a good omen. If Solomon had escaped, so also might Tom. And, as their anxiety on Solomon's account had all been dispelled by his restoration, so also might they hope that their anxiety about Tom would be dispelled. True, he had been lost to them for a much longer time, and his absence was certainly surrounded by a more terrible obscurity than any which had been connected with that of Solomon. Yet this one favorable circumstance served to show them that all might not be so dark as they had feared. Thus, therefore, they began to be more sanguine, and to hope that when they reached St. John, some tidings of the lost boy might be brought to them.

Solomon's exertions towards giving them a dinner were on this day crowned with greater success than had been experienced for some days past. Their exertions had given them an appetite, and they were able to eat heartily for the first time since Tom's departure.

The rest of the day passed very slowly with them. They retired early, and slept until midnight. At that time they waked, and went on deck, when they had the extreme satisfaction of seeing the vessel get under way. A moderate breeze was blowing, which was favorable, and though the tide was not yet in their favor, yet the wind was sufficient to bear them out into the bay. Then the boys all went below again, full of hope. The night passed away quietly, and without any incident whatever. They all slept soundly, and the dreams that came to them were pleasant rather than otherwise.

Awaking in the morning by daylight, they all hurried up on deck, and encountered there a new disappointment; for all around them they saw again the hated presence of the fog. The wind also had died away, and the vessel's sails flapped idly against her masts.

"Where are we now?" asked Bruce, in a despondent tone.

"Wal," said Captain Corbet, "as nigh as I can reckon, we're two or three miles outside of St. John harbor."

"How is the tide?"

"Wal, it's kine o' agin us, jest now."

"There doesn't seem to be any wind."

"Not much."

"Shall we get into St. John to-day?"

"Wal, I kine o' think we'll manage it."

"How soon?"

"Wal, not much afore midday. You see we're driftin away jest now."

"Don't you intend to anchor till the next rise of tide?"

"O, yes; in about ten minutes we'd ought to be about whar I want to anchor."

At this disheartening condition of affairs the boys sank once more into a state of gloom. In about ten minutes, as Captain Corbet said, the schooner was at anchor, and there was nothing to do but to wait.

"We'll run in at turn o' tide," said he.

Breakfast came, and passed. The meal was eaten in silence. Then they went on deck again, fretting and chafing at the long delay. Not much was said, but the boys stood in silence, trying to see through the thick fog.

"It was so fine when we left," said Bart, "that I thought we'd have it all the way."

"Wal, so we did--pooty much all; but then, you see, about four this mornin we run straight into a fog bank."

"Has the wind changed?"

"Wal, thar don't seem jest now to be any wind to speak of, but it kine o' strikes me that it's somethin like southerly weather. Hence this here fog."

After a few hours the vessel began to get under way again; and now, too, there arose a light breeze, which favored them. As they went on they heard the long, regular blast of a steam whistle, which howled out a mournful note from time to time. Together with this, they heard, occasionally, the blasts of fog horns from un-seen schooners in their neighborhood, and several times they could distinguish the rush of some steamer past them, whose whistle sounded sharply in their ears.

As they drew nearer, these varied sounds became louder, and at length the yell of one giant whistle sounded close beside them.

"We're a enterin o' the harbure," said Captain Corbet.

Hours passed away from the time the Antelope raised anchor until she reached the wharf. In passing up the harbor, the shadowy forms of vessels at anchor became distinguishable amid the gloom, and in front of them, as they neared the wharf, there arose a forest of masts belonging to schooners. It was now midday. Suddenly there arose a fearful din all around. It was the shriek of a large number of steam whistles, and seemed to come up from every side.

"Is that for the fog?" asked Bruce.

"O, no," said Bart; "those are the saw-mills whistling for twelve o'clock."

The boys had already completed their preparations for landing, and had changed their eccentric clothing for apparel which was more suited to making their appear-ance in society. Bart had insisted that they should go to his house, and wait until they might decide what to do; and the boys had accepted his hospitable invitation.

They stepped on shore full of hope, not doubting that they would hear news of Tom. They had persuaded themselves that he had been picked up by some vessel which was coming down the bay, and had probably been put ashore here; in which case they knew that he would at once communicate with Bart's people. They even thought that Tom would be there to receive them.

"Of course he will be," said Bart; "if he did turn up, they'd make him stay at the house, you know; and he'd know that we fellows would come down here in the hope of hearing about him. So we'll find him there all right, after all. Hurrah!"

But, on reaching his home, Bart's joyous meeting with his family was very much marred by the deep, dark, and bitter disappointment that awaited him and his companions.

They knew nothing whatever about Tom. Bart's father was shocked at the story. He knew that no boy had been picked up adrift in the bay during the past week. Such an event would have been known. He felt exceedingly anxious, and at once instituted a search among the coasting vessels. The search was a thorough one, but resulted in nothing. There was no one who had seen anything of a drifting boat. All reported thick fog in the bay.

The result of this search plunged Bart and his friends into their former gloom.

Other searches were made. Inquiries were sent by telegraph to different places, but without result.

The fate of the missing boy now became a serious question

As for Bart and his friends, they were inconsolable.

XVIII.

Down the Bay.--Drifting and Anchoring.--In the Dark, morally and physically.--Eastport, the jumping-off Place.--Grand Manan.--Wonderful Skill.--Navigating in the Fog.--A Plunge from Darkness into Light, and from Light into Darkness.

It was Saturday when Bart reached home. As much was done on that day as possible. Bart was in the extreme of wretchedness, and so eager was he to resume the search for his friend, that his father gave his permission for him to start off again in the Antelope. The other boys also were to go with him. They determined to scour the seas till they found Tom, or had learned his fate.

Mr. Damer also assured Bart that he would take the matter in hand himself, and would send out two schooners to go about the bay. In addition to this, he would telegraph to different places, so that the most extensive search possible might be instituted. Every part of the coast should be explored, and even the islands should be visited.

All this gave as much consolation to Bart and his friends as it was possible for them to feel under the circumstances.

As much as possible was done on Saturday, but the next day was an idle one, as far as the search was concerned. Bart and the boys waited with great impatience, and finally on Monday morning they left once more in the Antelope. It was about five o'clock in the morning, the tide was in their favor, and, though there was a head wind, yet be fore the turn of tide they were anchored a good distance down the bay.

"My idee is this," said Captain Corbet. "I'll explore the hull bay in search of that driftin boy. I'll go down this side, cross over, and come up on t'other. We'll go down here first, an not cross over till we get as fur as Quoddy Head. I think, while we air down thar, I'll call at Eastport an ask a few questions. But I must say it seems a leetle too bad to have the fog go on this way. If this here had ony happened a fortnight ago, we'd have had clear weather an fair winds. It's too bad, I declar."

They took advantage of the next tide to go down still farther, and by twelve o'clock on Monday night they were far down. Since leaving St. John they had seen nothing whatever, but they had heard occasionally the fog horns of wandering schooners, and once they had listened to the yell of a steamer's whistle.

"I've allus said," remarked Captain Corbet, "that in navigatin this here bay, tides is more important than winds, and anchors is more important than sails. That's odd to seafarin men that ain't acquainted with these waters, but it air a oncontrovar-tible fact. Most of the distressin casooalties that happen hereabouts occur from a ignorance of this on the part of navigators. They WILL pile on sail. Now, in clar weather an open sea, pile it on, I say; but in waters like these, whar's the use? Why, it's flyin clar in the face of Providence. Now look at me--do I pile on sail? Not me. Catch me at it! When I can git along without, why, I git. At the same time, I don't think you'll find it altogether for the good of your precious health, boys, to be a movin about here in the fog at midnight. Better go below. You can't do no good a settin or a standin up here, squintin through a darkness that might be felt, an that's as thick as any felt I ever saw. So take my advice, an go below, and sleep it off."

It was impossible to gainsay the truth of Captain Corbet's remarks, and as it was really midnight, and the darkness almost as thick as he said, the boys did go below, and managed to get to sleep in about a minute and a half after their heads touched the pillows.

Before they were awake on the following day the anchor was hoisted, and the Antelope was on her way again.

"Here we air, boys," said the captain, as they came on deck, "under way--the Antelope on her windin way over the mounting wave, a bereasting of the foamin biller like all possessed. I prophesy for this day a good time as long as the tide lasts."

"Do you think we'll get to Eastport harbor with this tide?"

"Do I think so?--I know it. I feel it down to my butes. Eastport harbure? Yea! An arter that we hev all plain-sailin."

"Why, won't the fog last?"

"I don't car for the fog. Arter we get to Eastport harbure we cease goin down the bay. We then cross over an steal up the other side. Then it's all our own. If the fog lasts, why, the wind'll last too, an we can go up flyin, all sails set; an I'll remuve from my mind, for the time bein, any prejudyce that I have agin wind at sails."

"Do you intend to go ashore at Eastport?"

"Yes, for a short time--jest to make inquiries. It will be a consolation, you know."

"Of course."

"Then I'll up sail, an away we'll go, irrewspective of tides, across the bay."

By midday the captain informed them that they were in Eastport harbor.

"See thar," said he, as he pointed to a headland with a light-house. "That thar is the entrance. They do call this a pootyish place; but as it's this thick, you won't hev much chance to see it. Don't you want to go ashore an walk about?"

"Not if we can help it. Of course we'll have to ask after poor Tom, but we haven't any curiosity."

"Wal, p'aps not--ony thar is people that find this a dreadful cur'ous place. It's got, as I said, a pootyish harbure; but that ain't the grand attraction. The grand attraction centres in a rock that's said to be the eastest place in the neighborin republic,--in short, as they call it, the 'jumpin-off place.' You'd better go an see it; ony you needn't jump off, unless you like."

Sailing up the harbor, the fog grew light enough for them to see the shore. The town lay in rather an imposing situation, on the side of a hill, which was crowned by a fort. A large number of vessels lay about at the wharves and at anchor. Here they went ashore in a boat, but on making inquiries could gain no information about Tom; nor could they learn anything which gave them the slightest encouragement.

"We've got to wait here a while so as to devarsefy the time. Suppose we go an jump off?" said the captain.

The boys assented to this in a melancholy manner, and the captain led the way through the town, till at last he halted at the extreme east end.

"Here," said he, "you behold the last extremity of a great an mighty nation, that spreads from the Atlantic to the Pacific, an from the Gulf of Mexiky to the very identical spot that you air now a occypyin of. It air a celebrated spot, an this here air a memorable momient in your youthful lives, if you did but know it!"

There was nothing very striking about this place, except the fact which Captain Corbet had stated. Its appearance was not very imposing, yet, on the other hand, it was not without a certain wild beauty. Before them spread the waters of the bay, with islands half concealed in mist; while immediately in front, a steep, rocky bank went sheer down for some thirty or forty feet to the beach below.

"I suppose," said the captain, "that bein Pilgrims, it air our dooty to jump; but as it looks a leetle rocky down thar, I think we'd best defer that to another oppor-toonity."

Returning to the schooner, they weighed anchor, set sail, and left the harbor. On leaving it, they did not go back the way they had come, but passed through a narrow and very picturesque channel, which led them by a much shorter route into the bay. On their left were wooded hills, and on their right a little village on the slope of a hill, upon whose crest stood a church.

Outside the fog lay as thick as ever, and into this they plunged. Soon the mo-notonous gray veil of mist closed all around them. But now their progress was more satisfactory, for they were crossing the bay, and the wind was abeam.

"Are you going straight across to Nova Scotia now?" asked Bart.

"Wal, yes; kine o' straight across," was the reply; "ony on our way we've got to call at a certain place, an contenoo our investergations."

"What place is that?"

"It's the Island of Grand Manan--a place that I allers feel the greatest respect for. On that thar island is that celebrated fog mill that I told you of, whar they keep grindin night an day, in southerly weather, so as to keep up the supply of fog for old Fundy. Whatever we'd do without Grand Manan is more'n I can say."

"Is the island inhabited?" asked Bruce.

"Inhabited? O, dear, yas. Thar's a heap o' people thar. It's jest possible that a driftin boat might git ashore thar, an ef so we'll know pooty soon."

"How far is it?"

"O, ony about seven or eight mile."

"We'll be there in an hour or so, then?"

"Wal, not so soon. You see, we've got to go round it."

"Around it?"

"Yes"

"Why?"

"Cos thar ain't any poppylation on this side, an we've got to land on t'other."

"Why are there no people on this side?"

"Cos thar ain't no harbures. The cliffs air six hundred feet high, and the hull shore runs straight on for ever so fur without a break, except two triflin coves."

"How is it on the other side?"

"Wal, the east side ain't a bad place. The shore is easier, an thar's harbures an anchorages. Thar's a place they call Whale Cove, whar I'm goin to land, an see if I can hear anythin. The people air ony fishers, an they ain't got much cultivation; but it's mor'en likely that a driftin boat might touch thar somewhar."

The Antelope pursued her course, but it was as much as three hours before she reached her destination. They dropped anchor then, and landed. The boys had already learned not to indulge too readily in hope; but when they made their inquiries, and found the same answer meeting them here which they had received in other places, they could not avoid feeling a fresh pang of disappointment and discouragement.

"Wal, we didn't git much good out of this place," said Captain Corbet. "I'm sorry that we have sech a arrand as ourn. Ef it warn't for that we could spend to-night here, an to-morry I'd take you all to see the fog mill; but, as it is, I rayther think I won't linger here, but perceed on our way."

"Where do we go next--to Nova Scotia?"

"Wal, not jest straight across, but kine o' slantin. We head now for Digby; that's about straight opposite to St. John, an it's as likely a place as any to make inquiries at."

"How long will it be before we get there?"

"Wal, some time to-morry mornin. To-night we've got nothin at all to do but to sweep through the deep while the stormy tempests blow in the shape of a mild sou-wester; so don't you begin your usual game of settin up. You ain't a mite of good to me, nor to yourselves, a stayin here. You'd ought all to be abed, and, ef you'll take my advice, you'll go to sleep as soon as you can, an stay asleep as long as you can. It'll be a foggy night, an we won't see a mite o' sunshine till we git into Digby harbure. See now, it's already dark; so take my advice, an go to bed, like civilized humane beings."

It did not need much persuasion to send them off to their beds. Night was coming on, another night of fog and thick darkness. This time, however, they had the consolation of making some progress, if it were any consolation when they had no definite course before them; for, in such a cruise as this, when they were roaming about from one place to another, without any fixed course, or fixed time, the progress that they made was, after all, a secondary consideration. The matter of first importance was to hear news of Tom, and, until they did hear something, all other things were of little moment.

The Antelope continued on her way all that night, and on the next morning the boys found the weather unchanged. Breakfast passed, and two or three hours went on. The boys were scattered about the decks, in a languid way, looking out over the water, when suddenly a cry from Pat, who was in the bows, aroused all of them. Immediately before them rose a lofty shore, covered in the distance with dark trees, but terminating at the water's edge in frowning rocks. A light-house stood here, upon which they had come so suddenly that, before they were over their first surprise, they were almost near enough to toss a biscuit ashore.

"Wal, now, I call that thar pooty slick sailin," exclaimed Captain Corbet, glancing at the lighthouse with sparkling eyes. "I tell you what it is, boys, you don't find many men in this here day an age that can leave Manan at dusk, when the old fog mill is hard at work, and travel all night in the thickest fog ever seen, with tide agin him half the time, an steer through that thar fog, an agin that thar tide, so as to hit the light-house as slick as that. Talk about your scientific navigation--wouldn't I like to see what one of them thar scientific captings would do with his vessel last night on sech a track as I run over! Wouldn't I like to run a race with him? an ef I did, wouldn't I make a pile to leave and bequeath to the infant when his aged parient air buried beneath the cold ground?"

While Captain Corbet was speaking, the schooner sailed past the light-house, and the thick fog closed around her once more. On one side, however, they could see the dim outline of the shore on their right. On they sailed for about a quarter of a mile, when suddenly the fog vanished, and, with scarce a moment's notice, there burst upon them a blaze of sunlight, while overhead appeared the glory of the blue sky. The suddenness of that transition forced a cry of astonishment from all. They had shot forth so quickly from the fog into the sunlight that it seemed like magic.

They found themselves sailing along a strait about a mile in width, with shores on each side that were as high as Blomidon. On the right the heights sloped up steep, and were covered with trees of rich dark verdure, while on the other side the slope was bolder and wilder. Houses appeared upon the shore, and roads, and cultivated trees. This strait was several miles in length, and led into a broad and magnificent basin.

Here, in this basin, appeared an enchanting view. A sheet of water extended before their eyes about sixteen miles in length and five in breadth. All around were lofty shores, fertile, well tilled, covered with verdurous trees and luxuriant vegetation. The green of the shores was dotted with white houses, while the blue of the water was flecked with snowy sails. Immediately on the right there appeared a circular sweep of shore, on which arose a village whose houses were intermingled with green trees.

Into this beautiful basin came the old French navigators more than two centuries ago, and at its head they found a place which seemed to them the best spot in Acadie to become the capital of the new colony which they were going to found here. So they established their little town, and these placid waters became the scene of commercial activity and of warlike enterprise, till generations passed away, and the little French town of Port Royal, after many strange vicissitudes, with its wonderful basin, remained in the possession of the English conqueror.

"Now," said Captain Corbet, "boys, look round on that thar, an tell me of you ever see a beautifuller place than this. Thar's ony one place that can be compared with this here, an that's Grand Pre. But for the life o' me, I never can tell which o' the two is the pootiest. It's strange, too, how them French fellers managed to pick out the best places in the hull province. But it shows their taste an judgment--it doos, railly."

It was not long before the Antelope had dropped anchor in front of the town of Digby, and Captain Corbet landed with the boys as soon as possible. There was as good a chance of Tom being heard of here as anywhere; since this place lay down the bay, in one sense, and if by any chance Tom had drifted over to the Nova Scotia shore, as now seemed probable, he would be not unlikely to go to Digby, so as to resume his journey, so rudely interrupted, and make his way thence to his friends.

Digby is a quiet little place, that was finished long ago. It was first settled by the Tory refugees, who came here after the revolutionary war, and received land grants from the British government. At first it had some activity, but its business soon languished. The first settlers had such bright hopes of its future that they regularly laid out a town, with streets and squares. But these have never been used to any extent, and now appear grown over with grass. Digby, however, has so much beauty of scenery around it, that it may yet attract a large population. On landing here, Captain Corbet pursued the same course as at other places. He went first to one of the principal shops, or the post office, and told his story, and afterwards went to the schooners at the wharves. But at Digby there was precisely the same result to their inquiries as there had been at other places. No news had come to the place of any one adrift, nor had any skipper of any schooner noticed anything of the kind during his last trip.

"What had we better do next?"

"Wal," said Captain Corbet, "we can ony finish our cruise."

"Shall we go on?"

"Yes."

"Up the bay?"

"Yes. I'll keep on past Ile Haute, an I'll cruise around Minas. You see these drifts may take him in a'most any direction. I don't see why he shouldn't hev drifted up thar as well as down here."

It was Wednesday when they reached Digby.

On the evening of that day the Antelope weighed anchor, and sailed out into the Bay of Fundy.

It was bright sunshine, with a perfectly cloudless sky inside, but outside the Antelope plunged into the midst of a dense and heavy fog.

XIX.

Tom's Devices.--Rising superior to Circumstances.--Roast Clams.--Baked Lobster.--Boiled Mussels.--Boiled Shrimps.--Roast Eggs.--Dandelions.--Ditto, with Eggs.--Roast Dulse.--Strawberries.--Pilot-bread.--Strawberry Cordial.

Meanwhile another day had passed away on Ile Haute.
When we last saw Tom he had succeeded in finding some clams, which he roasted in front of his fire, and made thus a very acceptable relish. This not only gratified his palate for the time, but it also stimulated him to fresh exertions, since it showed him that his resources were much more extensive than he had supposed them to be. If he had ever dreaded getting out of all his provisions, he saw now that the fear was an unfounded one. Here, before his eyes, and close beside his dwelling-place, there extended a broad field full of food. In that mud flat there were clams enough to feed him for all the rest of his life, if that were necessary. But what was more, he saw by this the possibility that other articles of food might be reckoned on, by means of which he would be able to relieve his diet from that monotony which had thus far been its chief characteristic. If he could find something else besides clams and biscuit, the tedium of his existence here would be alleviated to a still greater degree.

He spent some time in considering this subject, and in thinking over all the possible kinds of food which he might hope to obtain. Sea and land might both be relied on to furnish food for his table in the desert. The sea, he knew, ought to supply the following:--

    1. Clams,
    2. Lobsters,
    3. Mussels,

in addition to other things which he had in his mind. The land, on the other hand, ought to furnish something. Now that his attention was fairly directed to this important subject, he could think of several things which would be likely to be found even on this island, and the search for which would afford an agreeable amusement.

The more he thought of all this, the more astonished he was at the number of things which he could think of as being likely to exist here around him. It was not so much for the sake of gratifying his appetite, as to find some occupation, that he now entered eagerly upon putting this new project into execution. Fish, flesh, and fowl now offered themselves to his endeavors, and these were to be supplied by land, sea, and sky. This sudden enlargement of his resources, and also of his sphere of operations, caused him to feel additional satisfaction, together with a natural self-complacency. To the ordinary mind Ile Haute appeared utterly deserted and forlorn--a place where one might starve to death, if he had to remain for any length of time; but Tom now determined to test to the utmost the actual resources of the island, so as to prove, to himself what one unaided boy could do, when thus thrown upon his own intelligent efforts, with dire necessity to act as a stimulus to his ingenuity.

First of all, then, there was his box of biscuit, which he had brought with him.

To this must be added his first discovery on the island, namely, the clams. Nothing could be of greater importance than this, since it afforded not merely a relish, but also actual food.

The next thing that he sought after was lobsters, and he went off in search of these as soon as he could on the following day.

He waited till the tide was low, which was at about twelve o'clock, and then went down along the beach. At high tide, the water came close up to the foot of the lofty cliff; but at ebb, it descended for some distance, so that there was some sort of a beach even in places that did not promise any.

The beach nearest to where Tom had taken up his abode was an expanse of mud and sand; but passing along beyond this, on the north side, it became gravelly. About a hundred yards to the west, on this side of the island, he came to the place where he had tied his boat, on that eventful time when he had drifted here. Below this, the beach extended down for a long distance, and at the lowest point there were rocks, and sharp stones, and pebbles of every size. Here Tom began his search, and before he had looked five minutes, he found several lobsters of good size. A little farther search showed him that there was a large supply of these, so that, in fact, sufficient support might have been obtained for a whole ship's company. By the time that he had found a half dozen of these, and had brought them back to his hearth-stone, it had grown too dark to search for any more. Tom's search, however, had been so successful, that he felt quite satisfied; and though the day had passed without any change in the weather or any lifting of the fog, though he had listened in vain for any sound over the waters which might tell of passers by, though his signal had not been seen, and his bright burning fire had not been noticed, yet the occupation of thought and of action which he had found for himself, had been sufficient to make the time pass not unpleasantly.

His evening repast was now a decided improvement on that of the preceding day. First of all, he spread some clams in the hot ashes to roast; and then, taking the dipper which had been used for baling, he filled it with water, and placing this on the fire, it soon began to boil. Into this he thrust the smallest lobster, and watched it as the water bubbled around it, and its scaly covering turned slowly from its original dark hue to a bright red color.

His success thus far stimulated him to make some attempts at actual cookery. Removing some of the lobster from its shell, he poured out most of the water from the pan, and into what remained he again put the lobster, cutting it up as fine as he could with his knife. Into this he crumbled some biscuit, and stirred it up all together. He then placed it over the fire till it was well baked. On removing it and tasting it, he found it most palatable. It was already sufficiently salt, and only needed a little pepper to make it quite equal to any scolloped lobster that he had ever tasted.

His repast consisted of this, followed by the roast clams, which formed an agreeable variety.

Tom now felt like a giant refreshed; and while sitting in front of the evening fire, he occupied his mind with plans for the morrow, which were all directed towards enlarging his supply of provisions.

He awaked late on the next morning, and found the weather unchanged. He tried to quell his impatience and disappointment, and feeling that idleness would never do, he determined to go to work at once, and carry out the plans of the preceding day. It was now Thursday, the middle of the second week, and the fog had clung pertinaciously around him almost all that time. It was indeed disheartening, and idleness under such circumstances would have ended in misery and despair; but Tom's perseverance, and obstinate courage, and buoyant spirits enabled him still to rise above circumstances, and struggle with the gloom around him.

"O, go on, go on," he muttered, looking around upon the fog. "Let's see who can stand it longest. And now for my foraging expedition."

Making a hearty repast out of the remnants of the supper of the preceding evening, he went first to the shore, so as to complete his search there while the tide should be low. It was going down now, and the beach was all before him. He wandered on till he came to where there was an immense ledge of sharp rocks, that went from the foot of the precipice down into the bay. Over these he clambered, looking carefully around, until at last he reached the very lowest point. Here he soon found some articles of diet, which were quite as valuable in their way as the clams and lobsters. First of all, he found an immense quantity of large mussels. These were entangled among the thick masses of sea-weed. He knew that the flavor of mussels was much more delicate than that of clams or lobsters, and that by many connoisseurs these, when good and fresh, were ranked next to oysters. This discovery, therefore, gave him great joy, and he filled his pan, which he had carried down, and took them back to the shore. He also took an armful of sea-weed, and, reaching his camping-place, he threw the mussels in a hollow place in the sand, placing the sea-weed around them. In this way he knew that they would keep fresh and sweet for any reasonable length of time.

Returning to the ledges of rock, he walked about among them, and found a number of pools, some of which were of considerable size. These had been left by the retreating water; and in these hollows he soon saw a number of small objects moving about. Some of them he caught without much difficulty, and saw that they were shrimps. He had hoped to find some of these, but the discovery came to him like some unexpected pleasure, and seemed more than he had any right to count on. Beside the shrimps his other discoveries seemed inferior. There was a large number, and they could be caught without much trouble. He soon filled his pan, and brought these also to his camping-place. These he deposited in a little pool, which was on the surface of some rocks that lay not far from the shore. Over these he also laid some sea-weed.

The tide was now coming up, but Tom made a further journey to the beach, so as to secure something which he had noticed during his previous expedition. This was a marine plant called dulse, which, in these waters, grows very plentifully, and is gathered and dried by the people in large quantities. It was a substance of which Tom was very fond, and he determined to gather some, and dry it in the sun. Collecting an armful of this, he took it to the shore, and spread it out over the grass, though, in that damp and foggy atmosphere, there was not much prospect of its drying.

It was now about three o'clock in the afternoon, and Tom's researches along the shore were successfully terminated. He had found all the different articles that he had thought of and his new acquisitions were now lying about him.

These were,--

Clams,
Lobsters,
Mussels,
Shrimps,
Dulse.

As he murmured to himself the list of things, he smiled triumphantly.

But still there was work to be done. Tom intended to keep fashionable hours, and dine late, with only a lunch in the middle of the day. His explorations of the afternoon were to be important, and he hoped that they would be crowned with a portion of that success which had attended the work of the morning. He took, therefore, a hasty lunch of biscuit and cold lobster, washed down with water, and then set forth.

This time he turned away from the shore, and went to the top of the island. He carried in his hand a bit of rope, about a dozen feet in length, and went along the edge of the cliff as far as he could, turning aside at times to avoid any clumps of trees or bushes that grew too thickly. In front of him the line of cliff extended for some distance, and he walked along, until, at last, he came to a place where the gulls flew about in larger flocks than usual, almost on a line with the top of the rock. He had not noticed them particularly on his former walk along here; but now he watched them very attentively, and finally stood still, so as to see their actions to better advantage.

Tom, in fact, had made up his mind to procure some gulls' eggs, thinking that these would make an addition to his repast of great importance; and he now watched the motions of these birds, so as to detect the most accessible of their nests. He did not have to watch long. A little observation showed him a place, just under the cliff, not far away from him. Hastening forward, he bent over, and, looking down, he saw a large number of nests. They had been constructed on a shelf of rock immediately below the edge of the cliff, and the eggs were within easy reach. The gulls flew about wildly, as the intruder reached down his hands towards their nests, and screamed and shrieked, while some of them rushed towards him, within a few feet of his head, as though they would assail him and beat him off. But Tom's determination did not falter. He cared no more for the gulls than if they were so many pigeons, but secured as many eggs as he could carry. These he took with him back to his camp.

But he was not yet satisfied. He was anxious to have some vegetables; and over the open ground, among the grass, he had seen plants which were very familiar to him. There were dandelions; and Tom saw in them something that seemed worth more than any of his other acquisitions. Going forth in search of these, he managed to get his pan full of them. These he washed, and after cutting off the roots, he put them in the pan with water, and then set them over the fire to boil.

While they were boiling Tom went off once more, and found some wild strawberries. They were quite plentiful about here, and this was the season for them. He stripped a piece of bark from a birch tree, as the country people do, and formed from this a dish which would hold about a quart. This he filled after a moderate search.

He took the strawberries to his camp, and then, going back to the woods, he procured some more birch bark, out of which he made a half dozen dishes. It was now about five o'clock, and Tom thought it was time for him to begin to cook his dinner.

The dandelions were not quite cooked as yet; so Tom had to wait; but while doing so, he heated some stones in the fire. By the time they were heated, the dandelions were cooked; and Tom, removing the pan, put some shrimps and mussels in it, to boil over the fire. He then removed the stones, and placed one of the lobsters among them in such a way, that it was surrounded on every side in a hot oven. He then buried a few clams among the hot ashes, and did the same with three or four of the gulls' eggs.

One of the hot stones was reserved for another purpose. It was the largest of them, and was red hot when he drew it from the fire, but soon cooled down enough to resume its natural color, although it retained an intense heat.

Over this he spread some of the wet dulse, which soon crackled and shrivelled up, sending forth a rich and fragrant steam. In roasting this dulse, a large piece would shrink to very small proportions, so that half of Tom's armful, when thus roasted, was reduced to but a small handful.

After finishing this, he drew the gulls' eggs from the fire, and taking off the shells, he cut them in slices, and put them with the dandelions. Then he took the shrimps and mussels from the fire, and removing them from the pan, he separated them, and put them into different bark dishes. The clams were next drawn forth, and though rather overdone, they were, nevertheless, of tempting appearance and appetizing odor. Finally, the lobster was removed, and Tom contented himself with one of the claws, which he placed on a dish, reserving the remainder for another time.

And now the articles were all cooked, and Tom's repast was ready. He looked with a smile of gratification upon the various dishes which his ingenuity and industry had drawn forth from the rocks, and cliffs, and mud, and sand of a desert island, and wondered whether other islands, in tropical climates, could yield a more varied or more nutritious supply. He thought of other plants which might be found here, and determined to try some that seemed to be nutritious.

Here is the repast which Tom, on that occasion, spread before himself:--

1. Roast clams,
2. Baked lobster,
3. Boiled mussels,

4. Boiled shrimps,
5. Roast eggs,
6. Dandelions,
7. Dandelions with eggs,
8. Roast dulse,
9. Strawberries,
10. Pilot-bread.

In one thing only did Tom fall short of his wishes, and that was in the way of drinks. But before that dinner was finished, even this was remedied; for necessity, the great mother of invention, instigated Tom to squeeze about half of his strawberries into a little water. Out of this he formed a drink with a flavor that seemed to him to be quite delicious. And that made what Tom called,--

11. Strawberry cordial.

XX.

New Discoveries.--The Boat.--A great Swell.--Meditations and Plans.--A new, and wonderful, and before unheard-of Application of Spruce Gum.-- I'm afloat! I'm afloat!

Tom sat there over his banquet until late. He then went down to the beach, and brought up a vast collection of driftwood, and throwing a plenteous supply upon the fire, he lay down beside it, and looked out over the water, trying, as usual, to see something through the thick mist. The flames shot up with a crackle and a great blaze, and the bright light shone brilliantly upon the water. The tide was now up, and the boat was full before him. Tom fixed his eyes upon this boat, and was mournfully recalling his unsuccessful experiment at making her sea-worthy, and was waiting to see her sink down to her gunwales as she filled, when the thought occurred to him that she was not filling so rapidly as she might, but was floating much better than usual. A steady observation served to show him that this was no fancy, but an actual fact; and the confirmation of this first impression at once drove away all other thoughts, and brought back all the ideas of escape which he once had cherished.

The boat was admitting the water, certainly, yet she certainly did not leak quite so badly as before, but was floating far better than she had done on the night of his trial. What was the meaning of this?

Now, the fact is, he had not noticed the boat particularly during the last few days. He had given it up so completely, that it ceased to have any interest in his eyes. Raising his signal, building his house, and exploring the island had taken up all his thoughts. Latterly he had thought of nothing but his dinner. But now the change in the boat was unmistakable, and it seemed to him that the change might have been going on gradually all this time without his noticing it until it had become so marked.

What was the cause of this change? That was the question which he now sought to answer. After some thought he found a satisfactory explanation.

For a number of days the boat had been admitting the water till she was full. This water had remained in for an hour or more, and this process of filling and emptying had been repeated every tide. The atmosphere also had been wet, and the wood, thus saturated with water so frequently, had no chance of getting dry. Tom thought, therefore, that the wooden framework, which he had constructed so as to tighten the leak, had been gradually swelling from the action of the water; and the planks of the boat had been tightening their cracks from the same cause, so that now the opening was not nearly so bad as it had been. Thus the boat, which once had been able to float him for a quarter of an hour or more, ought now to be able to float him for at least double that time.

Tom watched the boat very attentively while the tide was up; and, when at length it began to retreat, and leave it once more aground, he noticed that it was not more than half full of water. If any confirmation had been needed to the con-clusions which he had drawn from seeing the improved buoyancy of the boat, it would have been afforded by this. Tom accepted this with delight, as an additional circumstance in his favor; and now, having become convinced of this much, he set his wits to work to see if some plan could not be hit upon by means of which the boat could once more be made sea-worthy.

Tom's indefatigable perseverance must have been noticed by this time. To make the best of circumstances; to stand face to face with misfortune, and shrink not; to meet the worst with equanimity, and grasp eagerly at the slightest favorable change,--such was the character that Tom had shown during his experience of the past. Now, once more, he grasped at this slight circumstance that appeared to favor his hopes, and sought to find some way by which that half-floating boat could be made to float wholly, and bear him away to those shores that were so near by. Too long had he been submitting to this imprisonment; too long had he been waiting for schooners to pass and to bring him help; too long had he been shut in by a fog that seemed destined never to lift so long as he was here. If he could only form some kind of a boat that would float long enough to land him on the nearest coast, all that he wished would be gratified.

As he thought over this subject, he saw plainly what he had felt very strongly before--that the boat could not be sea-worthy unless he had some tar with which to plaster over the broken bow, and fill in the gaping seams; but there was no tar. Still, did it follow that there was nothing else? Might not something be found upon the island which would serve the purpose of tar? There must be some such substance and perhaps it might be found here.

Tom now thought over all the substances that he could bring before his mind. Would clay do? No; clay would not. Would putty? No, and besides, he could not get any. What, then, would serve this important purpose?

Tar was produced from trees. Were there no trees here that produced some sticky and glutinous substance like tar? There was the resin of pine trees, but there were no pines on the island. What then? These fir trees had a sort of sticky, balsamic juice that exuded plentifully from them wherever they were cut. Might he not make some use of that? Suddenly, in the midst of reflections like these, he thought of the gum that is found on spruce trees--spruce gum! It was an idea that deserved to be followed up and carried out. Thus far he had never thought of spruce gum, except as something which he, like most boys, was fond of chewing; but now it appeared before his mind as affording a possible solution of his difficulty. The more he thought of it, the more did it seem that this would be adapted to his purpose. The only question was, whether he could obtain enough of it. He thought that he might easily obtain enough if he only took the proper time and care.

With this new plan in his mind, Tom retired for the night, and awaked the next morning by the dawn of day. It was still foggy; but he was now so resigned, and was so full of his new plan, that it did not trouble him in the slightest degree. In fact, he was so anxious to try this, that the sight of a boat landing on the beach, all ready to take him off, would not have afforded him an unmixed satisfaction.

He took his tin dipper, and went up at once into the woods. Here he looked around very carefully, and soon found what he wanted. He knew perfectly well, of course, how to distinguish spruce trees from fir, by the sharp, prickly spires of the former, and so he was never at a loss which trees to search. No sooner had he begun, than he was surprised at the quantities that he found. To an ordinary observer the trunk of the spruce tree seems like any other tree trunk--no rougher, and perhaps somewhat smoother than many; but Tom now found that on every tree almost there were little round excrescences, which, on being picked at with the knife, came off readily, and proved to be gum. Vast quantities of a substance which goes by the name of spruce gum are manufactured and sold; but the pure gum is a very different article, having a rich, balsamic odor, and a delicate yet delicious flavor; and Tom, as he filled his pan, and inhaled the fragrance that was emitted by its contents, lamented that his necessities compelled him to use it for such a purpose as that to which this was destined. After four or five hours' work, he found that he had gathered enough. He had filled his pan no less than six times, and had secured a supply which was amply sufficient to give a coating of thick gum over all the fractured place. The tide, which had already risen, was now falling, and, as soon as the boat was aground, and the water out of her, Tom proceeded to raise her bows, in precisely the same manner as he had raised the boat on a former occasion.

The next thing was to bring the gum into a fit condition for use. This he did by kindling the fire, and melting it in his tin pan. This would rather interfere with the use of that article as a cooking utensil, but now that Tom's mind was full of this new purpose, cooking and things of that sort had lost all attractions for him. As for food, there was no fear about that. He had his biscuit, and the lobster and shell-fish which he had cooked on the preceding day were but partially consumed. Enough remained to supply many more meals.

The gum soon melted, and then a brush was needed to apply it to the boat. This was procured by cutting off a little strip of canvas, about a yard long and six inches wide. By picking out some of the threads, and rolling it up, a very serviceable brush was formed.

Taking the gum now in its melted state, Tom dipped his brush into it, and applied it all over the broken surface of the bow, pressing the hot liquid in close, and allowing it to harden in the cracks. His first coating of gum was very satisfactorily applied, and it seemed as though a few more coatings ought to secure the boat from the entrance of the water. The gum was tenacious, and its only bad quality was its brittleness; but, as it would not be exposed to the blows of any hard substances, it seemed quite able to serve Tom's wants.

Tom now went down to the drift-wood and brought up a fresh supply of fuel, after which he melted a second panful of gum, and applied this to the boat. He endeavored to secure an entrance for it into all the cracks that did not seem to be sufficiently filled at the first application, and now had the satisfaction of seeing all of those deep marks filled up and effaced by the gum.

One place still remained which had not yet been made secure against the entrance of the water, and that was where the planks gaped open from the blow that had crushed in the bows. Here the canvas that was inside protruded slightly. Torn ripped up some of the canvas that was on the tent, and taking the threads, stuffed them in the opening, mixing them with gum as he did so, until it was filled; and then over this he put a coating of the gum. After this another pan, and yet another, were melted, and the hot gum each time was applied. This gave the whole surface a smooth appearance, that promised to be impenetrable to the water.

The gum which he had collected was enough to fill two more pans. This he melted as before, and applied to the bows. Each new application clung to the one that had preceded it, in a thick and quickly hardening layer, until at last, when the work was done, there appeared a coating of this gum formed from six successive layers, that was smooth, and hard, and without any crack whatever. It seemed absolutely water-tight; and Tom, as he looked at it now, could not imagine where the water could penetrate. Yet, in order to make assurance doubly sure, he collected two more panfuls, and melting this he applied it as before. After this was over, he made a torch of birch bark, and lighting this, he held the flame against the gum till the whole outer surface began to melt and run together. This served to secure any crevices that his brush might have passed by without properly filling.

The work was now complete as far as Tom could do it; and on examining it, he regretted that he had not thought of this before. He felt an exultation that he had never known in his life. If he, by his own efforts, could thus rescue himself, what a cause it would be always after to struggle against misfortune, and rise superior to circumstances!

As to the voyage, Tom's plan was the same that it had been on a former occasion. He would float the boat at high tide, and then push off, keeping her near the shore, yet afloat until ebb tide. Then, when the tide should turn, and the current run up the bay, he would put off, and float along with the stream until he reached land.

According to his calculations it would be high tide about two hours after dark, which would be some time after ten. He would have to be up all night; for the tide would not turn until after four in the morning. But that did not trouble him. He would have too much on his mind to allow him to feel sleepy, and, besides, the hope which lay before him would prevent him from feeling fatigue.

One thing more remained, and that was, to bring up a fresh supply of fuel. The night would be dark, and while floating in the boat, he would need the light of the fire. So he brought up from the beach an ample supply of drift-wood, and laid it with the rest.

When Tom's work was ended, it was late in the day, and he determined to secure some sleep before he began his long night's work. He knew that he could waken at the right time; so he laid himself down in his tent, and soon slept the sleep of the weary.

By ten o'clock he was awake. He found the water already up to the boat. There was no time to lose. He carried his box of biscuit on board, and filled his pan with water from the brook, so as to secure himself against thirst in case the boat should float away farther than he anticipated. Then he took his paddle, and got into the boat.

The water came up higher. Most anxiously Tom watched it as it rose. The fire was burning low, and in order to make more light, Tom went ashore and heaped an immense quantity of wood upon it. The flames now blazed up bright, and on going back again to the boat, the water was plainly visible as it closed around the bows.

Most anxiously he now awaited, with his eyes fastened upon the bottom of the boat. He had not brought the old sail this time, but left it over his tent, and he could see plainly. Higher came the water, and still higher, yet none came into the boat, and Tom could scarce believe in his good fortune.

At last the boat floated!

Yes, the crisis had come and passed, and the boat floated!

There was now no longer any doubt. His work was successful; his deliverance was sure. The way over the waters was open. Farewell to his island prison! Welcome once more the great world! Welcome home, and friends, and happiness!

In that moment of joy his heart seemed almost ready to burst. It was with difficulty that he calmed himself; and then, offering up a prayer of thanksgiving, he pushed off from the shore.

The boat floated!

The tide rose, and lingered, and fell.

The boat floated still.

There was not the slightest sign of a leak. Every hour, as it passed, served to give Tom a greater assurance that the boat was sea-worthy.

He found no difficulty in keeping her afloat, even while retaining her near the shore, so that she might be out of the way of the currents.

At length, when the tide was about half way down, he found the fire burning too low, and determined to go ashore and replenish it. A rock jutted above the water not far off. To this he secured the boat, and then landing, he walked up the beach. Reaching the fire, he threw upon it all the remaining wood. Returning then to the boat, he boarded her without difficulty.

The tide fell lower and lower.

And now Tom found it more and more difficult to keep the boat afloat, without allowing her to be caught by the current. He did not dare to keep her bows near the shore, but turned her about, so that her stem should rest from time to time on the gravel. At last the tide was so low that rocks appeared above the surface, and the boat occasionally struck them in a very unpleasant manner. To stay so near the shore any longer was not possible. A slight blow against a rock might rub off all the brittle gum, and then his chances would be destroyed. He determined to put out farther, and trust himself to Providence.

Slowly and cautiously he let his boat move out into deeper water.

But slowness and caution were of little avail. In the deeper water there was a strong current, which at once caught the boat and bore her along. Tom struggled bravely against it, but without avail. He thought for a moment of seeking the shore again, but the fear that the boat would be ruined deterred him.

There was a little wind blowing from the southwest, and he determined to trust to the sail. He loosened this, and, sitting down, waited for further developments.

The wind filled the sail, and the boat's progress was checked somewhat, yet still she drifted down the bay. She was drifting down past the north shore of the island. Tom could see, amid the gloom, the frowning cliffs as he drifted past. The firelight was lost to view; then he looked for some time upon the dark form of the island.

At last even that was lost to view.

He was drifting down the bay, and was already below Ile Haute.

XXI.

Scott's Bay and Old Bennie.--His two Theories.--Off to the desert Island.--Landing.--A Picnic Ground.--Gloom and Despair of the Explorers.--All over.--Sudden Summons.

It was on Wednesday evening that the Antelope passed from the sunshine and beauty of Digby Basin out into the fog and darkness of the Bay of Fundy. The tide was falling, and, though the wind was in their favor, yet their progress was somewhat slow. But the fact that they were moving was of itself a consolation. In spite of Captain Corbet's declared preference for tides and anchors, and professed contempt for wind and sails, the boys looked upon these last as of chief importance, and preferred a slow progress with the wind to even a more rapid one by means of so unsatisfactory a method of travel as drifting.

At about nine on the following morning, the Antelope reached a little place called Wilmot Landing, where they went on shore and made the usual inquiries with the usual result. Embarking again, they sailed on for the remainder of that day, and stopped at one or two places along the coast.

On the next morning (Friday) they dropped anchor in front of Hall's Harbor--a little place whose name had become familiar to them during their memorable excursion to Blomidon. Here they met with the same discouraging answer to their question.

"Wal," said Captain Corbet, "we don't seem to meet with much success to speak of--do we?"

"No," said Bart, gloomily.

"I suppose your pa'll be sendin schooners over this here same ground. 'Tain't no use, though."

"Where shall we go next?"

"Wal, we've ben over the hull bay mostly; but thar's one place, yet, an that we'll go to next."

"What place is that?"

"Scott's Bay.

"My idee is this," continued Captain Corbet: "We'll finish our tower of inspection round the Bay of Fundy at Scott's Bay. Thar won't be nothin more to do; thar won't remain one single settlement but what we've called at, 'cept one or two triflin places of no 'count. So, after Scott's Bay, my idee is to go right straight off to old Minas. Who knows but what he's got on thar somewhar?"

"I don't see much chance of that."

"Why not?"

"Because, if he had drifted into the Straits of Minas, he'd manage to get ashore."

"I don't see that."

"Why, it's so narrow."

"Narrer? O, it's wider'n you think for; besides, ef he got stuck into the middle of that thar curr'nt, how's he to get to the shore? an him without any oars? Answer me that. No, sir; the boat that'll drift down Petticoat Jack into the bay, without gettin ashore, 'll drift up them straits into Minas jest the same."

"Well, there does seem something in that. I didn't think of his drifting down the Petitcodiac."

"Somethin? Bless your heart! ain't that everythin?"

"But do you think there's really a chance yet?"

"A chance? Course thar is. While thar's life thar's hope."

"But how could he live so long?"

"Why shouldn't he?"

"He might starve."

"Not he. Didn't he carry off my box o' biscuit?"

"Think of this fog."

"O, fog ain't much. It's snow an cold that tries a man. He's tough, too."

"But he's been so exposed."

"Exposed? What to? Not he. Didn't he go an carry off that ole sail?"

"I cannot help thinking that it's all over with him?"

"Don't give him up; keep up; cheer up. Think how we got hold of ole Solomon after givin him up. I tell you that thar was a good sign."

"He's been gone too long. Why, it's going on a fortnight?"

"Wal, what o' that ef he's goin to turn up all right in the end? I tell you he's somewhar. Ef he ain't in the Bay of Fundy, he may be driftin off the coast o' Maine, an picked up long ago, an on his way home now per steamer."

Bart shook his head, and turned away in deep despondency, in which feeling all the other boys joined him. They had but little hope now. The time that had elapsed seemed to be too long, and their disappointments had been too many. The sadness which they had felt all along was now deeper than ever, and they looked forward without a ray of hope.

On Friday evening they landed at Scott's Bay, and, as old Bennie Griggs's house was nearest, they went there. They found both the old people at home, and were received with an outburst of welcome. Captain Corbet was an old acquaintance, and made himself at home at once. Soon his errand was announced.

Bennie had the usual answer, and that was, that nothing whatever had been heard of any drifting boat. But he listened with intense interest to Captain Corbet's story, and made him tell it over and over again, down to the smallest particular. He also questioned all the boys very closely.

After the questioning was over, he sat in silence for a long time. At last he looked keenly at Captain Corbet.

"He's not ben heard tell of for about twelve days?"

"No."

"An it's ben ony moderate weather?"

"Ony moderate, but foggy."

"O, of course. Wal, in my 'pinion, fust an foremust, he ain't likely to hev gone down."

"That thar's jest what I say."

"An he had them biscuit?"

"Yes--a hull box."

"An the sail for shelter?"

"Yes."

"Wal; it's queer. He can't hev got down by the State o' Maine; for, ef he'd got thar, he'd hev sent word home before this."

"Course he would."

Old Bennie thought over this for a long time again, and the boys watched him closely, as though some result of vital importance hung upon his final decision.

"Wal," said Bennie at last, "s'posin that he's alive,--an it's very likely,--thar's ony two ways to account for his onnat'ral silence. Them air these:--

"Fust, he may hev got picked up by a timber ship, outward bound to the old country. In that case he may be carried the hull way acrost. I've knowed one or two sech cases, an hev heerd of severial more.

"Second. He may hev drifted onto a oninhabited island."

"An oninhabited island?" repeated Captain Corbet.

"Yea."

"Wal," said Captain Corbet; after a pause, "I've knowed things stranger than that."

"So hev I."

"Air thar any isle of the ocean in particular that you happen to hev in your mind's eye now?"

"Thar air."

"Which?"

"Ile Haute."

"Wal, now, railly, I declar--ef I wan't thinkin o' that very spot myself. An I war thinkin, as I war a comin up the bay, that that thar isle of the ocean was about the only spot belongin to this here bay that hadn't been heerd from. An it ain't onlikely that them shores could a tale onfold that mought astonish some on us. I shouldn't wonder a mite."

"Nor me," said Bennie, gravely.

"It's either a timber ship, or a desert island, as you say,--that's sartin," said Captain Corbet, after further thought, speaking with strong emphasis. "Thar ain't a mite o' doubt about it; an which o' them it is air a very even question. For my part, I'd as soon bet on one as t'other."

"I've heerd tell o' several seafarin men that's got adrift, an lit on that thar isle," said Bennie, solemnly.

"Wal, so hev I; an though our lad went all the way from Petticoat Jack, yet the currents in thar wandorins to an fro could effectooate that thar pooty mighty quick, an in the course of two or three days it could land him high an dry on them thar sequestrated shores."

"Do you think there is any chance of it?" asked Bruce, eagerly, directing his question to Bennie.

"Do I think? Why, sartin," said Bennie, regarding Bruce's anxious face with a calm smile. "Hain't I ben a expoundin to you the actool facts?"

"Well, then," cried Bart, starting to his feet, "let's go at once."

"Let's what?" asked Captain Corbet.

"Why, hurry off at once, and get to him as soon as we can."

"An pray, young sir, how could we get to him by leavin here jest now?"

"Can't we go straight to Ile Haute?"

"Scacely. The tide'll be agin us, an the wind too, till nigh eleven."

Bart gave a deep sigh.

"But don't be alarmed. We'll go thar next, an as soon as we can. You see we've got to go on into Minas Basin. Now we want to leave here so as to drop down with the tide, an then drop up with the flood tide into Minas Bay. I've about concluded to wait here till about three in the mornin. We'll drop down to the island in about a couple of hours, an'll hev time to run ashore, look round, and catch the flood tide."

"Well, you know best," said Bart, sadly.

"I think that's the only true an rational idee," said Bennie. "I do, railly; an meantime you can all get beds here with me, an you can hev a good bit o' sleep before startin."

This conversation took place not long after their arrival. The company were sitting in the big old kitchen, and Mrs. Bennie was spreading her most generous repast on the table.

After a bounteous supper the two old men talked over the situation until bedtime. They told many stories about drifting boats and rafts, compared notes about the direction of certain currents, and argued about the best course to pursue under certain very difficult circumstances, such, for example, as a thick snow-storm, midnight, a heavy sea, and a strong current setting upon a lee shore, the ship's anchor being broken also. It was generally considered that the situation was likely to be unpleasant.

At ten o'clock Bennie hurried his guests to their beds, where they slept soundly in spite of their anxiety. Before three in the morning he awaked them, and they were soon ready to reembark.

It was dim morning twilight as they bade adieu to their hospitable entertainers, and but little could be seen. Captain Corbet raised his head, and peered into the sky above, and sniffed the sea air.

"Wal, railly," said he, "I do declar ef it don't railly seem as ef it railly is a change o' weather--it railly doos. Why, ain't this rich? We're ben favored at last. We're agoin to hev a clar day. Hooray!"

The boys could not make out whether the captain's words were justified or not by the facts, but thought that they detected in the air rather the fragrance of the land than the savor of the salt sea. There was no wind, however, and they could not see far enough out on the water to know whether there was any fog or not.

Bennie accompanied them to the boat, and urged them to come back if they found the boys and let him rest in Scott's Bay. But the fate of that boy was so uncertain, that they could not make any promise about it.

It was a little after three when the Antelope weighed anchor, and dropped down the bay.

There was no wind whatever. It was the tide only that carried them down to their destination. Soon it began to grow lighter, and by the time that they were half way, they saw before them the dark outline of the island, as it rose from the black water with its frowning cliffs.

The boys looked at it in silence. It seemed, indeed, a hopeless place to search in for signs of poor Tom. How could he ever get ashore in such a place as this, so far out of the line of his drift; or if he had gone ashore there, how could he have lived till now? Such were the gloomy and despondent thoughts that filled the minds of all, as they saw the vessel drawing nearer and still nearer to those frowning cliffs.

As they went on the wind grew stronger, and they found that it was their old friend--the sou-wester. The light increased, and they saw a fog cloud on the horizon, a little beyond Ile Haute. Captain Corbet would not acknowledge that he had been mistaken in his impressions about a change of weather, but assured the boys that this was only the last gasp of the sou-wester, and that a change was bound to take place before evening. But though the fog was visible below Ile Haute, it did not seem to come any nearer, and at length the schooner approached the island, and dropped anchor.

It was about half past four in the morning, and the light of day was beginning to be diffused around, when they reached their destination. As it was low tide, they could not approach very near, but kept well off the precipitous shores on the south side of the island. In the course of her drift, while letting go the anchor, she went off to a point about half way down, opposite the shore. Scarce had her anchor touched bottom, than the impatient boys were all in the boat, calling on Captain Corbet to come along. The captain and Wade took the oars.

It was a long pull to the shore, and, when they reached it, the tide was so low that there remained a long walk over the beach. They had landed about half way down the island, and, as they directed their steps to the open ground at the east end, they had a much greater distance to traverse than they had anticipated. As they walked on, they did not speak a word. But already they began to doubt whether there was any hope left. They had been bitterly disappointed as they came near and saw no sign of life. They had half expected to see some figure on the beach waiting to receive them. But there was no figure and no shout of joy.

At length, as they drew nearer to the east end, and the light grew brighter, Bart, who was in advance, gave a shout.

They all hurried forward.

Bart was pointing towards something.

It was a signal-staff, with something that looked like a flag hoisted half mast high.

Every heart beat faster, and at once the wildest hopes arose. They hurried on over the rough beach as fast as possible. They clambered over rocks, and sea-weed, and drift-wood, and at length reached the bank. And still, as they drew nearer, the signal-staff rose before them, and the flag at half mast became more and more visible.

Rushing up the bank towards this place, each trying to outstrip the others, they hurried forward, full of hope now that some signs of Tom might be here. At length they reached the place where Tom had been so long, and here their steps were arrested by the scene before them.

On the point arose the signal-staff, with its heavy flag hanging down. The wind was now blowing, but it needed almost a gale to hold out that cumbrous canvas. Close by were the smouldering remains of what had been a huge fire, and all around this were chips and sticks. In the immediate neighborhood were some bark dishes, in some of which were shrimps and mussels. Clams and lobsters lay around, with shells of both.

Not far off was a canvas tent, which looked singularly comfortable and cosy.

Captain Corbet looked at all this, and shook his head.

"Bad--bad--bad," he murmured, in a doleful tone. "My last hope, or, rayther, one of my last hopes, dies away inside of me. This is wuss than findin' a desert place."

"Why? Hasn't he been here? He must have been here," cried Bart. "These are his marks. I dare say he's here now--perhaps asleep--in the camp. I'll go--"

"Don't go--don't--you needn't," said Captain Corbet, with a groan. "You don't understand. It's ben no pore castaway that's come here--no pore driftin lad that fell upon these lone and desolate coasts. No--never did he set foot here. All this is not the work o' shipwracked people. It's some festive picnickers, engaged in whilin away a few pleasant summer days. All around you may perceive the signs of luxoorious feastin. Here you may see all the different kind o' shellfish that the sea produces. Yonder is a luxoorious camp. But don't mind what I say. Go an call the occoopant, an satisfy yourselves."

Captain Corbet walked with the boys over to the tent. His words had thrown a fresh dejection over all. They felt the truth of what he said. These remains spoke not of shipwreck, but of pleasure, and of picnicking. It now only remained to rouse the slumbering owner of the tent, and put the usual questions.

Bart was there first, and tapped at the post.

No answer.

He tapped again.

Still there was no answer.

He raised the canvas and looked in. He saw the mossy interior, but perceived that it was empty. All the others looked in. On learning this they turned away puzzled.

"Wal, I thought so," said Captain Corbet. "They jest come an go as the fancy takes 'em. They're off on Cape d'Or to-day, an back here to-morrer."

As he said this he seated himself near the tent, and the boys looked around with sad and sombre faces.

It was now about half past five, and the day had dawned for some time. In the east the fog had lifted, and the sun was shining brightly.

"I told you thar'd be a change, boys," said the captain.

As he spoke there came a long succession of sharp, shrill blasts from the fog horn of the Antelope, which started every one, and made them run to the rising ground to find out the cause.

XXII.

Astounding Discovery.--The whole Party of Explorers overwhelmed.--Meeting with the Lost.--Captain Corbet improves the Occasion.--Conclusion.

At the sound from the Antelope they had all started for the rising ground, to see what it might mean. None of them had any idea what might be the cause, but all of them felt startled and excited at hearing it under such peculiar circumstances. Nor was their excitement lessened by the sight that met their eyes as they reached the rising ground and looked towards the schooner.

A change had taken place. When they had left, Solomon only had remained behind. But now there were two figures on the deck. One was amidships. The schooner was too far away for them to see distinctly, but this one was undoubtedly Solomon; yet his gestures were so extraordinary that it was difficult to identify him. He it was by whom the blasts on the fog horn were produced. Standing amidships, he held the fog horn in one hand, and in the other he held a battered old cap which supplied the place of the old straw hat lost at Quaco. After letting off a series of blasts from the horn, he brandished his cap wildly in the air, and then proceeded to dance a sort of complex double-shuffle, diversified by wild leaps in the air, and accompanied by brandishings of his hat and fresh blasts of the horn. But if Solomon's appearance was somewhat bewildering, still more so was that of the other one. This one stood astern. Suddenly as they looked they saw him hoist a flag, and, wonder of wonders, a black flag,--no other, in short, than the well-known flag of the "B. O. W. C." That flag had been mournfully lowered and put away on Tom's disappearance, but now it was hoisted once more; and as they looked, the new comer hoisted it and lowered it, causing it to rise and fall rapidly before their eyes.

Nor did the wonder end here. They had taken away the only boat that the schooner possessed in order to come ashore, leaving Solomon alone. They had noticed no boat whatever as they rowed to land. But now they saw a boat floating astern of the Antelope, with a small and peculiarly shaped sail, that now was flapping in the breeze. Evidently this boat belonged to the new comer. But who was he? How had he come there? What was the meaning of those signals with that peculiar flag, and what could be the reason of Solomon's joy?

They stood dumb with astonishment, confused, and almost afraid to think of the one cause that each one felt to be the real explanation of all this. Too long had they searched in vain for Tom,--too often had they sunk from hope to despair,--too confident and sanguine had they been; and now, at this unexpected sight, in spite of the assurance which it must have given them that this could be no other than Tom, they scarce dared to believe in such great happiness, and were afraid that even this might end in a disappointment like the others.

But, though they stood motionless and mute, the two figures on board the Antelope were neither one nor the other. Solomon danced more and more madly, and brandished his arms more and more excitedly, and there came forth from his fog horn wilder and still wilder peals, and the flag rose and fell more and more quickly, until at last the spectators on the shore could resist no longer.

"G-o-o-o-o-o-o-o-o-d ger-ra-a-a-cious!"

This cry burst from Captain Corbet.

It was enough. The spell was broken. A wild cry burst forth from the boys, and with loud, long shouts of joy they rushed down the bank, and over the beach, back to their boat. The captain was as quick as any of them. In his enthusiasm he forgot his rheumatism. There was a race, and though he was not even with Bruce and Bart, he kept ahead of Pat, and Arthur, and Phil, and old Wade.

Hurrah!

And hurrah again!

Yes, and hurrah over and over; and many were the hurrahs that burst from them as they raced over the rocky beach.

Then to tumble into the boat, one after another, to grasp the oars, to push her off, to head her for the schooner, and to dash through the water on their way back, was but the work of a few minutes.

The row to the schooner was a tedious one to those impatient young hearts. But as they drew nearer, they feasted their eyes on the figure of the new comer, and the last particle of doubt and fear died away. First, they recognized the dress- -the familiar red shirt. Tom had worn a coat and waistcoat ashore at Hillsborough on that eventful day; but on reaching the schooner, he had flung them off, and appeared now in the costume of the "B. O. W. C." This they recognized first, and then his face was revealed--a face that bore no particular indication of suffering or privation, which seemed certainly more sunburnt than formerly, but no thinner.

Soon they reached the vessel, and clambered up; and then with what shouts and almost shrieks of joy they seized Tom! With what cries and cheers of delight they welcomed him back again, by turns overwhelming him with questions, and then pouring forth a torrent of description of their own long search!

Captain Corbet stood a little aloof. His face was not so radiant as the faces of the boys. His features were twitching, and his hands were clasped tight behind his back. He stood leaning against the mainmast, his eyes fixed on Tom. It was thus that he stood when Tom caught sight of him, and rushed up to shake hands.

Captain Corbet grasped Tom's hand in both of his. He trembled, and Tom felt that his hands were cold and clammy.

"My dear boys," he faltered, "let us rejice--and--be glad--for this my son--that was dead--is alive agin--"

A shudder passed through him, and he stopped, and pressed Tom's hand convulsively. Then he gave a great gasp, and, "Thar, thar," he murmured, "it's too much! I'm onmanned. I've suffered--an agonized--an this--air--too much!"

And with these words he burst into tears.

Then he dropped Tom's hand, and retreated into the cabin, where he remained for a long time, but at last reappeared, restored to calmness, and with a smile of sweet and inexpressible peace wreathing his venerable countenance.

By this time the boys had told Tom all about their long search; and when Captain Corbet reappeared, Tom had completed the story of his adventures, and had just reached that part, in his wanderings, where he had left the island, and found himself drifting down the bay. As that was the point at which Tom was last lost sight of in these pages, his story may be given here in his own words.

"Yes," said he, "you see I found myself drifting down. There was no help for it.

The wind was slight, and the tide was strong. I was swept down into a fog bank, and lost sight of Ile Haute altogether. Well, it didn't matter very much, and I wasn't a bit anxious. I knew that the tide would turn soon, and then I'd come up, and fetch the land somewhere; so I waited patiently. At last, after about--well, nearly an hour, the tide must have turned, and I drifted back, and there was wind enough to give me quite a lift; and so all of a sudden I shot out of the fog, and saw Ile Haute before me. I was coming in such a way that my course lay on the south side of the island, and in a short time I came in sight of the schooner. I tell you what it is, I nearly went into fits--I knew her at once. A little farther on, and I saw you all cutting like mad over the beach to my camp. I was going to put after you at first; but the fact is, I hated the island so that I couldn't bear to touch it again, and so I concluded I'd go on board and signal. So I came up alongside, and got on board. Solomon was down below; so I just stepped forward, and put my head over the hatchway, and spoke to him. I declare I thought he'd explode. He didn't think I was a ghost at all. It wasn't fear, you know--it was nothing but delight, and all that sort of thing, you know. Well, you know, then we went to work signaling to you, and he took the fog horn, and I went to the flag, and so it was."

"I don't know how we happened not to see your boat," said Bruce.

"O, that's easy enough to account for," said Tom. "I was hid by the east point of the island. I didn't see the schooner till I got round, and you must have been just getting ashore at that time."

During all this time Solomon had been wandering about in a mysterious manner; now diving below into the hold, and rattling the pots and pans; again emerging upon deck, and standing to listen to Tom and look at him. His face shone like a polished boot; there was a grin on his face that showed every tooth in his head, and his little twinkling black beads of eyes shone, and sparkled, and rolled about till the winking black pupils were eclipsed by the whites. At times he would stand still, and whisper solemnly and mysteriously to himself, and then, without a moment's warning, he would bring his hands down on his thighs, and burst into a loud, long, obstreperous, and deafening peal of uncontrollable laughter.

"Solomon," said Tom, at last, "Solomon, my son, won't you burst if you go on so? I'm afraid you may."

At this Solomon went off again, and dived into the hold. But in a minute or two he was back again, and giggling, and glancing, and whispering to himself, as before. Solomon and Captain Corbet thus had each a different way of exhibiting the same emotion, for the feeling that was thus variously displayed was nothing but the purest and most unfeigned joy.

"See yah, Mas'r Tom--and chil'n all," said Solomon, at last. "Ise gwine to pose dat we all go an tend to sometin ob de fust portance. Hyah's Mas'r Tom habn't had notin to eat more'n a mont; an hyah's de res ob de blubbed breddern ob de Bee see double what been a fastin since dey riz at free clock dis shinin and spicious morn. Dis yah's great an shinin casium, an should be honnad by great and strorny stivities. Now, dar ain't no stivity dat can begin to hole a can'l to a good dinna, or suppa, or sometin in de eatin line. So Ise gwine to pose to honna de cobbery ob de Probable Son by a rale ole-fashioned, stunnin breakfuss. Don't be fraid dar'll be any ficiency hyah. I got tings aboard dat I ben a savin for dis spicious an lightful cobbery. Ben no eatin in dis vessel ebber since de loss chile took his parter an drifted off. Couldn't get no pusson to tetch nuffin. Got 'em all now; an so, blubbed breddern, let's sem'l once more, an ole Solomon'll now ficiate in de pressive pacity ob Gran Pandledrum. An I pose dat we rect a tent on de sho oh dis yah island, and hab de banket come off in fust chop style."

"The island!" cried Tom, in horror. "What! the island? Breakfast on the island? What a horrible proposal! Look here, captain. Can't we get away from this?"

"Get away from this?" repeated the captain, in mild surprise.

"Yes," said Tom. "You see, the fact is, when a fellow's gone through what I have, he isn't over fond of the place where he's had that to go through. And so this island is a horrible place to me, and I can't feel comfortable till I get away out of sight of it. Breakfast! Why, the very thought of eating is abominable as long as that island is in sight."

"Wal, railly, now," said Captain Corbet, "I shouldn't wonder if thar was a good deal in that, though I didn't think of it afore. Course it's natral you shouldn't be over fond of sech, when you've had sech an oncommon tough time. An now, bein' as thar's no uthly occasion for the Antelope to be a lingerin' round this here isle of the ocean, I muve that we histe anchor an resume our vyge. It's nigh onto a fort-night since we fust started for Petticoat Jack, and since that time we've had rare and strikin vycissitoods. It may jest happen that some on ye may be tired of the briny deep, an may wish no more to see the billers bound and scatter their foamin spray; some on ye likewise may be out o' sperrits about the fog. In sech a case, all I got to say is, that this here schooner'll be very happy to land you at the nighest port, Scott's Bay, frincense, from which you may work your way by land to your desired haven. Sorry would I be to part with ye, specially in this here moment of jy; but ef ye've got tired of the Antelope, tain't no more'n's natral. Wal, now,--what d'ye say--shall we go up to Scott's Bay, or will ye contenoo on to Petticoat Jack, an accomplitch the riginal vyge as per charter party?"

The boys said nothing, but looked at Tom as though referring the question to him.

"As far as I am concerned," said Tom, who noticed this reference to him, "it's a matter of indifference where we go, so long as we go out of sight of this island. If the rest prefer landing at Scott's Bay, I'm agreed; at the same time, I'd just as soon go on to Petitcodiac."

"An what do the rest o' ye say?" asked the captain, somewhat anxiously.

"For my part," said Bruce, "I think it's about the best thing we can do."

The others all expressed similar sentiments, and Captain Corbet listened to this with evident delight.

"All right," said he, "and hooray! Solomon, my aged friend, we will have our breakfast on board, as we glide past them thar historic shores. Pile on what you have, and make haste."

In a few minutes more the anchor was up, and the Antelope was under way.

In about half an hour Solomon summoned them below, where he laid before them a breakfast that cast into the shade Tom's most elaborate meal on the island. With appetites that seemed to have been growing during the whole period of Tom's absence, the joyous company sat down to that repast, while Solomon moved around, his eyes glistening, his face shining, his teeth grinning, and his hips moving, as, after his fashion, he whispered little Solomonian pleasantries to his own affectionate heart. At this repast the boys began a fresh series of questions, and drew from Tom a full, complete, and exhaustive history of his island life, more particularly with regard to his experience in house-building, and housekeeping; and with each one, without exception, it was a matter of sincere regret that it had not been his lot to be Tom's companion in the boat and on the island.

After breakfast they came up on deck. The wind had at length changed, as Captain Corbet had prophesied in the morning, and the sky overhead was clear. Down the bay still might be seen the fog banks, but near at hand all was bright. Behind them Ile Haute was already at a respectful distance, and Cape Chignecto was near.

"My Christian friends," said Captain Corbet, solemnly,--"my Christian friends, an dear boys. Agin we resoom the thread of our eventfool vyge, that was brok of a suddent in so onparld a manner. Agin we gullide o'er the foamin biller like a arrer shot from a cross-bow, an culleave the briny main. We have lived, an we have suffered, but now our sufferins seem to be over. At last we have a fair wind, with a tide to favor us, an we'll be off Hillsborough before daybreak to-morrer. An now I ask you all, young sirs, do you feel any regretses over the eventfool past? I answer, no. An wan't I right? Didn't I say that that thar lad would onst more show his shinin face amongst us, right side up, with care, in good order an condition, as when shipped on board the Antelope, Corbet master, from Grand Pre, an bound for Petticoat Jack? Methinks I did. Hence the vally of a lofty sperrit in the face of difficulties. An now, young sirs, in after life take warnin by this here vyge. Never say die. Don't give up the ship. No surrender. England expects every man to do his dooty. For him that rises superior to succumstances is terewly great; an by presarvin a magnanumous mind you'll be able to hold up your heads and smile amid the kerrash of misfortin. Now look at me. I affum, solemn, that all the sufferins I've suffered have ben for my good; an so this here vyge has eventooated one of the luckiest vyges that you've ever had. An thus," he concluded, stretching out his venerable hands with the air of one giving a benediction,--"thus may it be with the vyge of life. May all its storms end in calms, an funnish matter in the footoor for balmy rettuspect. Amen!"

It was a close approach to a sermon; and though the words were a little incoherent, yet the tone was solemn, and the intention good. After this the captain dropped the lofty part of a Mentor, and mingled with the boys as an equal.

This time the voyage passed without any accident. Before daybreak on the following morning they reached Hillsborough, where Mrs. Watson received them with the utmost joy. In a few days more the boys had scattered, and Bart arrived home with the story of Tom's rescue.

The Codes Of Hammurabi And Moses
W. W. Davies

QTY

The discovery of the Hammurabi Code is one of the greatest achievements of archaeology, and is of paramount interest, not only to the student of the Bible, but also to all those interested in ancient history...

Religion   **ISBN:** *1-59462-338-4*   **Pages:132**
MSRP $12.95

The Theory of Moral Sentiments
Adam Smith

QTY

This work from 1749. contains original theories of conscience amd moral judgment and it is the foundation for systemof morals.

Philosophy   ISBN: *1-59462-777-0*   **Pages:536**
MSRP $19.95

Jessica's First Prayer
Hesba Stretton

QTY

In a screened and secluded corner of one of the many railway-bridges which span the streets of London there could be seen a few years ago, from five o'clock every morning until half past eight, a tidily set-out coffee-stall, consisting of a trestle and board, upon which stood two large tin cans, with a small fire of charcoal burning under each so as to keep the coffee boiling during the early hours of the morning when the work-people were thronging into the city on their way to their daily toil...

Childrens   ISBN: *1-59462-373-2*   **Pages:84**
MSRP $9.95

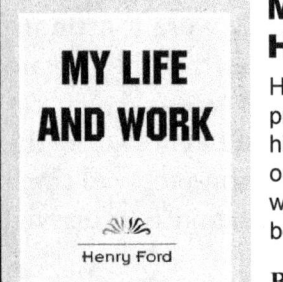

My Life and Work
Henry Ford

QTY

Henry Ford revolutionized the world with his implementation of mass production for the Model T automobile. Gain valuable business insight into his life and work with his own auto-biography... "We have only started on our development of our country we have not as yet, with all our talk of wonderful progress, done more than scratch the surface. The progress has been wonderful enough but..."

Biographies/   ISBN: *1-59462-198-5*   **Pages:300**
MSRP $21.95

The Art of Cross-Examination
Francis Wellman

QTY

I presume it is the experience of every author, after his first book is published upon an important subject, to be almost overwhelmed with a wealth of ideas and illustrations which could readily have been included in his book, and which to his own mind, at least, seem to make a second edition inevitable. Such certainly was the case with me; and when the first edition had reached its sixth impression in five months, I rejoiced to learn that it seemed to my publishers that the book had met with a sufficiently favorable reception to justify a second and considerably enlarged edition. ..

Pages:412

Reference   ISBN: *1-59462-647-2*   *MSRP $19.95*

On the Duty of Civil Disobedience
Henry David Thoreau

QTY

Thoreau wrote his famous essay, On the Duty of Civil Disobedience, as a protest against an unjust but popular war and the immoral but popular institution of slave-owning. He did more than write—he declined to pay his taxes,   and was hauled off to gaol in consequence. Who can say how much this refusal of his hastened the end of the war and of slavery ?

Law   ISBN: *1-59462-747-9*   **Pages:48**

MSRP $7.45

Dream Psychology Psychoanalysis for Beginners
Sigmund Freud

QTY

Sigmund Freud, born Sigismund Schlomo Freud (May 6, 1856 - September 23, 1939), was a Jewish-Austrian neurologist and psychiatrist who co-founded the psychoanalytic school of psychology. Freud is best known for his theories of the unconscious mind, especially involving the mechanism of repression; his redefinition of sexual desire as mobile and directed towards a wide variety of objects; and his therapeutic techniques, especially his understanding of transference in the therapeutic relationship and the presumed value of dreams as sources of insight into unconscious desires.

Pages:196

Psychology   ISBN: *1-59462-905-6*   *MSRP $15.45*

The Miracle of Right Thought
Orison Swett Marden

QTY

Believe with all of your heart that you will do what you were made to do. When the mind has once formed the habit of holding cheerful, happy, prosperous pictures, it will not be easy to form the opposite habit. It does not matter how improbable or how far away this realization may see, or how dark the prospects may be, if we visualize them as best we can, as vividly as possible, hold tenaciously to them and vigorously struggle to attain them, they will gradually become actualized, realized in the life. But a desire, a longing without endeavor, a yearning abandoned or held indifferently will vanish without realization.

Pages:360

Self Help   ISBN: *1-59462-644-8*   *MSRP $25.45*

QTY

The Rosicrucian Cosmo-Conception Mystic Christianity *by Max Heindel*   ISBN: *1-59462-188-8* **$38.95**
The Rosicrucian Cosmo-conception is not dogmatic, neither does it appeal to any other authority than the reason of the student. It is; not controversial, but is; sent forth in the, hope that it may help to clear...   *New Age/Religion 646*

Abandonment To Divine Providence *by Jean-Pierre de Caussade*   ISBN: *1-59462-228-0* **$25.95**
"The Rev. Jean Pierre de Caussade was one of the most remarkable spiritual writers of the Society of Jesus in France in the 18th Century. His death took place at Toulouse in 1751. His works have gone through many editions and have been republished...   *Inspirational/Religion Pages 400*

Mental Chemistry *by Charles Haanel*   ISBN: *1-59462-192-6* **$23.95**
Mental Chemistry allows the change of material conditions by combining and appropriately utilizing the power of the mind. Much like applied chemistry creates something new and unique out of careful combinations of chemicals the mastery of mental chemistry...   *New Age Pages 354*

The Letters of Robert Browning and Elizabeth Barret Barrett 1845-1846 vol II   ISBN: *1-59462-193-4* **$35.95**
by Robert Browning and Elizabeth Barrett   *Biographies Pages 596*

Gleanings In Genesis (volume I) *by Arthur W. Pink*   ISBN: *1-59462-130-6* **$27.45**
Appropriately has Genesis been termed "the seed plot of the Bible" for in it we have, in germ form, almost all of the great doctrines which are afterwards fully developed in the books of Scripture which follow...   *Religion/Inspirational Pages 420*

The Master Key *by L. W. de Laurence*   ISBN: *1-59462-001-6* **$30.95**
In no branch of human knowledge has there been a more lively increase of the spirit of research during the past few years than in the study of Psychology, Concentration and Mental Discipline. The requests for authentic lessons in Thought Control, Mental Discipline and...   *New Age/Business Pages 422*

The Lesser Key Of Solomon Goetia *by L. W. de Laurence*   ISBN: *1-59462-092-X* **$9.95**
This translation of the first book of the "Lernegton" which is now for the first time made accessible to students of Talismanic Magic was done, after careful collation and edition, from numerous Ancient Manuscripts in Hebrew, Latin, and French...   *New Age/Occult Pages 92*

Rubaiyat Of Omar Khayyam *by Edward Fitzgerald*   ISBN:*1-59462-332-5* **$13.95**
Edward Fitzgerald, whom the world has already learned, in spite of his own efforts to remain within the shadow of anonymity, to look upon as one of the rarest poets of the century, was born at Bredfield, in Suffolk, on the 31st of March, 1809. He was the third son of John Purcell...   *Music Pages 172*

Ancient Law *by Henry Maine*   ISBN: *1-59462-128-4* **$29.95**
The chief object of the following pages is to indicate some of the earliest ideas of mankind, as they are reflected in Ancient Law, and to point out the relation of those ideas to modern thought.   *Religion/History Pages 452*

Far-Away Stories *by William J. Locke*   ISBN: *1-59462-129-2* **$19.45**
"Good wine needs no bush, but a collection of mixed vintages does. And this book is just such a collection. Some of the stories I do not want to remain buried for ever in the museum files of dead magazine-numbers an author's not unpardonable vanity..."   *Fiction Pages 272*

Life of David Crockett *by David Crockett*   ISBN: *1-59462-250-7* **$27.45**
"Colonel David Crockett was one of the most remarkable men of the times in which he lived. Born in humble life, but gifted with a strong will, an indomitable courage, and unremitting perseverance...   *Biographies/New Age Pages 424*

Lip-Reading *by Edward Nitchie*   ISBN: *1-59462-206-X* **$25.95**
Edward B. Nitchie, founder of the New York School for the Hard of Hearing, now the Nitchie School of Lip-Reading, Inc, wrote "LIP-READING Principles and Practice". The development and perfecting of this meritorious work on lip-reading was an undertaking...   *How-to Pages 400*

A Handbook of Suggestive Therapeutics, Applied Hypnotism, Psychic Science   ISBN: *1-59462-214-0* **$24.95**
by Henry Munro   *Health/New Age/Health/Self-help Pages 376*

A Doll's House: and Two Other Plays *by Henrik Ibsen*   ISBN: *1-59462-112-8* **$19.95**
Henrik Ibsen created this classic when in revolutionary 1848 Rome. Introducing some striking concepts in playwriting for the realist genre, this play has been studied the world over.   *Fiction/Classics/Plays 308*

The Light of Asia *by sir Edwin Arnold*   ISBN: *1-59462-204-3* **$13.95**
In this poetic masterpiece, Edwin Arnold describes the life and teachings of Buddha. The man who was to become known as Buddha was born as Prince Gautama of India but he rejected the worldly riches and abandoned the reigns of power when... Religion/History/Biographies Pages 170

The Complete Works of Guy de Maupassant *by Guy de Maupassant*   ISBN: *1-59462-157-8* **$16.95**
"For days and days, nights and nights, I had dreamed of that first kiss which was to consecrate our engagement, and I knew not on what spot I should put my lips..."   *Fiction/Classics Pages 240*

The Art of Cross-Examination *by Francis L. Wellman*   ISBN: *1-59462-309-0* **$26.95**
Written by a renowned trial lawyer, Wellman imparts his experience and uses case studies to explain how to use psychology to extract desired information through questioning.   *How-to/Science/Reference Pages 408*

Answered or Unanswered? *by Louisa Vaughan*   ISBN: *1-59462-248-5* **$10.95**
Miracles of Faith in China   *Religion Pages 112*

The Edinburgh Lectures on Mental Science (1909) *by Thomas*   ISBN: *1-59462-008-3* **$11.95**
This book contains the substance of a course of lectures recently given by the writer in the Queen Street Hall, Edinburgh. Its purpose is to indicate the Natural Principles governing the relation between Mental Action and Material Conditions...   *New Age/Psychology Pages 148*

Ayesha *by H. Rider Haggard*   ISBN: *1-59462-301-5* **$24.95**
Verily and indeed it is the unexpected that happens! Probably if there was one person upon the earth from whom the Editor of this, and of a certain previous history, did not expect to hear again...   *Classics Pages 380*

Ayala's Angel *by Anthony Trollope*   ISBN: *1-59462-352-X* **$29.95**
The two girls were both pretty, but Lucy who was twenty-one who supposed to be simple and comparatively unattractive, whereas Ayala was credited, as her Bombwhat romantic name might show, with poetic charm and a taste for romance. Ayala when her father died was nineteen...   *Fiction Pages 484*

The American Commonwealth *by James Bryce*   ISBN: *1-59462-286-8* **$34.45**
An interpretation of American democratic political theory. It examines political mechanics and society from the perspective of Scotsman James Bryce   *Politics Pages 572*

Stories of the Pilgrims *by Margaret P. Pumphrey*   ISBN: *1-59462-116-0* **$17.95**
This book explores pilgrims religious oppression in England as well as their escape to Holland and eventual crossing to America on the Mayflower, and their early days in New England...   *History Pages 268*

QTY

The Fasting Cure *by Sinclair Upton*   ISBN: *1-59462-222-1* **$13.95** ☐

In the Cosmopolitan Magazine for May, 1910, and in the Contemporary Review (London) for April, 1910, I published an article dealing with my experi-
ences in fasting. I have written a great many magazine articles, but never one which attracted so much attention... New Age/Self Help/Health Pages 164

Hebrew Astrology *by Sepharial*   ISBN: *1-59462-308-2* **$13.45** ☐

In these days of advanced thinking it is a matter of common observation that we have left many of the old landmarks behind and that we are now pressing
forward to greater heights and to a wider horizon than that which represented the mind-content of our progenitors... Astrology Pages 144

Thought Vibration or The Law of Attraction in the Thought World   ISBN: *1-59462-127-6* **$12.95** ☐

by William Walker Atkinson   Psychology/Religion Pages 144

Optimism *by Helen Keller*   ISBN: *1-59462-108-X* **$15.95** ☐

Helen Keller was blind, deaf, and mute since 19 months old, yet famously learned how to overcome these handicaps, communicate with the world, and
spread her lectures promoting optimism. An inspiring read for everyone... Biographies/Inspirational Pages 84

Sara Crewe *by Frances Burnett*   ISBN: *1-59462-360-0* **$9.45** ☐

In the first place, Miss Minchin lived in London. Her home was a large, dull, tall one, in a large, dull square, where all the houses were alike, and all the
sparrows were alike, and where all the door-knockers made the same heavy sound... Childrens/Classic Pages 88

The Autobiography of Benjamin Franklin *by Benjamin Franklin*   ISBN: *1-59462-135-7* **$24.95** ☐

The Autobiography of Benjamin Franklin has probably been more extensively read than any other American historical work, and no other book of its kind
has had such ups and downs of fortune. Franklin lived for many years in England, where he was agent... Biographies/History Pages 332

Name	
Email	
Telephone	
Address	
City, State ZIP	

☐ **Credit Card**   ☐ **Check / Money Order**

Credit Card Number	
Expiration Date	
Signature	

Please Mail to: *Book Jungle*
PO Box 2226
Champaign, IL 61825
or Fax to: *630-214-0564*

ORDERING INFORMATION

web*: www.bookjungle.com*
email*: sales@bookjungle.com*
fax*: 630-214-0564*
mail*: Book Jungle PO Box 2226 Champaign, IL 61825*
or PayPal *to sales@bookjungle.com*

Please contact us for bulk discounts

DIRECT-ORDER TERMS

20% Discount if You Order
Two or More Books
Free Domestic Shipping!
Accepted: Master Card, Visa,
Discover, American Express

www.ingramcontent.com/pod-product-compliance
Lightning Source LLC
Chambersburg PA
CBHW080728020726
47503CB00010B/2833